To Guru :)

From Yaya

Ophelia's Curse

Tina Griffith

authorHOUSE

AuthorHouse™
1663 Liberty Drive
Bloomington, IN 47403
www.authorhouse.com
Phone: 1 (800) 839-8640

© 2019 Tina Griffith. All rights reserved.

No part of this book may be reproduced, stored in a retrieval system, or transmitted by any means without the written permission of the author.

Published by AuthorHouse 07/10/2019

ISBN: 978-1-7283-1286-6 (sc)
ISBN: 978-1-7283-1285-9 (e)

Print information available on the last page.

Any people depicted in stock imagery provided by Getty Images are models, and such images are being used for illustrative purposes only. Certain stock imagery © Getty Images.

This book is printed on acid-free paper.

Because of the dynamic nature of the Internet, any web addresses or links contained in this book may have changed since publication and may no longer be valid. The views expressed in this work are solely those of the author and do not necessarily reflect the views of the publisher, and the publisher hereby disclaims any responsibility for them.

☙ ❧ ☙ ❧ ☙ ❧ ☙

The moon was bright and full, the stars were twinkling like diamonds, and dusk was beginning to cool the air. All around them was a soft, distinct fluttering sound of leaves being kissed by the wind, as birds of all sizes, came and went from their cozy nests. The sky above was clear, but on the ground, a light fog was crawling its way to the spot where Jayla and Bill were sitting. With a faint hooting sound coming from their left, and the warmth and beauty of a fire roaring nearby, this was a lovely beginning to a romantic evening.

At first, their date seemed to be going quite well, but then Jayla became a little too aggressive.

Bill Turken liked women and wasn't afraid of a little role playing, so he got himself cozy and waited to see just how far she would go. Less than ten minutes later, it became painfully clear that her frisky intentions were bordering on life-threatening. Bill was no longer happy and was now fearing for his life.

☙ ❧ ☙ ❧ ☙ ❧ ☙

CHAPTER ONE

August 29, 1999

Deep in the bowels of the large and lush Schilling Forest, came the first of many deathly screams from a man who knew that he was about to die. "HELP!" he cried, over and over again with great intensity. Sadly, he knew that the nearest house was a good fifteen minutes away, but he didn't want to give up hope. His stomach lurched into his throat as he wished for someone to wake him from this unbelievable nightmare. "SAVE ME!" he called as loud as he could.

Suddenly, the same terrified feeling he got whenever he sat down on the dentist's chair, rushed to every pore in his body. The dreaded, cold and clammy feeling of anxiety, took over his mind as quickly as the hair on the back of his neck stood up. "HELP!" he screamed, again and again in a high-pitched voice. He was shaking uncontrollably now, the color of his face had turned ashen, and beads of sweat were dotting his upper lip and forehead.

Leaning over the wide-eyed and terrified little man, was a beautiful, dark-haired woman named Jayla. Her thick hair hung in long graceful curls over her shoulders, and her magnetic eyes beckoned you to find her irresistible. Her figure was curvy and magnificent, and her hips tapered into long straight legs. The black velvet dress which clung to her body, heightened the translucence of the apricot and milky color of her skin. Her beauty was intoxicating, and she had an intelligent face and charm to match, but Bill would soon learn that her heart held grudges which her lips dared not speak.

Unbeknownst to him, she was actually a gypsy-witch in disguise, and she was currently enjoying his huge spike of uneasiness.

As Jayla stared into the balding man's anxious face, she remembered how patient she had been, while waiting for just over a year for this special moment to arrive. Not only had she pretended to be loving and tender to him during their private moments, but she had also fulfilled every one of his nasty wishes.

It suddenly made her sick to her stomach to recall all that they had done, and now that she no longer needed to be someone who she was not, she turned into an ugly wicked force that was not to be reckoned with.

The 37-year old man was panting and sweating like crazy, he had tremors in his voice, and he was whimpering relentlessly. None of this matched his appearance from an hour ago, when his hair had been perfectly combed and styled, his shirt had been freshly ironed, and he was proudly wearing brand new pants and polished shoes. In that moment he was sitting on the ground, his pants were wrinkled and dirty, his shirt had been ripped open, and his face was blotchy from crying.

The spiteful witch looked at him with utter hate, while she summoned every vile thought that she had about him, to come to the surface. Every dirty deed that she had done to him or with him, also came bubbling up to the forefront of her mind. And with it, came an ungodly turmoil of painful emotions, which fueled her rising anger and gave her more than enough power to cast her current spell.

"Please don't kill me!" Bill cried, with absolute panic in his voice. His feet were bound together with rope, his hands were tied behind his back, and his heart was racing in his chest. While tears of absolute fear were pouring down his cheeks, he felt as if he was sinking into a giant pool of quicksand and would never be seen again.

The short but husky, broad shouldered man, who once worked for a loan shark and tortured people for a living, was now on the other end of an intimidating delivery. "I thought you loved me", he stated, as if his words were going to alter her plans. Bill was more scared than he wanted to admit, but he knew he must try to appeal to the gentle side of her soul. "I thought we were going to have a long and happy life together. Isn't that what we had always talked about?" he asked with tenderness.

His state of mind was anything but calm, and for a brief second, he lost his head and became brave. "This is going a little too far. Do you even know what you're doing?" He then watched as the features on her face distorted, and she became almost unrecognizable.

An evil smirk fell upon Jayla's face, for she had no intention of having a long life with him or any other man on this earth. And despite what he thought, she knew full-well what she was doing, for she had executed this premeditated routine many times before today.

"Do you need money?" he asked with reckless abandonment. His voice was breaking and his lips were trembling beyond control. "I've got some hidden, and I will give you all that I have!" he promised.

A nearby owl hooted, as if it had been laughing at Bill's poor attempt to soothe the beast within the witch's body.

Bill tried to ignore the disrespectful mocking of the large bird, and continued his pitiful plea bargaining. "Jayla? Honey?" His words were streaked with desperation as he implored her to spare his life, just as all of his victims had done to him when he was about to kill them. "Ple-e-a-a-s-e!" he begged, while the sound of his own heartbeat thrashed in his ears.

Jayla leaned in closer to his face, and as her amusement echoed all around them, she giggled. "I don't need your money, you silly fool. I just need you to die." Her forest green eyes glistened with delight as the words hissed out of her mouth.

"Wh-hat?" he stammered. His thoughts were racing a mile a minute, and then he was hit with the sensation of information coming much too quickly for him to process. "No, no, wait!" he screamed with absolute insistence.

Jayla straightened her posture while she cackled unkindly. "There's no need to wait, my dear", she announced in a voice that was devoid of all emotion. "For the time has come." With dramatic flair, she retrieved something from her over-sized front pocket. A second later, she released some fine red powder into the brooding flames.

Panic took over his body as Bill tried to get up, but Jayla pushed him back down with the bottom of her shoe. "Stay right where you are, Billy boy; the party's just getting started."

A loud POOF exploded from the fire, and the shattering sound vibrated against all the trees in the forest. It was followed by a large grey puff of smoke, which began to rise into the air like a giant snake.

"Please!" Bill cried. "I beg you!" He had never been so frightened in his whole entire life, and he was now on the verge of becoming hysterical. "I don't want to die! Whatever I did or didn't do, I'm sorry." His eyes were bulging out of their sockets, but they were not blinking, and the muscles in his body began to break out in uncontrollable shivers.

Jayla's mind was not on the lowly male before her, but on how the deadly substance was becoming one with the air. She steered it towards her current victim with her hands, while making sure not to get in its deadly path.

Bill's eyes kept an intense grasp of the woman before him, but he couldn't help but wonder if he was going to be burned alive. Suddenly, he heard a small shuffling of footsteps coming from behind a tree on his right. "Hello?" he called loudly, hoping that someone had come to save him. His heart dropped into his stomach when he saw that it was just a curious deer walking away from the ominous death scene. A second later, a brash rustling sound came from overhead. Bill looked up to see a stocky black bird fly out from between the branches of a tall tree. "Ka-Kaw" it laughed, as it flew away into the night.

Bill lowered his chin to his chest while his body tightened with total despair. "H-E-L-P!" he screamed into the cool air, even though he knew that no-one could hear him. And because he was fearful that his time on this earth was limited, he decided to try another approach.

"Listen!" he begged nicely. "If you let me go, I promise not to tell anyone anything – not your name or where you live - not anything! Just please, please let me go!" In that moment, he was beyond terrified, as if he was about to be thrown into a pool of hungry piranhas.

Jayla stopped stirring the charred pieces of wood, and watched as the man before her was living his last seconds of life. She had no emotional or physical tie to him, and she didn't care what he thought of her.

Bill's breathing was starting to become labored, and just like that, his voice was no longer as strong as it used to be. While a look of confusion covered every inch of his face, he fought to understand why he was beginning to feel calm, and why his will to fight had lost some of its power. Everything around him felt like it was moving further and further away, and he soon found himself drifting off to sleep.

As she watched him die, Jayla's mouth broke into a nimble smile, for she could see that the deadly potion was taking effect. And when the energy had finally drained out of the large man's body, the features on Jayla's face turned stern and unforgiving.

The moment when the atmospheric continuum was at its peak, and the sun was sitting in a perfect triangle with the earth and the moon, the witch stretched out her arms and her shoulders automatically hunched forward. Without missing a beat, her fingers, which had mysteriously gnarled and lengthened, moved in the air while they spread apart. In a piercing voice that vibrated as she spoke, she stared at the body of her target and began to recite the first verse of a startling spell.

> A soul I need, a soul I take
> After which, your body will bake
> Come to me, come inside
> Your dark soul I will abide

The winds twitched and swirled on high speed, as an eerie, ghostly sound swam through the forest. Meanwhile, the molecules in the air started pulsating as they took on a strange scent of lilacs and sage.

Jayla continued to stare into Bill's motionless face as she recited the next verse.

> With the full moon up high
> And all the stars in the sky
> Leave his body, reside in mine
> Heed these words and all will be fine

Suddenly, clouds appeared and grew dark and bizarre. Lightning cracked loudly across the heavens, and the ground shook wildly beneath her feet.

Bill's lifeless body fell sideways onto the ground, which was the signal that his soul was ready to leave and that Jayla should prepare herself to receive it.

For the past 16 months and 13 days, she had shown him phony smiles, let him listen to her pretend laughter, given him a false friendship, and made love to him to keep him interested. And now, this was the moment when she would be rewarded for all of her efforts.

As she delivered the final verse of the transference spell, her body stiffened. She took a deep breath, she raised her chin, closed her eyes, and pinned her arms tightly against her sides.

> Move it now, let it be free
> I command you, so mote it be

With baited breath, and the delicate sound of firefly wings beating all around her head, she waited for the dark soul to begin its journey.

Bill's soul rose out of his dead body and floated over to Jayla. As it entered into the top of her skull, she automatically shivered from its cool temperature. As it sunk further down her torso, it slowly coupled itself with her own composition.

It took less than two minutes for the transfer to be complete, and when it was over, Jayla opened her eyes.

She had instantly gained the darkness of his personality, and the core of her being would now have to fight the evil of his soul, so that both souls could merge as one.

As the beautiful gypsy-witch pondered the new attitude in her body, her stillness was broken by a strange noise.

Directly in front of her, the fire hissed and popped as if it was alive. The fright of this brought Jayla back to reality, and it made her jump to attention. Realizing that she had no time to waste, she took the corpse and placed it into the middle of the large flames. She then stood back and watched to make sure that all traces of it were burned to a crisp.

During those long and tedious hours, she flexed her fingers and toes, and she reveled in how much softer her skin and hair had become since she woke up that morning.

She also noticed that her extraordinary senses, which include the normal 5 that mortals have, plus *proprioception, complete conscious awareness, a variety of split receptors in her skin, acute echo location, and *synaesthesia, were all very much heightened.

---

*Proprioception - is the sense of the relative position of one's own parts of the body and strength of effort being employed in movement.

*Synaesthesia - the ability to feel a very strong and involuntary connection between the stimulus and the sense that it triggers.

Sadly, Jayla knew that it wouldn't last. Judging by how she felt, she would need to recharge her life source in less than 19 months.

The gypsy witch sighed as she looked up at the sky, and she could tell by the position of the moon, that she could close her eyes for at least six hours. After making herself comfortable on the blanket, Jayla encouraged her body to rest.

While she slept, her body was able to relax, and her witchly appearance reverted back to how it was when she first walked into the Schilling Forest with Bill Turken.

Time ticked by and it was finally morning, and with the dawn of a new day, came a new opportunity for her to gain another soul. Because the remains of Bill Turken had been completely turned into dust, Jayla could now make her way back to her village.

CHAPTER TWO

October 24, 2000

It was 7:28 on Monday morning, and like the rest of the country, the inmates of the Broken Hill Prison were preparing for their workday. Unbeknownst to the outside world, the decade's old, maximum-security penitentiary housed 203 men, and Roger Casem was one of them.

Little did he know that when he woke up that morning, that his current state of life was about to change. Or furthermore, that he would die a horrible and unexpected death, before the week was over.

The slender man snuffed out the last bit of his 2nd cigarette, into a disfigured, disposable, aluminum ashtray. All around him were the unhappy grunts and shouts of angry men who felt that they were wrongfully imprisoned, as well as the strong voices of guards who were correcting the inmates when they were being intentionally disruptive. The shuffling of feet and the sounds of grown men crying, while being unsettling, was quite normal in the uninviting and depressing facility.

As his hollow brown eyes scanned the unexciting large room, his body shuddered at the coolness in the stale air. And as much as he didn't like it, summer had ended and the world was now heading into fall – his least favorite season of all.

Roger looked up and took notice of how much more of the ugly green paint had peeled off the walls since last year at this time. He then looked down at the tiles beneath his feet, and noted that they were the same ones that have been on the floor since his second stint at the prison. 'Some things will never change', he decided in his head. The muscles in his body automatically cringed in agreement. Seconds later, the putrid smell of urine and fresh vomit wafted into his nostrils, and he knew that he was not going to miss this place, or the people, at all.

This was Roger's 5th time in prison, but he wanted to make it his last; he hated it there, as if *that was something to question, and he decided that he would do whatever it took to never come back again.*

A man who had brutally accosted Roger just a few weeks ago, walked by his chair, and they purposely didn't make eye contact. The man was obviously on a mission, and because of the blind hatred which was clearly flaunted all over his scruffy face, Roger knew enough to make himself seem small and invisible. Once the burly inmate was far enough away, Roger breathed a sigh of relief.

The appalling living conditions that he couldn't endure for any long period of time, and the unspeakable things which he had gone through in the past, is what made him want to get out of jail. All of it continues to haunt him on a daily basis, but mostly at night, when he laid his head down on the pillow and tried to go to sleep. The shocking details of each event usually kept his mind active 24/7, but sadly, it was never enough to make him want to go straight.

Being thrown into jail and being let out again, was an exhausting ride, but it was an emotional roller coaster that he knew he might never get off of.

Roger looked up at the round clock on the wall by the stairs, and he hoped that he had just enough time to finish a third Export A. He placed the unfiltered cigarette in between his lips and reached for the lighter. Once the end was lit, he took a long drag, and then exhaled it slowly. His eyes were now fixed and looking at nothing in particular, his right hand was positioned firmly on his right knee, and that leg was bouncing up and down as if it had too much energy flowing through it.

The unkempt man was rightfully nervous, because he honestly didn't know how his day was going to turn out. Frustration had been building up in his body because a huge decision was about to be made, and it meant that his life was hanging in the balance. Unfortunately, he had no say-so in the outcome and this was driving him crazy.

Roger took another long drag on his cigarette and then exhaled it slowly, but his mind wouldn't release the over-active muscles in his body from vibrating.

The 35-year old man was going up against the parole board, and they were going to decide if he would be eligible to get out of jail early. If they said yes, he could be on the outside in 48 hours. If they rejected his appeal, he would have to stay put for another twelve months and two days. Because he'd already spent a good part of the last twenty years locked inside of a 7' x 10' bleak and damp cell, he hoped for them to say yes.

As sweat began to dot his naturally oily forehead, Roger tried to convince himself that everything would turn out ok.

BANG

Every fiber in his body sprang to attention from the loud noise, and his thoughts were now ruthlessly diverted.

SMASH

The heads of everyone in the room spun around at the same time, while their hearts raced at full speed and their eyes widened as far as they could go.

A chair had been pushed away by the back of an angry inmate's knees, and it was screeching across the floor like nails on a chalkboard. The stranger did not start the fight, but he vowed to step in, if and when it was needed.

"I'm going to kill you!" Simon growled, as he leaned headfirst towards the man sitting opposite him. His eyes had narrowed and his gravelly voice had anger weaving all through it. His calloused hands were reaching forward, in a frenzied hope of grabbing the tattooed neck of the hated inmate.

"Not if I kill you first!" Richard shouted, in a voice that sounded like death warmed over. The features on his weathered face were now twisted almost beyond recognition.

CRASH

Two long tables had been violently flipped over by three other monstrous looking men, and chairs were being broken from extreme tempers.

As they all lashed out at each other, teeth were broken, skin was being ripped open, eyes and ears began to bleed, and bones were now poking out of their joints.

Surprisingly, these five men looked like they were killing each other, but no-one was stopping what was happening.

It was a habit for the guards to watch but not get involved too early, so that the inmates could tire themselves out; it made it easier for them to be controlled after they had liberated some of their pent-up hostility.

Because Roger had been on the wrong end of some of those fights many times in the past, he was frantic and desperately wanted to get out of the unsafe area. He dropped his cigarette on the floor while he stood up very slowly, and placed his open hands high in the air. He then motioned to the Corrections Officer that he was ready to leave the room.

After the officer acknowledged his request, he signaled for the Prison Officer to escort inmate #926591 back to his cell. Once Roger had been taken out of the room and the doors had been slammed shut, the Corrections Officer began the lockdown.

After hitting the emergency button on the wall next to his shoulder, the senior officer blew his whistle loud and long. He and the three other officers then raced unsympathetically towards the disorderly men.

The sirens were blaring thunderously loud to all who could hear, weapons had come out of their mysterious hiding places, and many more officers were rushing to get to the high priority area.

Even though the guards were trying to break up the horrific small war, the five inmates continued clawing, shouting, and engaging in the hostile combat with each other.

It didn't take long before the armed men became caught in the forceful blows and intensifying blood-bath of what the frustrated inmates were delivering. Blow after blow, the guards and inmates took their punishment, and bravely stood their ground. Knuckles and feet connected with razor-sharp accuracy, on the muscles and bones of any man who got in the way. Foreheads banged into faces with cruel force, oxygen supply was cut off by a strong upper arm, and dirty nails dug into moist flesh until blood oozed out from a deep gaping hole.

BANG

The blast from the Walther PPQ M2 pistol was sharp and deafening, and alerted everyone in that area that playtime was over.

"That's enough!" the Corrections Officer shouted with absolute authority. He placed his expensive black weapon back into its holster, and as uneasiness crept through his veins, he proudly supervised the next few minutes with semi-confidence.

Out of the fifteen guards who had rushed into the rowdy area, one had been brutally injured and two others had to be given moderate medical attention. After their wounds had been attended to by the prison medical staff, the injured guards were sent to a private area of the building where they could rest.

As for the five inmates, one was dead and two others needed to have gashes sewn up and bones set. After they were attended to, they were transported to the make-shift hospital area in the prison. The other two were less injured and could still walk, so they were handcuffed and thrown into a cavernous place called, 'The Hole'. This was a small, dark, cold, concrete room in the basement, with no ventilation and not much human contact. As ironic as it sounds, prisoners were sent there to cool down.

After an inmate had been thrown into one of those rooms, his fellow inmates prayed for him to get out alive. Sometimes they made it and sometimes they did not – it mostly hung on the temperament of the officer who was standing guard. If he liked you, he gave you a little slack, but if you had pissed him off in the past, he made sure that your time in 'The Hole' was not pleasant at all.

Once the energy-charged room had been emptied of guards and inmates, the cleaning staff were ordered to come and make everything presentable again.

While everyone was doing what they were paid to do, the Corrections Officer marched himself to the warden's office, to file his report of another unexpected incident.

Meanwhile, Roger was only steps away from his cell on the second floor. All around him were the loud and angry voices of the men who had been locked in their cells against their will. Their disparaging grunts and groans were echoing throughout the entire building, and until they all quieted down, the inmates would remain locked up until further notice.

Officer Seth Hiros had the honor of walking Roger to his cell that day. They had been friendly for the past ten years, and they often spoke about things that were happening on the inside and outside of the 130-year old prison.

"I guess this is you", the officer stated. The uniformed man undid the handcuffs and watched Roger go into his small room. He then made extra sure that the cell door was firmly locked. "Good luck today", he added with total sincerity.

"Thanks", Roger replied. He then threw him the infamous Boy Scout's salute.

Officer Seth returned the gesture, and winked as he placed his left hand on his belt. He then made his way back to the East Wing on the first floor.

As Roger sat motionless on the edge of his bed, his mind began to drift. He knew at least three of the five men who were involved in the frightening ruckus, and he also knew what kind of disturbing punishment they would suffer when everything calmed down. His muscles flinched at the mere thought of all that awaited those inmates, but instead of focusing on that upsetting situation, Roger decided to spruce himself up for the important meeting with the parole board.

As he shaved, he noticed the many scars on his face and neck from his lifetime of drugs and physical abuse. Though he tried to ignore the obvious imperfections, his eyes couldn't help but examine each and every one of the dreadful marks. And apart from the few pothole acne scars on his cheeks and forehead, the other mementoes were crude reminders of a very difficult life. All of them made him feel ugly, but each one gave him a story to tell.

Minutes later, after Roger was dressed, he got down on his knees. With his chin raised towards the sky, he prayed to God. He made it clear how much he wanted to get out of jail, and he promised to change his ways. After saying Amen and making the sign of the cross on his chest, he brushed the fabric near his knees and sat on the bed. After inhaling a few large breaths of air into his lungs, he was now ready to go to the meeting.

A guard arrived 10 minutes later, and after handcuffing Roger's hands behind his back, the repeated offender was escorted to the meeting room.

A minute after he got there, four older men in dark suits burst in through a secret door. As they all sat down on the other side of a ten foot table, not one of them made eye contact with the inmate before them. There were no pleasant formalities or introductions offered, but the grey haired man in the middle did ask Roger if he knew why he had been brought before the committee.

"Yes, sir", he said in a strong, clear voice. "I do."

Roger was trying to keep the muscles in his face slack, while he maintained good eye contact with whoever was speaking. By doing this, he hoped to convince the committee that he was compliant, and that he was listening carefully to every word which was being spoken.

"Good", the man in the middle cautioned. All four gentlemen looked at each other with a significant glance, and then gave a knowing nod to Roger. "Okay, we can begin."

"We have studied your records and believe that you have tried to be a model inmate", the gentleman on the end stated. "Because of that, we see no reason why you shouldn't be released earlier than it was originally ordered."

"Providing that you understand that we don't want to see you in here again", the man on the other end of the table added bleakly. He leaned his upper body forward, placed an apathetic look upon his face, and began tapping the lead point of his pencil against the table. He then waited for Roger to respond.

The ambience in the room grew tense as the first man spoke again. "Because you've been in here many times over the past two decades, I strongly agree with that suggestion."

Roger, who was perspiring from every sweat gland in his body, tried not to show any emotion. "You won't", he replied loudly, with reverence in his voice.

The only man who had not spoken up until now, took his turn. After scrunching up his face and inhaling a dreaded long sigh, he began to read his list of demands. "You will not be permitted to carry a weapon, commit an act of violence, or drive a car. You are not to use drugs – pharmaceutical or otherwise – without the written consent of your parole officer." He stopped talking in order to increase the power behind his next statement. "You will need to get yourself a real job, because we won't be supporting you on the outside." He tapped the tip of his index and middle fingers on the desk and continued. "You need to stay in touch with your parole officer two times a day, and you cannot leave the state for any reason. Is that clear?"

Roger, whose hands had been locked in a tight fist on his lap, nodded in an obedient manner. His legs were beginning to cramp from sitting rigid for so long, and a fluttery feeling was starting to spread through his chest.

"Hello?" The only man with glasses asked. "We need to hear your answer."

"Can you honestly say that you understand everything which has been said here today?" another men asked.

"Yes, sir." As he spoke, Roger could feel that his internal temperature and heartbeat were rising.

The committee talked among themselves for a few minutes, and then they all closed their binders at the same time.

"We will submit our recommendations to Warden Campbell in the morning", the man in the middle explained.

"If he signs you out, you should be released within 48 hours", the man on the far left stated.

"Thank you", Roger sighed. He closed his eyes and bent his head forward, to show them his utmost appreciation for discharging him. "Thank you very much."

It was in that exact moment, when a guard, who now stood directly behind Roger, nudged him in the back of his neck. This startled him, and made him stand up and wait silently, while all four men left the room. Roger was then escorted out through a different door and taken to his cell.

Several minutes after his cell door had been locked, Roger laid himself down on the bed. After taking his first deep breath in an hour, he knotted his fingers behind his head, stared at the wall by his feet, and let his mind wander. It didn't take long after that, before he had a déjà vu moment.

Roger knew the inside of the prison better than he knew the outside world. He was well aware of every inch of his cell, most of the names of the guys who were incarcerated with him, and how to avoid getting raped or beaten up when he was out in the yard or in the shower area. That had been Roger's life since he was a teenager, but now that he had the possibility of getting out, he decided that it was time to go straight.

CHAPTER THREE

August 30, 1999

It was morning, and as Jayla made her way through the winding dirt path of the Schilling Forest, the sun was beginning to rise in the east. And while the bright ball of energy was about to warm the earth, it stilled the hearts of all those who would rather dwell in the shroud of shadows.

Bright flickers of undemanding light were peeking through the crumbling veil of night, and as most witches and gypsies know, this looming daybreak lessened the power of all spells which need to be performed under the frivolous face of the full moon.

The gypsy-witch was very aware that she had to hasten her steps, so she raised her hands and cupped them outwards, as if to brighten the way of the path. This simple spell also enabled the low-hanging branches to lift up, and encouraged the generously endowed bushes to squish themselves into tinier balls. This in turn, made her journey quicker and easier.

While Jayla walked towards the entrance of the natural jungle, her thoughts reflected on why she had to live her life by killing men. As the depressing visions appeared in her mind, the ugly feeling of hate pushed strongly against her chest.

She was filled with a great deal of melancholy at how much she loathed the thought of being cursed, and she wanted nothing more than to be rid of the hopelessness which she suffered with, each and every day of her adult life.

As she stepped over the threshold between forest and meadow, her chin dropped to her chest, her iridescent eyes began to tear up, and it wasn't long before the delicate tears of salty water began to run down her flushed cheeks.

She was in a hurry and did not see the beauty of the meadow before her. Had she looked, she would have seen the morning sun sparkling on the droplets of water which were clinging to the long blades of grass. The light made it look like expensive jewels were growing in the pasture of lush greenery, but in her haste, she stepped over them as if they were nothing.

"Time is running out", a strong male voice whispered. The eerie announcement had come from behind her right shoulder, and it seemed to beckon her to hurry along.

Jayla was not afraid, for she knew that her father was always watching and guiding her steps. She wished that he was still alive so that he could advise her in every situation, but sadly, Lemnor had been viciously murdered by a mighty sorcerer in a horrendous battle of, 'who had the stronger power'.

"I'm hurrying, Papa", she called to the air around her. Once her feet touched the hardened soil in the withering meadow, she searched for the small path that led to the village. After grabbing her long colorful skirt with tight fists, she picked up her pace. Her mind, however, remained focused on the reasons behind this gruesome and exhausting, perpetual ritual of killing men in order to stay alive.

Jayla knew for a fact, that if her father had not died, she and her mother would never have come to the gypsy village. More importantly, she would not have met Ophelia.

Without truly wanting to, Jayla flashed upon the day when Ophelia placed the morbid curse upon her. It ultimately doomed her to a split life, and an endless pursuit of fading beauty – something which she still despises each and every day.

Upon learning of her husband's death, Petra May, a Solitary Pagan Witch, took her young daughter to the Village of Torin, which sat just outside of the Schilling Forest. There, in the large clearing, lived a group of thirty gypsies and eight witches. All of them were dressed in vibrant rags and sang happy tunes, while the rest of the world suffered through wars, criminal activity, and unnecessary destruction.

Mother and child were welcomed into the group with open arms, and they were immediately given a 2-bedroom home to live in, and plenty of food to eat. Every morning, Petra May taught her 4-year old little girl the ways of being a witch, just as her descendants had done to her. Every afternoon, Jayla was being cultured on how to be a gypsy.

Jayla relished sitting at the knee of the older ladies, and she listened happily to their delightful stories of long ago. As the years went by, she learned how to use her magic to make spells and potions. And even though it was not part of her lessons, she also discovered how to sew and cook like the simple folk, who lived in the neighbouring villages.

The little girl had always had a wonderful disposition, and she displayed the beauty of a thousand angels. And because she was a natural witch, and she carried the blood of a brilliant sorcerer in her veins, everyone assumed that she could end up being a very powerful individual. However, nobody could have predicted that her life would turn out to be so challenging, and it was all because of one jealous and stubborn teenage girl.

Ophelia and her family came to the village when Jayla was nine years old. The girls had an instant connection, and were often found laughing and talking well into the night. Years later, when their bodies changed from childhood to womanhood, other things changed as well.

By her fourteenth birthday, Ophelia had turned into a bit of a wild child; she became untamed and did not like to adhere to rules. She dropped out of her daily lessons, and stopped helping out around her home and village.

Jayla, on the other hand, was tidy, calm, kind, and thoughtful. She had an eagerness to know everything that could be taught, and she helped out whenever and wherever she could.

When it came to boys, Ophelia wanted them all to fall madly in love with her, while Jayla couldn't care less about falling in love with anyone. As far as Ophelia was concerned, this was Jayla's best quality, and with Jayla out of the way, Ophelia would have more boys to choose from.

The girls soon began to spend a little time apart, but they never fully lost the last thread of their solid bond of friendship.

On the day after Jayla's sixteenth birthday, a family of four boys moved into the village. The two older sons were destined to marry two gypsy girls, while the youngest son was not old enough to even shave. This left a potential courtship with Rune, who was the only other boy in the family.

Rune Hallewell was a handsome lad of eighteen. He was tall, had curly brown hair that fell to his shoulders, and he walked with a swagger that most grown men would have loved to achieve. To the naked eye, he was very much a lady's man, but in his heart, he hoped to wed before he turned twenty-one.

Ophelia had done her best to entice him, and she was by his side every chance that she could get.

While he was always friendly towards her, Rune was not interested in anything that she was offering.

Ophelia could feel his resistance and was determined not to give up. Despite his refusal of her advances, she continued to ease her way into his heart - whether he wanted her to or not.

Rune was polite and smiled in her direction, and pretended to listen to whatever she had to say. After a while though, this was proving to be too much for him to bear, so he began to avoid her.

With Ophelia spending all of her time chasing Rune, Jayla had to find other things to keep herself busy. Little did Jayla know that Rune had developed a crush on her, and that he was using every possible motive he had, to spy on the beautiful girl with the dark hair and perfectly-shaped green eyes.

The first time he saw Jayla, he swooned – a fact that he would never admit to anyone. She was hanging clothes in her backyard and the wind was playing with her dress and her hair. From where he stood, he could hear her humming a tune, and no matter how hard he tried, he couldn't take his eyes off of her.

Jayla was busy with her chores, but she had detected that someone was nearby. Because the stranger didn't seem to pose a threat, Jayla kept her senses heightened and continued on with her work.

Ophelia happened to be walking by, and she saw Rune staring at Jayla. She became instantly jealous and rushed to his side. "Hi, Rune. Want to go for a walk with me?" She batted her eyes in his direction, as if that would lure him away.

"Uh, no, but thank you", he stated kindly. He was surprised that she kept showing up, and wished that she would stop following him.

As she wrapped her hands around his upper arm she whispered, "But we won't be gone long." She was acting possessive and wanted the world to know that he was hers, and hers alone.

Rune closed his eyes and lowered his face towards the ground. He was not interested in the freckle-faced girl, but decided to treat her thoughtfully, as he had always been taught to do. "I'd love to hang out with you today, but I can't", he stated in a friendly voice. His eyes wandered back to where Jayla was standing, and then they shifted to Ophelia. He was nervous that he had been caught staring, and his body exploded with anxiety. "I-I'm sorry", he stammered. "I have to go."

Ophelia's heart sank in her chest as she watched Rune dash off. Once he was out of sight, she turned and glared at her best friend.

Ophelia had blind rage coursing through her bones, but she tried to contain her emotions when she realized that Jayla had not paid any attention to Rune. It was quite clear that he was smitten with her, but it was also clear that Jayla didn't seem to care. That left Ophelia to believe that she still had a chance with the foolish young man.

Over the next few months, the red-head chased him non-stop, and appeared in places where he thought he was completely alone. She even challenged him to conversations that he had no interest in having. And sadly, at most of those 'chance meetings', Ophelia had caught Rune mooning over Jayla.

"I have no interest in him", Jayla promised, when Ophelia confronted her. She had been caught in Ophelia's angry mind games many times in the past, and she knew firsthand the vicious outcomes and how to avoid them.

Ophelia's jealousy caused her to become blind with anger, and she couldn't hear the sincere words which her best friend was saying.

"Please, listen to me!" she begged sternly. Jayla grabbed Ophelia by the shoulders and looked her straight in the eyes. "I am not interested in any boy from this village", she promised wholeheartedly. "Please, believe me!"

Ophelia was too full of rage to feel the sting of truth behind the pleading words, and after ripping herself free from Jayla's grip, she stormed away.

This left Jayla standing in an emotional pool of shock. They had had several fights before, but never had Jayla ever felt the wrath of hatred in Ophelia's eyes as she did today.

As the weeks went by, Ophelia's blood was boiling more and more with unwarranted anger. She was no longer interested in captivating Rune in order to create a relationship, but to win an emotive battle between herself and Jayla.

Day in and day out, Ophelia walked around with her hands in fists and her body filled with tense muscles. She also bared her teeth like a mean dog, while she grunted at anyone who dared to speak or look in her direction. Her large brown eyes were always full of suspicion, and she tried every trick in the book to get Rune to notice her. This included a powerful, well-known love spell, which her grandmother said, 'brought grama and grampa together'.

While this was all delightful in theory, Ophelia soon learned that the affection which Rune had for Jayla, was much more powerful than anything that Ophelia or others could conjure up.

And when she had finally had enough, and Ophelia felt that she had no other choice, she confronted him head-on. "Just so you know", she cautioned strongly. "I will not escape your advances forever." She purposely threatened him in a seductive manner, as she moved her curvy body closer to his. "I know how to make you smile and sweat, and I can keep you happier than you've ever been in your whole entire life."

"WOW!" Rune declared in alarm. He was not interested in Ophelia, and after her shocking display of unlady-like, aggressive behavior, he now knew that he needed to tell her his true thoughts, or leave the village forever.

Jayla had perfect peripheral vision, and she could feel emotions building a mile away. She knew what Rune thought of her, and she loved that he kept it to himself. She hadn't counted on Ophelia stepping in to make everything worse, but she did know that her friend wanted to have Rune all to herself.

On this particular day, Jayla could see that the two of them were having a heated discussion. Because she wanted nothing to do with either of them in that moment, she pretended to keep reading her book of spells.

Rune was scared of this aggressive teenager, and it showed on his face and in his body language. He constantly felt imprisoned by Ophelia, because he kept being backed into a corner and he didn't know how to get out. Without thinking, his eyes automatically redirected themselves to Jayla, and he was suddenly filled with an overwhelming passion to be with her. His eyes softened as he studied the fullness of her ample breasts and generously curved and slightly parted lips, and then he slowly undressed her in his mind. Forgetting for a second that Ophelia was standing mere inches away from him, he became totally mesmerized by the only other girl in the immediate area.

As Ophelia turned to look at her best friend, her eyes narrowed and her heart rate went up. As she turned her attention back to Rune, she crossed her arms tightly across her chest, and wondered when this man would stop ogling a girl who didn't want anything to do with him.

Rune was completely caught up in his private fantasy, and he even tried to envision what it would be like to kiss Jayla and hold her in his arms.

Because she now knew how strong his feelings for Jayla were, Ophelia realized that she would have to do something drastic in order to make sure that they would never be together. The angry teenager took a deep breath, and enforced the deadliest power in her soul to rise up to the surface. Then, with unbelievable strength, she struck him as hard as she could.

Before he knew what was happening, Rune felt something solid slam into the side of his face.

Jayla's head swung around just in time to see Ophelia hit him. Shock made her suck her breath into her throat, but she dared not blink or move, for fear of what Ophelia would do or say.

A second later, Jayla watched as Ophelia walked away.

When Rune opened his eyes, he wasn't quite sure what had happened, and because Jayla was cooing him to awareness and trying to make him comfortable, he didn't care that his face felt like it had exploded or that he was laying on the cold ground.

"Are you alright?" she asked tenderly, as she hovered over his aching body.

"I-I don't know, but I think so." He tried to lift his head, but Jayla convinced him to lie still. He wanted to feel his face, but she encouraged him not to.

"Don't touch", she ordered, as she gently brushed a few strands of hair off of his forehead.

Several of the elders heard what had happened and came over to assess the situation. When they were done with their quick evaluation, they picked him up and encouraged him to walk. Before they got too far, Rune stopped them.

"Jayla", he sighed, through tears of joy and pain. "Thank you for being so kind to me." He stared at her as if he was imparting a hidden message, and then he smiled as he let the elders take him home.

Jayla smiled, but it was with friendship. "You're welcome, but it's not necessary." She knew how he felt about her and she was flattered, but she was not in love with him. She cared about him as a person and she wished him well in life – that's it.

Unfortunately, Ophelia was consumed with an uncontrollable madness and that's not how she saw the situation. In her mind, she envisioned Jayla rushing over to Rune and act like a doting nurse to him. She even saw them both smile, which caused her to conjure up all kinds of vile thoughts and images.

Before too long, Ophelia's mind was spinning out of control and she was believing things that were simply not true. She soon realized that Rune would never be hers, so she decided that both he and Jayla would have to pay for breaking her heart.

That night, while everyone was sleeping, Ophelia slipped into Rune's home and stood by the side of his bed. She gave herself a few minutes to gaze into his handsome face, and then wondered what it would have been like, had he picked her over Jayla.

Jayla woke up with a mysterious sensation creeping all over her body. She could sense that danger was somewhere close by, but she couldn't detect who it was aimed at.

She sat up and tried to become more aware of her surroundings. She then pressed her index and middle fingers into her temples and concentrated on the eerie sensation. And while she couldn't pin-point the source, she was able to find the direction that it was coming from.

When she was ready, Ophelia opened her hand and blew a strange powder into Rune's face. She wore a look of great amusement as she watched him cough and fan away the strange aroma near his nose, and then he rolled over and tried to go back to sleep. Once he had settled down, Ophelia ascended to her full height, spread her hands out in front of her, and proceeded to say the hideous words which would end his life.

Rum Deedle Bi Nu
Now I know just what to do
Realizing that you will never be mine
Your life on earth has no more time

Fobra Diba Icka So
It's now time for you to go
Die my friend and be in pain
For loving you was quite insane

Rune's eyes sprang wide open, while he suffocated in the same air which he used to be able to breathe.

Jayla could feel the terrifying emotions skipping through the airwaves, and she could also feel that Ophelia was somehow attached to this devastating trouble. She was quite familiar with Ophelia's bad temper, and because of what had happened a few hours ago, Jayla hoped that the fear which was rippling all around her, had nothing to do with Rune.

As Jayla concentrated on his soul, her mind was telling her that he was at home. She was still restless and suspected that something dreadful was happening, but because she could tell that he was in bed and sleeping, she tried to make herself go back to sleep.

Ophelia watched with delight from behind her evil eyes, and once Rune was gone from this world, her lips formed into an evil, satisfying smile. She then slipped out of his room and went back to her own home.

After Ophelia put on her nighty, she laid in her bed and devised another plan – one to make Jayla regret the day when Rune first laid his eyes on her.

By morning, the jealous red-head knew the exact punishment that she would dish out. Because excitement ruled her heart, rather than have breakfast, Ophelia gathered the ingredients needed to make her potion.

Even before her eyes were open, Jayla could feel something unsettling lurking in the air. It was different from the night before, but it was still mean and decidedly undeserved. Furthermore, she could tell that it was going to affect her in a very bad way.

It was Jayla's turn to be scared and she wished that she had not been alone. Her mother was busy at a witch's coven, but it was soothing that they could always communicate through mental telepathy.

Jayla took a deep breath while she sat crossed-legged on her bed, and tried to gather her thoughts before she told her mother what was happening. When she was finished describing the horrid details of the story, her mother responded.

"My beautiful child", she began. Petra May's voice seemed to whisper on the wind as it breezed through Jayla's home. "I can feel the black cloud which you are speaking of, and it frightens me to no end." She hesitated, as if to gather her own thoughts, and then she continued. "Beware of the heinous act that is about to touch our lives, and please let Chevelle know everything that is happening. In her 189 years as a witch, she has seen and heard it all, and she will know how to help you."

"I will go right away", *Jayla promised, as she jumped off the bed.*

"And I will make my way back to your side", *her mother replied.*

Jayla's eyes were brimming with tears as her heart filled with sorrow. "Thank you, mama", she sighed. Jayla instantly felt the loving spirit of her mom all around her, and both of them were comforted with the fact that they would see each other before the sun fell on the earth that night.

Petra May went back to the meeting, but made excuses for why she needed to leave earlier than she had planned. Minutes later, she placed a *speed spell on her vehicle, and began to drive home.

After getting dressed, Jayla ran to the adorned home of Chevelle Boda. She was not the oldest person in the village, but she was indeed the wisest, and after Jayla revealed what was in her

---

*a speed spell enables the driver to hit all the green lights, while magically moving all the other cars out of the way.

heart, the kind lady was all too eager to give her some sound advice.

The first thing the kind old witch did, was to light a large black candle. She placed it on the small end table beside her favorite chair, and it seemed to give the room an enormous glow of warmth and protection.

Jayla knew that this candle had the power to neutralize negative energies which were cast upon a victim from outside forces, and when she saw Chevelle light it up and make it the focal point in the room, this gave her great comfort. She was beginning to relax now, and sat herself down by Chevelle's feet.

"Because we are gypsies and witches, we don't dabble in black magic - only white", the older lady stated strongly. "Most of us start out to do white magic, but if we are doing it with the wrong intentions, it will turn grey very quickly."

Jayla nodded as if she understood everything that Chevelle was saying. And as her eyes widened and her mind opened, she was ready to absorb even more knowledge.

Chevelle continued. "If evil finds its way into the spell, the magic will turn black –

that's not what we do." Suddenly, the wise woman stopped speaking and appeared to be staring off into space. It appeared as if she was looking at nothing, but in reality, she was visualizing the emotional storm that was brewing off in the distance. When she blinked, Jayla knew that Chevelle had found the culprit.

"I know the one who wants to harm you, and while I can't reverse the potion that she is conjuring up, I can alter its route." Chevelle stood up and went to look for her seventy-five year old book of magic. Once she found it, she returned to her great grandmother's over-sized rocker and sat down.

She muttered as she flipped through the pages, and stopped when she found what she had been looking for. "Here it is", she sighed happily.

Jayla lifted her body off the back of her heels and was peering into the book like a cat full of curiosity. She couldn't read the words because it was in a different language, but there were pictures which she could follow, and they almost made sense.

While she softly mumbled everything that she was reading, the overgrown fingernail of Chevelle's left index finger, was floating under the words in the spell.

It was incoherent to Jayla, but she knew that Chevelle was well-aware of what she was doing.

On the other side of the village, Ophelia was stirring her poisonous mixture through the rapidly boiling bubbles. The scent was appalling, and anyone who dared enter the twenty foot radius, immediately covered their noses and retreated. This made Ophelia laugh, for the brew still had another hour to boil before it would achieve its crowning glory.

Chevelle stood up and reached her arms out in front of her. With her eyes closed and all of her concentration placed on the correct enunciation of the words, she cast the pre-alteration spell.

> Riker Duker Thomas Dee
> Listen to what I say to thee
> When once we are ready,
> we shall begin
> To alter the spell and help her therein
>
> Keep Jayla alive, but adjust her fate
> There really is no time to wait
> Ophelia must suffer for
> her dastardly deed
> For we don't tolerate hatred and greed

A bright light flashed in every corner of the house, bringing with it a source of energy that changed into something which Chevelle could carry in her hands. It was round and smaller than a tennis ball, but it contained more power than the Roman Catholic Church did, back in Medieval Times.

As Chevelle placed the gleaming ball into the large pocket in the front of her dress, Jayla thanked her dear friend for helping. She then bid the older woman good-bye. But just before she closed the door, she turned and added, "I pray that you will feel the malice when it comes close, and that you will watch out for me."

Chevelle smiled and nodded, for she loved Jayla and would never let any harm come to her. "I will, my child. Never fear."

Jayla watched the old woman wink with both eyes, and then she made her way home.

After entering the small familiar building, she closed and locked the front door. After placing a protection spell around her home, Jayla had nothing more to do but wait, and for the first time in her life, she felt quite helpless.

"It will be alright, my child", Lemnor whispered, from somewhere off in the distance.

Jayla held her breath and hoped that her father was right.

"Always beware, though", he continued. "There will be some precarious moments which you will have to step through, but please know that you will overcome them with the help of my undying love."

Jayla nodded while her face lit up. "Thank you. That makes me feel better." She inhaled some air until her lungs were full, and then exhaled it as slowly as possible.

The minute Jayla left her side, Chevelle began walking around the village. After explaining the situation to all who would listen, she enlisted their help.

Petra May could feel her daughter's anxiety rising, and she whispered from her heart so that only Jayla could hear. "I'm on my way, darling."

Jayla suddenly felt enveloped inside of her mother's warm hug. It was a safe and calm place to be, but she knew it would not last long; danger was coming and she needed to be mentally prepared for Ophelia's arrival.

Ophelia had been stirring the liquid in a clockwise manner, and once the potion was ready, she took the large ladle out and placed it on the counter. She then focused her entire attention on the image of Jayla's face, while pointing into the belly of the hot pot. As she moved her finger counter clockwise around the outside perimeter, she began to hum.

It wasn't long before the molecules in the quivering energy of the icky substance had been changed, and the frightening bubbles were beginning to calm down. Once the potion was as still as ice, Ophelia recited the words to her spell;

Do as I say and not as I do
Today is the day which you will rue
You will die before the sun goes down
And I can then wear the crown

For I am the queen of all I see
And I rule the way I want things to be
You have been nothing but
a thorn in my side
And this is something, I
can no longer abide

A large explosion of light hovered over the potion, and then crystal-like drops sprinkled back into the pot. Ophelia smiled, for she now knew that the potion was ready.

Ophelia wiped her hands down the sides of her pants, and while continuing to picture Jayla in her mind, she whispered, "I can't wait to tell you about your bleak future." Ophelia threw her head back and cackled with joy, for she was anxious to see the surprised look which will arise on Jayla's face.

Because of her uncanny abilities, Jayla could hear the echoes of the gruesome laughter off in the distance, and it made her skin ache with worry.

"Don't trust her!" a male voice ordered from somewhere in the room. The tone was loud and sad, and begged Jayla to listen.

Jayla was certain that it was Rune's voice, but how could that be? "Rune?" she called, as she looked around. She was hopeful that he might be hiding behind a couch or a wall.

"I'm here in spirit, but I don't have much time", he said softly. "My last wish was to give you a warning."

Jayla's eyes widened in horror as she realized that Ophelia had done something to hurt Rune. The mere thought that he might have died unnecessarily, made her want to cry, but she knew that she needed to stay strong because she might be the next one to be harmed.

Serena Storm, Gwendolyn White, and Elwin Depraysie were among the witches and gypsies who stood proud beside Chevelle. And with her sister, Iba Boda, also by her side, she was now fully prepared to amend the curse which Ophelia was about to cast.

As is the rule, none of them could come in between Ophelia and Jayla, even though they all wanted to. And because it is well-known that there is power in numbers, they were all there to give this adjustment spell extra strength.

As they all waited nearby, none of them could show themselves until the misery had been placed upon Jayla's head. Carpathia Crow would then recite the despicable incantation, so that Jayla could have a chance at happiness... however fleeting.

The poisonous brew was ready, and so was Ophelia. With extreme caution, she removed a little more than a thimble of the potion and placed it into a small glass container. After setting a lid on the top, she made her way to Jayla's home.

"Jayla!" she called, once she had arrived. "Can you come out for a second?"

Jayla was already a bundle of nerves when she heard Ophelia calling to her. She had placed a protection spell around the perimeter of her home, but she knew that she would not be safe once she stepped off her property. She also knew that she couldn't avoid what was about to happen, so she did as Ophelia asked.

Once the front door opened, Jayla took a deep breath, and then got herself ready to face her future. "Ophelia", she stated calmly. She was quite intimidated, but showed her friend an unwavering stance. "It's nice to see you."

"I've come to give you something." Ophelia's voice was soft and almost childlike, and the personality she chose to bring forward, begged Jayla to trust her. "Can you come all the way outside?"

Even without Jayla's witchly power, she knew that something grave was about to fall upon her shoulders. She could have prevented what was going to happen, but in her heart, she couldn't believe that her friend would ever do her any harm.

Jayla stepped over the threshold, and then made her way over to where Ophelia was standing. Her eyes were wide and held great concern, while her heart was pounding in her chest; she could sense, that whatever happened next, was going to brutally impact the rest of her life.

"Look! I have a peace offering for you!" she lied. Ophelia held her hand out and showed Jayla the shiny glass container. "Isn't it pretty?"

Jayla leaned forward and peered into Ophelia's open hand. And while she could see something shiny resting there, she wasn't sure what was inside the object.

As Ophelia was handing the vial to her friend, she cleverly loosened the lid so that the liquid could leak out. "It's yours!" she cheered.

As Jayla reached out to receive it, every bone and muscle in her body shivered with fright. "Don't touch it!" a familiar voice screamed. To her surprise, the voice in question had come from inside of her own head.

As Ophelia released the object, the evil gypsy knew full-well that the poison would seep into Jayla's skin quite quickly, and that she would die within minutes.

Chevelle and the others were wide-eyed and anxious, as they held their breath and watched as the gruesome scene played out. And just as the cylinder landed into Jayla's hand, Carpathia stood up and spit out the words which would change the original path of Ophelia's spell.

Dum Deedle Do and Dumb Deedle So
From the skies above, I
think you should know
Not all will be what it looks like to you
Because death is not what Jayla is due

Dial back the power on the evil spell
Bounce it off the Lilura Bell
Ophelia should be punished,
and times three
For all she has done, so mote it be

With perfect timing, Chevelle reached into her pocket and then slammed the sparkly ball of magic to the ground. After it exploded, she stood back and watched as thousands of strands of colored energy, snaked its way through the air.

The ground shook with such a mighty roar, that it felt as if the earth had suddenly stopped turning. Surprisingly, the shock of the intense movement only affected Jayla and Ophelia, and it caused them to fall to the ground with a great thud.

From just out of reach, everyone watched as the heavens opened up and shot a thunder bolt of lightning towards Ophelia's heart. This knocked her unconscious, but the force of the jolt woke Jayla up.

"Where am I?" she questioned, after she opened her eyes.

The elders gathered around her, comforting her with murmurs of sadness, and telling her all that had happened. They also advised her of her sad future, and then instructed her on how she could still live a full life.

While Jayla was perplexed and angry with what Ophelia had done, she understood the reasons why, and tried to forgive her. With Chevelle's help, Jayla stood up, and after thanking each person for what they had contributed, she let a few of them walk her home.

Ophelia was out cold for at least an hour, and when she woke up, she was completely dazed and confused.

Melusina Gravestone opted to stay with the uncaring teen, and after Ophelia opened her eyes, the much older witch was only too happy to tell her of her dilemma.

Ophelia had grown up under the watchful eye of Melusina, and she had always had a sweet relationship with her. Today though, there was nothing sweet in Melusina's eyes, and it gave Ophelia a huge cause to worry.

Melusina stood up and towered over the heartless girl, and while waving her pale bony hands in the air, she dished out Ophelia's punishment.

"You have brought enormous sadness and fear to all those around you, so you are now doomed to a life of silence. From this moment on, I declare that you will not be able to speak, and you will no longer be able to hear what people are saying to you."

A clap of thunder smashed through the air, enforcing the power of the ruling. In that same instance, Ophelia's hearing and ability to speak, were stripped from her list of senses.

Melusina looked up and spread her arms out to the sides as she continued. "Because you have taken a life, we will be taking yours." *Her voice was loud and strong, and booming across many acres of land.* "You are hereby banished from this village, and any other village for up to one thousand miles away."

The girl's eyes widened with fear, as she brought her hands up to her ears and touched them from every angle. She could feel the skin, but she could not hear her own hair crunch between her finger tips. As she tried to speak, her lips moved but nothing came out. It was so heartbreaking, that Ophelia could feel her soul wilting from sadness.

Melusina lowered her arms and stared into Ophelia's young face.

Ophelia was embarrassed by the look in Melusina's cold and uncaring eyes, and she suddenly became painfully shy.

As the young girl struggled with the reality of her fate, the older witch watched unsympathetically.

Ophelia was confused that the woman who she had always identified as her friend, was being entertained by her plight. When she could taste the hatred which seethed through her veins, she no longer wanted to be in Melusina's company. And because she had been told to leave, that's what she was going to do.

According to Melusina, Ophelia was last seen sobbing while running away as fast as she could. It gave the older woman no joy to see the distraught teenager fading into the distance, and she knew that she needed to stay brave and still.

By the time Petra May had come home, Jayla had said thank you to all who had helped her survive her difficult ordeal. And as soon as she saw her mother's face, Jayla raced into her open arms and cried difficult tears against the older woman's matronly chest.

It was now time for Petra May to say thank you, and she did so with a great deal of gratitude and love. She then took her daughter home to rest.

Early the next morning, it was decreed by her mother and the elders, that Jayla would be taught the spell of transference. Months later, once she had perfected the deadly incantation, the village filled with male strangers. These men arrived under the pretense that they would be married off to the girl of their choice. In reality, they were there for Jayla to practice on.

It didn't take long before she became quite skilled in the art of moving a dead soul from out of a man's body and getting it to come into her own. The strong group of gypsies and witches were delighted when they could go back to tending their own lives again, but swore to always be there, if and when Jayla ever needed them.

Jayla's memories stopped clouding her brain, for she was now walking into her front door. As she stood in her living room area, she realized that she had been able to live a reasonably normal life, despite the terrible curse which had been placed upon her as a teenager.

Throughout the years, there were many times when Jayla wanted to give up, but she stuck to what had been 'her normal', in hopes that there might be an end to this unfair lifestyle, sometime in her future. Until then, she almost enjoyed the marginal rush of adrenaline which she received, whenever she performed the transference spell. It didn't give her a high, so much as it was a sense of achievement; taking a bad element out of this world to allow herself the beauty and time which she obtained in return.

The beautiful gypsy-witch tilted her head downward, and silently wished that her mother and Chevelle were still there to see how she was doing. Sadly, they had died a few months apart, and not that long ago. Those experiences had crippled Jayla and left her heartbroken to the max, but they also made her stronger and more defiant about what Ophelia had done to her.

As Jayla lifted her head up and looked around her living room, she took a long deep breath of air into her lungs. As she exhaled, she decided that she was proud of all that she had accomplished in the past few years, and she would not look backwards with any regret.

Jayla took a long moment to roll her neck from side-to-side and front-to-back. She shook her shoulders and arms until they felt loose, and then, while in a standing position, she raised each knee to her chest, ten times each. Once her muscles were limber and the blood was flowing through her body at a quicker speed than before, she felt more prepared for what lay ahead.

CHAPTER FOUR

October 24, 2000

The word 'straight' was still embedded in Roger's mind when he woke up from his nap, and it didn't take long until he remembered that Marlowe's face had appeared in his dreams.

Marlowe Perkins had been his best friend throughout childhood, but he was also someone who Roger had learned to hate with a vengeance.

As Roger stood up and got ready to go to the cafeteria for supper, memories of his teen years flooded his mind.

From elementary school to middle school, Roger had been in love with a little girl named, Molly Waters. They were neighbours, but because she was three years younger than Roger and Marlowe, Marlowe only knew of her brother, Colton.

In front of Colton and Marlowe, Roger acted boyish and tough like they did, but when he was alone with Molly, he was timid and playful, and he did whatever she wanted them to do.

To him, their chemistry was magical and their personalities were so in sync, you'd think they had been born as identical twins. To Molly, he was a playmate – nothing else. To him, they only had eyes for each other.

Roger smiled as he recalled each and every one of the vivid details of their time together, but it didn't take long before his emotions got the better of him. Suddenly, he recalled that fateful day when everything in his life changed, and an overwhelming anger quickly took the place of his modest reminiscing.

It started with Roger welcoming Molly to her new environment:

She was a freshman in high school and he was telling her which hallways to use for 'this and that'. He was smiling from ear-to-ear as he reveled in the joy of having her at 'his school'. And because she was now 15 years old, he couldn't wait until the day when he could ask her out on a date.

When Marlowe saw Roger talking and laughing with the cute girl, he became full of pubescent curiosity. After he turned the collar up on his shirt and smoothed his hair with the palm of his hands, he walked over to find out who she was. Even before their quick introduction, Marlowe could tell that there was something going on between Roger and Molly, so he made sure to get in between them.

Marlowe exaggerated his strut and oozed his powerful charm towards the beautiful blonde haired girl. "Well, hello."

Molly turned her body all the way around, and she smiled with the look of a teenage girl who was about to meet her famous singing idol. "Hello", was all that came out of her mouth. She was young and impressionable, and she immediately fell under his spell. Seconds later, she was giggling as she graciously accepted his advances – much to Roger's dismay.

"Marlowe, this is Molly. Molly, this is Marlowe." Roger was nervous about making the introductions, but he wasn't sure why.

After a minute of small talk, and the flash of electricity which sparked between the two new friends, Roger watched as Marlowe put his arm around Molly's shoulder. His lower jaw had popped open and his blood was beginning to boil. He was stunned to the core and now frozen to the spot.

Molly couldn't believe that a boy like Marlowe could be interested in her, so she batted her eyes and played right into his hands.

"I'm going to show her around the school", Marlowe insisted, even though he could see that this was making his friend angry.

Roger's eyes widened, because he saw that as his job. He had been her friend for as long as he could remember, and he had always thought that they would end up together.

Roger was beginning to panic, for he felt like his whole world was crumbling right before his eyes and there was nothing he could do to stop it.

"See you around!" Marlowe called, as he guided Molly to her first class. He had the look of the devil on his face, and he took great pleasure in Roger's downcast expression.

Watching Marlowe walk off with Molly as if they were a couple, sent Roger on a spiral road to emotional hell. All the muscles in his chest tightened and he suddenly felt like he couldn't breathe. He knew that he wasn't blinking, and when the bell rang and he should have been going to his first class, he stayed right where he was.

Even though that took place many years ago, Roger lowered his head in grief; he remembered that day and that moment so well. He was surprised to find that the pain was still as fresh now as it was back then, and that's probably why he tried not to think about her or Marlowe.

Marlowe was tall and sturdy, and always came off as a tough guy - a Grade A bully who never backed down from a battle of fists. Roger knew that he would never be able to fight Marlowe and win, even if he called upon Colton and his friends to help. To him, his only option was to keep quiet like a mouse and avoid any trouble.

A scowl grew across Roger's adult face, because he hated how he used to be. Since high school, he has tried so hard to push all the elements of his former self into a small ball, and keep it locked in a forgotten corner of his heart. Unfortunately, today they were leaping out of their protected vault, hoping to be noticed.

Roger went home from school early that day, and because he couldn't bear to see the two of them together again, he told his mother that he was sick. This had him in bed for the rest of the week. But on his first day back at school, when he saw Marlowe and Molly standing at her locker, he couldn't believe the amount of emotional and physical pain that was swimming in his belly.

Before they could see him, he ran out of the giant front doors of the large brick building, and cried all the way home. He was only 15 years old, and not only had his heart been ripped out of his chest, but he felt like a first class fool.

It didn't take long before Roger dropped out of school and began wandering the streets, and he soon found some new friends to hang out with. They were a little older than he was and a little rough around the edges, and most of them were pretty shady characters. Before too long, they had taught him how to smoke, do drugs, live on the streets, and steal in order to survive.

From then on, Roger had unknowingly started his education in and out of the prison walls.

All this talk about Molly was making Roger ache with misery; he didn't realize how much he had missed her until that very moment. Throughout the years, he had tried not to think about her, but now that he was getting out and he had vowed to go straight, he decided that it was time to check in on her.

Roger had kept tabs on Marlowe and Molly through the neighbourhood grapevine, and he knew that they had gotten married after she had finished high school.

According to Roger's mother, who had visited him once every few months or so for the past two years, Marlowe now owned a small business.

Roger was well-aware that he tuned out a lot of what his mother had said, because she could blubber on and on about things that he didn't care about. But he just remembered her talking about Marlowe, so he would use that as an opening when he called him later in the day.

Truth be told, it was really Molly who Roger wanted to see and know about, but because he needed Marlowe's help, he would have to renew their friendship first.

Roger shivered with awareness at the thought that he would get to see Molly again. As he sat on his bed, he could envision her enchanting smile. If he listened closely, he could almost hear her laughter.

It was always a full body response, with arm movement and tears, and he usually found himself laughing right along with her.

His mind wandered, and although he knew she would be older, he wondered if she still looked the same.

Roger imagined how his life would have turned out, had he and Molly ended up as a couple. That uplifting thought was deflated by the realization that Marlowe got to sleep with her every night, and it threw Roger into an unpleasant mood.

Deep-seeded anger was starting to seep into his soul, as the ugly images of them being together, flowed into his mind. Roger closed his eyes tight and shook his head no, because he needed to get those images out of his brain. He knew he had to put all of his faith and energy into the fact that Marlowe could help him when he got on the outside. But once the pieces of the puzzle were put into their proper places, Roger would then make sure that Marlowe got what he deserved. After that, Roger would work on making Molly *his* bride.

Now that the plan for the rest of his life had been created, Roger felt better. And just as

Roger sighed with relief, a buzzer rang loudly to announce the opening of the cell doors.

As he stood up and stepped out of his cramped quarters, he smiled at the thought of getting out of jail. At the sound of the second buzzer, Roger stood tall and stiff, and he inhaled a rather large amount of air into his lungs. On command, he turned his body to the left and exhaled slowly, and then began the long trek to the cafeteria.

As Roger walked in a single-file along with the other inmates, Jayla's face appeared before him in glorious color. "Oh, God!" he stated wildly. "I forgot all about her!" He took a second to think, and then he made his decision. "I'll have to call her when I get back from supper, and I'll call Marlowe first thing in the morning."

During the next twenty-five minutes, Roger's mind worked on how to break up with Jayla. He had no intention of keeping her in his life after he got out of jail, even though she was different; out of all the girls he had met while being behind bars, she was the one who he liked the most.

Every time Roger got locked up, he went online and contacted women through the Prison Chat Lines. He picked a new girl for every prison sentence he had, and disposed of them just before he got out. While they dated, the women brought him baked goods and visited with him often, so he put up with their unpolished personalities and trivial conversations.

He used these women for sex and to relieve the boredom, and once he was out of prison, he deleted their contact information and they never spoke again.

To this day, Roger did not know any of their names or what any of them looked like, and that's how he wanted his life to continue.

When supper was over, Roger made his way over to the lounge area. To his surprise, the line to use the phone was long, but because this was important, Roger decided to wait.

Roger had purposely not told Jayla that he was going before the Parole Board, because he honestly felt that it was none of her business. To him, she, and the many others before her, had voluntarily taken on the role of being his girlfriend. These ladies didn't get to have his money or the rest of his life, and he made sure to disappear the minute he was set free.

So what was the advantage to being Roger's lover? "None", he laughed when he was asked. "I'm the only one who has benefits."

Roger's mouth broke into a Cheshire cat's smile as he inched his way to the front of the line. He was very happy about starting a new life, and he couldn't wait to see Molly again. "But first things first", he whispered with a sinister lilt in his voice. He then concentrated on how he was going to break up with Jayla.

Roger knew it wasn't going to be easy, for a part of him really liked her, but if he wanted to have any kind of a relationship with Molly, he had to take Jayla out of his life.

In his mind's eye, Roger could see Jayla's beautiful face, and he could feel her full lips and soft cheeks as if they were kissing in that exact moment. Unfortunately, this interesting mental image was making it harder for him to dismiss her.

Under any other circumstances, he would have liked to keep Jayla in his life, but if there was even the slightest chance that he could be with Molly, then he needed to tell her good-bye. Still, Jayla was a very sensuous and exciting woman. What made it worse, is that if he had a check list for everything that he ever wanted in a partner, Jayla would fit each and every item.

Roger's mind drifted back to the moment when they met, and he fondly remembered how his breath sucked into the back of his throat the first time he saw her.

All eyes were on her when she walked into the visitor's area, including those of the guards and the cleaning staff. She was tall and walked with her head held high, and acted genuinely pleased when they were introduced.

He was in awe, and couldn't believe what an absolute vision of loveliness Jayla was. With wide eyes, and his jaw lowered and almost touching his chest, he watched her nod at a few people as she slowly moved her voluptuous body towards his.

After she sat down, they shared an unending and easy banter, and she often brought her hand up to stifle her girly giggles. The sound of her laughter was enchanting, and it made everyone around her feel warm. He loved the enjoyment he saw in her eyes, especially when they met his. And when they said good-bye, and she walked away in long, purposely seductive strides, everyone stopped talking and stared in her direction.

Roger felt an electrifying shudder reverberate throughout his entire body when she left, but it stopped when a gentle nudge from a nearby guard, brought him back from his daydreams.

Because of Jayla, Roger quickly became the envy of his fellow inmates, but they also joked that it wouldn't last. "You're far too ugly for her!" they teased cruelly. But when her visits became habitual, they all backed off in shock.

Roger moaned with full recollection of how exciting her body felt against his – clothed or naked. And when they finally got to have their first conjugal visit, he couldn't believe how skilful she was.

Her touch was soft and clever. Her movements were well-practised, and he could tell that she was capable of even more than she was delivering. She was always competent, and seemed fulfilled of what she was doing to him and with him. Plus, there was no doubt that she gave him more than she received.

Roger found himself blushing at the memory of their first time together, and he could suddenly feel a bulge growing behind his zipper. He shook his left leg in order to reduce the size of his thickening member, because he knew full-well that he needed to change his thoughts to a different topic, or receive the unwanted attention from one of his prison buddies. And as much as he didn't want *that* to happen, his priceless memories of her carried on without his permission, because she truly was a very captivating female.

Her tongue explored him as if it was meant to dance all over his body, and she never tired of any of the activities that defined the word 'sex'.

She was like an animal; she was eager to please, her mood automatically changed with her environment, and while she purrs when she's happy, she seems to be the type who can strike you dead with one strong look.

Roger was third in line from the phone now, and his mind continued to wander. After thinking about Jayla in such a passionate way, he questioned if getting rid of her was indeed the right thing to do. But then what would happen to Molly? He couldn't be with her if Jayla was his girlfriend.

As tough as this decision was, Roger knew that he could only choose one of them.

He pulled out the piece of paper with Jayla's number and flattened it out with his fingers. 'Should he call?' he wondered. The number was right there, and the quarter was burning a hole in the palm of his other hand.

"Next!" the guard shouted sharply.

Roger only had one man in front of him now, and his nerves were starting to fray. His mind was flipping with erratic thoughts and irrational fears, while his ears seemed to have developed an acute ability to hear things that should have seemed impossible.

A coin dropped from somewhere behind him and it made him jump, and in order to look like nothing was wrong, Roger pasted a fake smile on his tense lips. He was clearly nervous about making the wrong decision, and the awkward situation made him want to throw up.

Time was ticking away, and the more he contemplated the phone call, the more Roger decided that he really did want to be with Molly.

While he trusted that Jayla would understand, a part of him wished that he could keep Jayla on the side - even for a little while longer. Sadly, the wiser part of his brain knew that that wouldn't work.

How could Roger possibly know, that breaking it off with Jayla would not only end their relationship, but that it would end his life?

CHAPTER FIVE

August 30, 1999

Jayla was mentally and physically exhausted by the time she finally reached her home. Although she wanted to, she didn't dare rest, for Jayla knew that her time was limited.

As she stroked her cat's fur with one hand, Jayla logged onto the Prison Chatline with the other. As her eyes scanned all the profile pictures, her mind sifted through all the men's information with a fine-toothed comb. Eventually she had been able to reduce the long list of criminals, to one stunning man.

Roger Casem would be getting out of prison, around the same time when Jayla would need to have another soul inhabit her body. He was tall, he had a dark past, and from his history, she concluded that he would be able to give her the power and life force which she craved.

She reached out first, and they established a bond quite quickly. This was no surprise to Jayla, for she left nothing to fate. Before the month was over, emails were sent, phone calls were made, and they had been able to meet face-to-face in the prison's humble and undecorated meeting room.

She had used all of her physical and mental powers to ensure that he would be undeniably attracted to her, and it made her heart swell when he seemed pleased by what he saw. A conjugal visit was scheduled for a few weeks later, and it was then when Jayla knew that she had her newest conquest, tightly secured in the palm of her hand.

After she got home from their two hours of perfectly orchestrated lovemaking, a sinister smile spread quickly across her full lips. As she marked the date of his release on her kitchen calendar, she sighed with total gratification. "Once you are free from the daunting chains of this life, I will take your wretched soul as my own", she chuckled in a very ominous manner.

Jayla took a step back to admire the large red heart on the day and month in question. As her eyes lit up, her heart skipped a cheerful beat, and the amusement of Roger's demise echoed joyfully all around her.

CHAPTER SIX

October 24, 2000

While Roger was waiting to place the call to announce the end of their relationship, Jayla was in her large and colorful vegetable garden. She was selecting ripe ingredients for that night's supper, when an unsettling cold rush, enveloped her entire being. Her innate ability sensed that it was Roger who was thinking about her, but she didn't know why. Jayla stopped what she was doing and concentrated solely on him.

She could hear him saying her name as if it was blowing in the wind. However, she couldn't make out the entire sentence, because the emotions attached to the words kept wavering back and forth. Unfortunately, this was making it hard for her to interpret what he was trying to tell her.

It was all so frustrating and she didn't want to guess at what he wanted, so she decided that there was nothing she could do until she spoke with him directly.

Roger was rehearsing what he was going to say, but he truly wished that he didn't have to say good-bye to her.

"Next!" the guard shouted.

After standing in line for 22 minutes, it was finally Roger's turn to use the phone. As he picked up the receiver and dialed the first number, a ghastly chill washed over his body.

Jayla Remic was very pretty, of average height and weight, and she wore brightly colored clothing that she made herself. She was one of the first women to answer his ad on the Prison Chat Lines last year, but she neglected to disclose the fact that she had magical powers.

Roger found no need to ask her or any of the ladies any questions pertaining to their background. He also didn't ask what they did for a living, how old they were, if they had any children, or where they were born. All he wanted was a companion for a short while, but it had to be the right companion. For example: The girls had to have large breasts, a nicely shaped bottom, long hair, and they should be clean in appearance. He then used them for as much as they were willing to give, and Jayla was no exception.

Little did Roger know that Jayla had purposely sought him out instead of the other way around, for she needed him more than he needed her. She had an agenda to follow, so she gladly tolerated everything that happened between them - no matter how disgusting the situation might seem in that moment.

All of the men she picked held no importance to her; it was only their soul that she was after. And once she received the very core of their being, their bodies were disposed of while her life went forward.

As the clock ticked away, the uncontrollable feeling of Roger being all around her, grew stronger and stronger. From the deepest essence of her psyche, Jayla could tell that he was consumed with a need to talk with her, but why? 'Was he hurt?' she wondered. She quickly decided that he better not be, because she needed to be there when he drew his last breath.

Meanwhile, Roger continued to dial one number after another.

Jayla could feel his persistence, but she didn't know why. As she tried to figure it out, her mind went into total panic alert and she began to pace back and forth while wringing her hands. She wished that she could call and ask him if everything was ok, but she knew the rules - no phone calls were allowed from the outside on the weekdays.

The last number was dialed and now Roger was waiting for the lines to connect.

When her phone rang, Jayla nearly jumped out of her skin. As she reached for the receiver, she was immediately aware of who was on the other end. "Hello?"

"Hi, Jayla. It's Roger", he said quietly. His voice was soft, but his words were cautioning her to hear every syllable. "We need to talk."

Everything in Jayla's body began to coil around her, and her fright was growing tighter and tighter by the second. "I'm listening", she said. Her breath caught in her throat, her eyes went wide, and she could feel the muscles in her heart begin to pound a stronger beat.

Roger closed his eyes and lowered his head, as he searched for the right way to say good-bye. But after hearing her sweet voice, he suddenly didn't want her to go away. This confused him because he'd never had trouble dumping a girl before today.

"Roger?" Jayla could hear the background noise of cell block 39, and she was getting the impression that Roger was struggling with something of grave importance. "Are you still there? Is everything ok?" She could feel his apprehension, but didn't understand what it was all about.

"Uh, yah", he mumbled. For some reason, the words which he had rehearsed, wouldn't come out of his mouth.

Roger didn't know what it was about Jayla that was so different, but he suddenly had trouble letting her go. But if he wanted to be with Molly, he knew he would have to.

Roger cleared his throat and began again. "Jayla", he said, as he tried to add more power to his voice. He could feel a wave of awkwardness rise up around him, and he knew that he needed to get a firm grip of what was supposed to happen. After he made himself stand tall, he took a deep breath, and then let the words tumble out of his mouth. "I have something to talk to you about."

Jayla became horrified, and it was in that instant when everything became clear to her. 'Was he trying to tell me that it was over?' she wondered.

Anger was her first emotion, denial was her second. 'He will not leave me!' her mind screamed, and she immediately conjured up a mighty spell.

A second later, Jayla had gathered up all of her power and was now focusing on Roger's face. Her shoulders hunched forward, her eyebrows pushed together, and there was now a wild red color glistening in her extraordinarily shiny eyes. She took an enormous breath while her eyelids narrowed, and the fingers on her right hand arched and quickly spread apart. Her hand then flew to within an inch of the mouth piece of the receiver.

Not surprisingly, a disturbing tingling feeling began playing all over the shapely body of the gypsy-witch, as she prepared to cast her wicked spell. With her fingers dancing in the air and in a voice that was utterly gruesome, she muttered an incantation of innate forgetfulness towards his ears.

> With every cell in your body and soul
> You will forget what once was your goal
> Remember the love attached to my name
> And everything will remain the same

There was an immediate moment of ultimate confusion that followed, for while Roger remembered dialing a phone number, he had no memory of who he was calling.

After the incantation left her lips, everything in Jayla's face and body softened. "It's very nice to hear from you, Roger", she said sweetly, but her voice was beckoning him to say good-bye.

Roger was completely dumbfounded. He immediately recognized Jayla's voice, but he wasn't sure why he had called her. "Yah, uh...I think I just wanted to say Hi."

"Well, it's always wonderful to hear from you", she replied. "I'll see you soon, ok?"

"See you soon", he agreed. He hung up the phone and sauntered back to his cell in a daze, not fully aware of what had just happened.

As soon as their short but productive call had ended, the anxious woman jumped into action. She immediately dismissed her supper plans, and gathered all of her ingredients in order to concoct a potion to keep Roger close. "I've wasted too much time on you to let you go that easy, my pet", she cackled firmly into the air.

"Now I've got to do what I can, in order to keep you interested."

As the raven-haired beauty stirred her disgusting mixture, she placed her diced ingredients into the big pot. All the while, her insides were awakening with excitement over the prospect of receiving more power. The added bonus was, that she would make Roger regret that he had almost refused anymore of her advances.

With anger rising from the very core of her body, she vowed, "I need your soul and I will have it - with or without your consent."

Roger was the second man who tried to dump her in all her years on Earth, but Jayla was wise enough to know that he probably wouldn't be the last.

"Poor Benny Maverick", she sighed wearily, as her mind drifted back to that time period.

He called her from prison and tried to end their relationship on the phone. Jayla was young, and stunned to the core that this was happening. She cried and begged him to change his mind, but he only laughed at her attempt to use her girlish emotions against him. Once she came to her senses, Jayla fought like crazy for him to agree to one last meeting.

Benny was a conceited bastard, and he expressed great amusement at the thought of her wanting to be with him. After contemplating the idea of using her one more time, he finally gave in. "Sure", he chuckled in an appalling manner. "You can pick me up and drive me to my brother's house. Then you can take the next hour to showing me how much you've missed me."

He was a nasty man who snorted when he laughed, and this made her hate him even more.

Jayla was relieved that he had said yes, and instantly projected the trait of a woman with perfect behavior. "Thank you, sweetheart", she sighed. "I'll see you soon!"

Benny chuckled as he hung up, and wondered if he could finally fulfill his lifelong wish of being the only man in a threesome. Because of how desperate Jayla had sounded on the phone,

Benny had no doubt that she would say yes, which made him glow from extreme happiness.

When the receiver left her tight-fisted hand, Jayla's mood went from pretending to be nice, to being downright angry. The two sides of her brain merged into a battle of wits, as Jayla vowed to be ready for revenge.

Saturday came and Jayla was more prepared than ever. She looked like a high-class hooker, complete with too much make-up and poufy hair, and she posed seductively while she waited for him to walk out of the prison gates.

Benny smiled when he saw her, and because she looked so appetizing, he could feel his 'little me' growing hard.

Jayla ran towards him and wrapped her arms around his thick neck. "Hi, baby", she cooed.

Benny loved the kitschy reunion, and showed his appreciation with a mischievous grin. "Hi, gorgeous." He was happy with what he saw and was now delighted that he had agreed to see her. As he pressed his round body up against hers, his heart began to thump to the rhythm of romance.

Jayla let his sausage-like fingers wander around her body, while she kissed him passionately on the mouth. But at the same time as his fat lips were enjoying the cherry-flavored scent of her shiny lipstick, Jayla couldn't help but smile, for he was secretly being poisoned by the ingredients which the lipstick was made from.

After their lingering hello, Jayla opened the passenger door and suggested that they leave.

Benny loved that she was anxious to begin their lovemaking session, and he grabbed her ass before she got too far away from him. "Oh, baby. I can't wait until we're alone."

Jayla was disgusted that he had seized her right butt cheek, but continued to smile as she walked to the driver's side of the car. "Me, too", she replied in a happy tone. After turning the key, she began to drive down the street.

"Maybe we could pull over to the side of the road and see what happens?" Benny began

fondling himself with his right hand while he uttered the lewd suggestion. When they made eye contact, he moved his eyebrows up and down in a provocative manner, while saturating his unflattering lips with his tongue.

Jayla's entire body cringed at the unappealing sight. "That's a good idea", she replied with fake excitement. She knew that they would be pulling over to the side of the road soon, but not for the reason that he was implying.

"Mmm... Don't I know it!" With his left hand eagerly caressing her upper right thigh, Benny watched out the window for the perfect spot to stop. It didn't take long before he broke out in a sweat and started to feel strange, but he chalked it up to them driving in a quick speed on a gravelly road. As time passed, he began to show signs that he was struggling to breathe.

From out of the corner of her right eye, Jayla watched him with a frosty disregard.

"Something's wrong", he mumbled, through anxiety filled, tiny gasps of breath. His eyes were shockingly wide open, the color of his skin

was more grey than white, and he was pointing to his throat while continually grabbing her arm. "Help me!"

Jayla ignored his pleas, and instead, pressed her foot even harder on the gas pedal.

The end of Benny's life took mere minutes, and his death was slow and painful. Not surprisingly, that made it all more worthwhile to Jayla.

His oversized body had slumped forward in the same moment when she had spotted the perfect area to pull the car over. After she turned the motor off, Jayla walked to the passenger side of the car. She then opened the door and got prepared to chant the spell of transference.

Benny's soul left his body and rushed into hers, as if it had been waiting to do that for a long time.

Jayla felt the new power almost immediately. Minutes later, she even looked and felt better all over. Without hesitating for too long, she shut the passenger door, climbed back into the driver's seat, and then drove them both to the outer edge of the Schilling Forest. And there, in the large clearing, Jayla cooked his limp body, just as she had done with the other inmates. And after it had been burned to a crisp, she took the ashes and buried them in her garden.

A day later, she was back on the Prison Chat Lines to find another victim.

"Poor, Benny", she repeated, as she remembered his last moments. Her sentiment was not sincere in any way, because she truly felt that he had it coming.

Jayla took a minute to blink away all memories of her former victim, and then placed all of her focus on the potion which she was making for Roger to consume.

While Jayla was busy in her kitchen, Roger was laying in his bed. He was confused and was staring up at the ceiling, while contemplating everything that had just happened. And no matter how hard he tried, he couldn't recall what he wanted to talk to Jayla about.

After some time had passed, he decided to forget about her, and instead, placed all of his attention on trying to get hold of Marlowe. It didn't take long before Roger drifted into a deep sleep, and before he knew it, it was morning.

Throughout the night, Jayla had finished cooking up a scary concoction for her emergency visit with Roger. On the stroke of 7am, she had already showered and changed, and was now on her way to see her current victim.

Because she knew that the guards would have a problem with visitors wanting to come into the facility outside of visiting hours, she had devised the perfect way to work around that problem.

Jayla's goodies were baked with a strong wafting agent, so that when anyone raised the cloth, the powerful scent would travel straight to their nostrils. In turn, the odor would render that person to be without the ability to function normally. Their brains would run on automatic pilot, and with no recognition that anything was even wrong. This would give her an hour of free reign to see Roger, and it would allow them to have a much-needed conjugal visit.

As she drove towards the Broken Hill Prison, Jayla had to laugh. "After locking ourselves away for an hour, Roger will clearly stay smitten with me", she stated happily to the air around her.

She parked her vehicle, made her way past the first two sets of guards, and then she began to walk towards the visiting area. It was hard for Jayla not to giggle as she watched everyone who had dared to smell her goodies, move around like zombies. Including Mr. Rylan, the warden's newest assistant, who had been called because Warden Campbell was unavailable.

Mr. Rylan had seen Jayla in the prison at least a dozen times, and he was only too happy to rush to the visitor's area when he was told that she was looking for special permission to see an inmate. Unfortunately, Mr. Rylan didn't stand a chance; once he saw her beauty up close, and after he sniffed the delicious aroma from the delectable muffins, he was under her spell. "Let her through!" he commanded fiercely.

Jayla smiled while batting her bright and captivating eyes in his direction, and then she cooed as she thanked him. She also made it a point to brush up against the front of his body as she walked into the next room, which made Mr. Rylan blush, and have even more inappropriate thoughts about her.

And as Jayla sat down and waited for Roger to arrive, Mr. Rylan politely excused himself and rushed to Warden Campbell's private bathroom. Once he got there, he locked the door. The winded man then took matters into his right hand, and proceeded to entertain himself for the next several minutes.

Roger was shocked to learn that he had received a visitor, but he allowed himself to be escorted to the visiting area. When he arrived, he was more than surprised to see his current girlfriend. "What are you doing here?" he questioned with a bright smile, and in a voice that was an octave higher than he normally spoke.

Jayla could see that he was happy to see her, and this made her smile. "I couldn't wait until Saturday", she stated truthfully.

Roger's eyebrows shot to the top of his forehead. Her statement made him giggle inwardly, because he was being released tomorrow and would not be in jail on Saturday.

Jayla loved that Roger was happy to see her, and she continued with her plan. She pushed the basket of goodies towards him and opened the lid. "I made you something, in hopes that we could spend a little time together", she added softly. "I promise that I will make it worth your while." She slowly ran her tongue around the full circumference of her mouth, in case he didn't understand the meaning of what she was suggesting.

As much as Roger wanted to dismiss it, there was definitely a mutual flare of chemistry between them. But he was suddenly very nervous, and moved his head as he looked fearfully around the room.

Roger knew full well that today was not a visitor's day, plus, conjugal visits had to be planned and approved by the warden.

Jayla could see that disbelief and hesitation were confusing his thoughts, so as she fanned the delicious aroma of the muffins toward his face, she spoke up. "Mr. Rylan said it was ok, if that's what you're worried about."

Jayla had a hunch that Mr. Rylan was keeping himself busy, and that there was no threat that Roger could get hold of him at that moment.

A curious look spread across Roger's face. "He did?" That didn't sound right, and as much as he wanted to bypass the rational part of his mind and believe her, he couldn't.

Her lips parted on a soft, indrawn breath as she leaned towards him. "He did", she stated with total conviction.

Roger was feeling a little more than surprised by all that was happening, and he tilted his head to the side as if to question that Mr. Rylan had actually given his approval.

"Do you want me to prove it to you?" Without waiting for him to answer, Jayla stood up, and by sensuously moving her hips from side to side, she sauntered over to the young officer who had brought Roger into the room. After placing her hand gently against his right cheek, she asked, "Don't you think I deserve to spend a little cuddly time with my man?" She positioned her brightly painted lips next to his and purred like a happy kitten. She then licked his tightly closed lips with the pointed tip of her long tongue, while the inexperienced officer quivered uncontrollably in his freshly-polished boots.

Under the guard's standard uniform was a simple man, with normal physical needs. He was a virgin, but should anyone ask, he was not. He had never kissed a girl before, let alone been this close to a provocative one such as Jayla. So when she patted his cheek with her hand, his skin trembled at her touch. And when her warm tongue caressed his lips, he could feel a small amount of hot liquid spilling into his underwear.

"Of course you do", the officer replied boldly. As he melted into the green pool of her gorgeous eyes, he could feel his body relaxing in a state of warm bliss. A second later, the officer turned and aimed his next words towards Jayla's boyfriend. "Roger! Stand up and let's go!" He whipped out the key to the handcuffs which were tied around Roger's hands, and then ordered the other officer to escort the couple to the honeymoon suite.

"Thank you, sir", Jayla whispered, and then she walked over and stood next to Roger.

As they left the room and walked down the hallway, Roger's head was spinning with how any of this was even possible. But because he was about to get sex in the middle of the week, he wasn't going to object too loudly.

"We're here!" the guard announced happily, once they had arrived at the well-known room.

"Thank you", Jayla murmured towards the young officer, and she gave him a muffin as a reward for his kindness.

The man blushed and tipped his hat as he replied, "You're welcome. You guys have a good time."

Jayla winked in his direction and stated, "Oh, we will, honey." She turned and looked at Roger, and was awakened by the thrill that he still seemed to have an intriguing hint of danger about him.

After the door was closed, Jayla put all of her things down on the nearby chair. After locking eyes with her intendent, she walked towards him. "Alone, at last", she sighed. She wrapped her arms around his neck, and in a playful manner, she touched her nose against his.

Roger was still a little nervous, because it all seemed so surreal. With the way the guards and Mr. Rylan were acting, and now, with how Jayla was being a little more aggressive than usual, it was all quite odd to him.

"I've missed you", she lied. It was quite obvious that she was trying her best to get him aroused, and by the change in his breathing and the slight bulge in his pants, she could see that it was working. Her eyes began a seductive analysis of each and every spot on his face, while her lower body made sure to press up tightly against his.

For a brief moment, he held her gaze, and then he began to feel an offbeat flutter in the pit of his stomach. Because of his renewed interest in Molly, his mind was trying to refuse Jayla's advances. And as much as Roger was fighting the attraction, he was definitely getting turned on.

Jayla could sense Roger's reluctance, so she walked across the 3' squared fleece rug and reached into the basket to retrieve a muffin. "Look what I made for you", she teased. She brought it closer to his eyes and nose so that he couldn't help but be tempted.

Roger took one look at the delectable treat, and he couldn't bear not to have one little bite.

Because Jayla couldn't have him say no, she patted the soft muffin against Roger's lips. Thankfully, this was enough to push him over the edge.

"Fine!" he stated firmly, and he grabbed it with two hands.

Jayla watched him with sheer delight, and she soon found that his ruggedness and surprising aggressive power were enticing her. For a brief moment, she had become lost in the throes of being human. As soon as she realized what was happening, she remembered that she was on a deadly mission and she couldn't veer off track for even a moment. She cleared her head of all nonsense and continued on with her plan.

As she watched his teeth sink into the slightly warm and moist baked item, an infectious grin heated the room. "Eat, my love", Jayla whispered softly, in a slow and encouraging manner.

"It's delicious!" he muttered joyfully, and then he took another bite.

Jayla watched him swallow, and then she relished the fact that he would now be hers for as long as she needed him to be.

Roger felt lightheaded and strange within seconds after the mouthful of moist softness went down his throat, but it was a good strange, and he wasn't sure that he wanted to stop the happy sensations.

Up until that moment, it was as if Roger had been somewhat immune to the crippling aroma of the spiked muffins. But now that the morsels of food were going inside of his body, the magic was able to take control of his thoughts.

"How are you feeling, honey?" Jayla asked, but just by looking into his eyes, she already knew the answer.

Roger tried to speak, but his mind was too confused to form a sentence. He looked down at his hands, and while his fingers looked like a starfish with oddly placed legs, his own body was feeling more relaxed than it had in years.

Roger instantly thought back to the last time when he had felt so spaced out, and it didn't take long for him to decide that it was when he had had a little too much weed. And the more he remembered about that day, the more reason there was to chuckle out loud.

Jayla smiled at the notion that he was now ready to be seduced, so she began the daring act... slowly and very methodically.

Once he understood what she was doing, Roger shouted his approval. "I'm all yours!" He wore a silly smile on his face as he closed his eyes and let his head fall backwards. He automatically placed his feet 18" apart, and spread his arms out to the sides so that she could have better access to whatever she wanted. "Take me!" he declared happily.

Jayla was pleased by his total obedience. After she removed every stitch of clothing from Roger's body, she then removed her own. Once they were both naked, she ordered him to take a step forward, but just enough so that their bodies were almost touching.

Roger was filled with such a happiness, that he was eager to obey her commands with no reluctance.

Having him so close, cluttered Jayla's mind with a hundred thoughts. She was there to ensure that he would not leave her before it was time, and yet, it was now her who did not want him to leave.

Roger could feel the heat of her curvaceous hips all the way down to his toes, and it made him want to plow the primitive field of her body with amazing vigour. He suddenly felt like a super hero who had come, not from the stars, but from a dimensional rift in the galaxy. He felt strong and was poised for capture, but he would accept being her slave, if Jayla asked it to be so.

As they stood tummy-to-tummy, their eyes were locked and pleading for someone to make the first move. Their emotions were running high, while their minds whispered in the universal language that only lovers could understand.

He had an earthy male scent which drove Jayla crazy, while Roger could smell the woman under the delicate perfume. He looked into her eyes and whispered her name, while a breathy little moan escaped through her pouty lips.

Neither had intended to fall in love, but both of them were reeling with thoughts which they couldn't fathom. And though their time together was limited, they remained content to stand in the exquisite harmony of what was about to play out.

'Could it be that Roger was trying to crack the hard shell that I have built all around me?' she wondered unconsciously. Jayla pondered this question and others, as she stared into the enlarged pupils of his stunning eyes.

While they had made love before, Roger's mind confessed that today seemed to be new and very different. This odd and simple notion sent a shiver up his spine, and spread goose bumps to his entire body.

Jayla began breathing in deep, soul-drenching mouthfuls, after realizing that what she was feeling for him in that moment, might be more than just sexual desire. But that would be impossible, for she was not able to have a normal life. Or was she?

When Roger saw her face light up, he searched behind her eyes as his own expression changed to hungry lust. His entire focus was now on making wild and passionate love to the beautiful woman before him, but he wanted to take his time.

Because desire flared in his eyes and sweat was beginning to dot his skin, Jayla bit her lips in order to hold back a whimper. She hadn't counted on getting excited, but she could feel herself letting him have all that he wanted to take.

After they both took another step closer, Jayla could feel his hardness straining toward her. It was aching for release and begging to be touched, and she could see that a little fluid had already leaked out from its round tip.

Roger didn't mind that she had noticed, because in fact, it made him even more anxious to probe the silky heat between her thighs.

They stood silent as their breath mingled, and then moved quickly and worked as a collective unit. They each brought their hands forward and laced their fingers firmly together. Their eyes were now locked and their thoughts had become one; they both couldn't wait to get immersed in the sexual heat of animal gratification.

In a move he'd never made before in his life, Roger expressed an interest in wanting to press her body up against the wall. Without waiting for her to reply, he raised her hands up high in the air and tried to walk their bodies across the room.

Jayla shook her head no, for she wanted to use the double-sized bed. To ensure that he would comply, she buried her face into the soft curve of his neck and kissed him in a way that removed his free will.

Roger closed his eyes and moaned, for she was nibbling on his skin and working her way down. He winced when he felt her sharp little bites, and reluctantly removed his hands from hers and began to weave his fingers through her long thick hair.

As her teeth scraped his shoulder, it was quite clear that she had won that round. Jayla took a step backwards to admire his flawed face.

As he stared at her lush and red lips, he found it impossible to resist her. "God, you're beautiful",

Roger stated happily, and then he studied her body as if it were a priceless work of art.

Jayla couldn't help but smile as she glowed in her appreciation of his compliment.

Suddenly, his arms reached out and tightened possessively around her back. He desperately wanted her, and he wanted her to have no doubt that he would get what he was after.

Jayla could feel the power under his fingers, and as she gazed into his cunning eyes, she could feel the intense heat radiate off each and every one of his rippling muscles.

Without giving her a warning, Roger lifted her up into his strong arms and carried her to the bed. And while doing so, an unexpected gasp escaped from his lips, as the awareness that he was about to be inside of her, grew stronger.

She could sense what he was thinking, and her smile widened in approval. As her warm body was placed on the mattress, she inhaled a deep breath of anticipation.

Roger reached out, and ever so lightly, he ran the tip of his index finger from the top of her breast bone to the bottom.

Her creamy skin tingled at his touch, while his loving caress ignited something within her - something that she thought was long dead.

Jayla hardly ever grew this excited, but Roger's caress was actually making her tremble.

Their eyes locked, and seconds later, their mouths mated – it was their first kiss of the day and it was magical. The glow of desire quickly became the bonfire of lust that consumed them both, and neither could have imagine the limits of their mutual attraction to one another.

Roger tasted her lips as if it was the first time, and as her plump mouth pillowed his, it brought them both closer to arousal.

His tongue soon found its way inside of her eager mouth, and dueled with hers for several minutes. They were discovering great joy in the velvet darkness of the room, and then the sensual kiss ended as quickly as it had begun.

Jayla felt dizzy and gasped for air when she felt Roger nuzzling her earlobe. He moved without giving her notice, and laid intense kisses on her neck. He then trailed his lips to both of her cheeks, and landed his hot mouth back onto hers again.

It had been two months since they had had sex and he was beyond motivated, but there was something in the back of his mind telling him that he shouldn't be doing this. Not surprisingly, his loins were now a firestorm of passion and he decided not to stop.

Jayla didn't know what had come over her, but she was eager for Roger to explore her body again and again. While he kissed the white flesh between her ample breasts, she placed his right hand at the apex of her thighs. She then clenched her teeth together as her eyes closed tightly, and she let her head fall backwards in confused pleasure.

Roger was only too happy to accommodate her, so he fondled her until he heard her moan continually. He then reached further into the most womanly part of her, and he didn't stop until he felt the heat of her entire body grow even warmer.

Jayla felt some of his fingers move against the soft tuft of dark curls between her legs, while another one or two fingers were inside and stroking her deep and slow. She had lost all sense of reality in that moment, for she was drowning in throbbing decadence.

Roger knew that he was being mischievous, and he decided to keep it up for another minute before he would tantalize her with his experienced tongue.

Jayla began to writhe beneath him, calling out his name and begging him not to stop. He disobeyed and released his hand rather suddenly, and the bold swipe of his warm tongue against her cool skin, sent her spinning into pleasure's welcoming arms. It was hopeless for her to think of anything but what was happening in those delicious few minutes, and then she received the ultimate naughtiness of her first orgasm of the day.

When Roger felt her thighs tighten around his head, he smiled, for he knew what was happening.

Jayla came in cascading waves, one right after another, and it was somewhat difficult for her to catch her breath.

Roger raised his head to watch, as the soul-shattering orgasm robbed her of her senses. He could see that the spine-tingling climax reverberated throughout every part of her body, and he couldn't help but giggle when she began to shriek like a madwoman.

"OH, MY GOD!" she called loudly.

Roger watched in envy, and now wanted an orgasm to consume his own body. As soon as she was ready, he climbed on top of her sweaty and limp figure to begin his own journey.

Jayla was pleasantly exhausted, but spread her legs in order to receive him.

He wedged himself in between her thighs like he belonged there. Then, with his right hand, he reached for his rigid shaft and stroked it against the wet furnace of her loins. He paused briefly, and then slowly entered the swollen moist gates.

Jayla was bold and insistent, and wanted him to hurry and get inside. And once he was all the way in, she guided his pace with her hips.

Now fueled to new heights, the couple bucked and thrashed until they pummeled each other to the very edge. Excitement was building where they were joined, and it was soon followed by a hot and sticky release.

Roger closed his eyes and his body went taut, as a toe-curling orgasm rippled through his entire body.

With her heart pounding and her warm and sweaty body quivering, Jayla wondered about the last time when she had truly enjoyed herself with a man. Because the question threatened to weaken her happy mood, she decided not to feel guilty for the relief which she was currently experiencing.

Minutes later, they surrendered themselves into each other's arms, and rested before starting again.

When their hour was up, a guard knocked loudly on the door. "Time to go!" he ordered sternly. "The two of you have been locked away long enough, but I'll give you three more minutes to get dressed before I drag you out!"

They were both blissfully happy and felt fully alive, as they hugged each other one more time. Then they got dressed and walked towards the door.

As they said good-bye, Jayla positioned Roger until his body was standing directly in front of hers. "I wrote you something and I want you to hear it. Are you ready?" she asked, with hope and joy flashing in her eyes.

Jayla thought she needed to evoke an extra boast to what had happened between them today, and like any natural spirit, she bargained with boldness on whether or not she could perform a spell right to his face.

Roger wasn't sure what it was that she wanted him to hear, but he planted his feet firmly on the ground and listened. "I'm ready", he promised.

She made sure to lock eyes with the man who regarded her compassion as primitive and erotic, and then stated the following verse:

> Set aside your silly emotions
> And allow me to install some new notions
> From now on you'll think of me
> In every way to infinity

Jayla pushed her lips onto his, as an insurance that he would obey.

Roger returned the kiss, and he suddenly had an overwhelming feeling of love in his heart for the woman before him. He took a step closer and grabbed her shoulders, and then let his hungry lips rain a few passionate kisses on her bruised mouth.

The door to the room opened, and this officially ended their time together.

While Roger was walking back to his cell, Jayla was driving herself back to her home. They were both smiling, each for their own reasons, and they both felt like they had just won the lottery.

As they lay their heads down on their pillows that night, they each felt better than they had 24 hours earlier.

Jayla was now encouraged that Roger would not break up with her in the near future, but she was shocked by the tantalizing feeling of warmth that had crept over her body.

It was true that he had a strange kind of animal magnetism that drew her to him, but she knew better than to become powerless over a scarlet web of desire. It was also true that she needed his soul, but she did not need a mate for life. She truly didn't want to become a creature that revelled in the plain and simple craving of carnal pleasure, but even though she wanted to push the raw need aside, she couldn't help but be thrilled at the thought of him moving inside of her.

Roger didn't know what had prompted Jayla's surprise visit, but he was more than delighted that she had somehow convinced the guards to let them go to the honeymoon suite. And as he thought about her spectacular body, his fingers yearned to touch every part of her again.

As she laid quiet in her bed, Jayla's mouth could still taste him, and it was making her happier than she had been in a very long time. There was a certain glow about her now, as her energy danced and sparkled in the dark.

"Calm your urges and stay on course", a voice echoed.

Jayla bolted into a sitting position, as her eyes desperately searched the room. "He's only in your life for one reason", the voice stated calmly.

It took her a few seconds to realize that it was her soul who was speaking. Some people might call it a prudent sense of self, because it could superimpose beyond space and time. Jayla knew this heightened sense of conscious awareness as wisdom, and it came from her being a great witch.

Jayla automatically closed her eyes and lowered her face. "You are right, of course", she replied to no-one. She laid herself down and rested her head on her pillow again. It was then when she realized that she had gotten carried away with the silly idea that she could have a normal life. The plain truth was that Jayla only needed Roger to keep her alive, and not as a loving mate.

With this cold and contemptuous logic ringing in her ears, all the yearnings in her body recoiled in haste. And as an ugly emptiness covered her body like a thick comforter, she rolled onto her side and unwillingly cried herself to sleep.

Meanwhile, Roger was laying in his prison bed and had just stroked himself to another orgasm. He then rolled onto his side, and fell into a deep and satisfying sleep.

CHAPTER SEVEN

October 26, 2000

Jayla woke up feeling confident that her plan to keep him close had worked, but now there was a strange knot sitting in the core of her stomach. Because the beautiful gypsy-witch had an incredible amount of perception, she knew that this was a sign that something was not right.

As her smooth olive skin stretched insecurely over her high cheekbones, she was determined to find out what was going on, and she would not fall short of using all of her powers to do it.

Roger woke up wearing a curious smile. He couldn't help thinking about all that he had done with Jayla, and he couldn't wait until he saw her again.

Because she had made him so happy, Roger decided to deal with Marlowe right away, and he would keep Jayla until he got out of prison.

After breakfast, Roger looked through the white pages and wrote down all of the phone numbers that belonged to Marlowe Perkins. He then made his way to the lounge. As soon as a phone was free, he called the first number on the list. Unfortunately, that number was out-of-order.

The next four phone numbers were answered, but not by the person who Roger was looking for. He dialed the sixth number, but when Roger heard Marlowe's voice on the answering machine, his throat closed up, his eyes grew wide, and his skin began to crawl with extreme hatred.

Since he loathed leaving messages, Roger slammed the cheap black phone into its plastic cradle and gladly went back to his cell. As he walked through the loud and heavily secured area, he had an overwhelming urge to hit something.

Roger wanted nothing to do with Marlowe, but he also knew that Marlowe could help him once he got on the outside of the heavily guarded walls.

Roger dragged an open hand through his unruly hair and grunted loudly. "God, I hate that guy", he insisted, but no-one was listening. He was angry, his muscles were tight, and he felt trapped like a caged animal. Still, he had no other choice but to try calling Marlowe again.

By the time he arrived at his cell, Roger had calmed down; he understood that he needed to push his emotions aside if he wanted to be with Molly. He just wish that they didn't live in the same home.

His heart softened as he thought about seeing her, and he couldn't wait until they started their life together.

Just then, Jayla's face appeared before him. Because he had been with her yesterday, and he knew her warm and willing body very well, he let his thoughts linger on the shrewd woman who brandished the charms of an imaginative sex goddess. A minute later, he wondered if he could keep both Jayla and Molly in his life.

He smiled as he let the idea swirl around in his head, until he realized that he could not. Feeling somewhat defeated, he scowled and let himself fall backwards onto his overused, twin size bed.

Jayla was sitting cross-legged on the carpeted floor of her living room. She was waist-high in old tattered books, and was looking for anything that could help her. The books were strewn about in complete disarray, and each one was opened to a certain page which talked about strange knots within the body. The paragraph under a particular colorful diagram, suggested that the placement of Jayla's knot determined that a lie was about to unfold. But not just any lie; a momentous fabrication of words that could ultimately change her immediate future.

Jayla was furious by this information, and as her hands clenched and her eyes widened, adrenaline rushed throughout her entire body. Driven by the belief that she was about to be mistreated, she had to know more.

With the inherent strength from her father and *The Craft of the Wise powers from her mother, Jayla was about to undertake the disturbing task of finding out who the person is that wants to harm her.

Meanwhile, it was 10am and Marlowe was busy meeting his mistress at their usual spot – the corner of Trinity Blvd and Sandstone Drive. They had come in different cars and from opposite ends of the city, and within seconds after parking, the prudent lovers ran into each other's welcoming arms.

They met several months ago, while both of them were taking classes at night school. They had formed a bond and decided to go out for coffee, and three weeks later, they ended up in a motel.

Marlowe enjoyed his time with Louise, but he was not in love with her; those weekly meetings were the only thing which was keeping him sane and happy.

---

*The Craft of the Wise is another way to say Witchcraft, but it's so much more than just magic.

It had been a long time since anyone had appreciated her, and Louise could feel herself starting to fall in love with Marlowe. At the same time, she began to develop a hatred for her husband, Jack.

After their affectionate hello, Marlowe and Louise walked hand-in-hand to the next block, and then checked into the not-so-elegant, Brimley Hotel. Once the elevator doors had closed, Marlowe took a few minutes to study his younger fellow student.

He loved her soft voice, her attractive body, and her eagerness to enjoy life to the fullest. He adored how her long flowing, blonde hair cascaded over her shoulders, and how she held onto each and every word that he said. He also loved how unshakable she was in the art of role playing.

Today he was the authoritative teacher, and she was the timid student who needed to be taught a lesson. Her punishment was for lack of obedience. To redeem herself, she needed to do everything he asked her to do, and without question.

They arrived on the 4th floor at 10:07am, and went to their assigned room. After locking the door, their personalities changed: no longer were they Marlowe and Louise. Now they were Mr. Freeman and Tiffany Jones.

"Are you ready to begin?" he asked quietly, but with total authority. With his hands on his hips, he was staring her down as if he was 2 feet taller than she was.

Louise began to portray the illusion of total innocence to a 'T'. She sucked her bottom lip into her mouth, opened her eyes really wide, and slowly nodded her head in response to his question.

"Good!" he praised, and then he lowered his hands to where they naturally hung. "I will need you to take off every bit of clothing that you have on", he ordered kindly.

Before she exhaled her next breath, Louise began doing what she was told to do. When she was completely naked, Marlowe placed his hands on her shoulders and asked her to sit on the edge of the bed.

Louise was quiet as she watched Marlowe get undressed, and she became silently giddy when he walked over and stood directly in front of her.

Using his hands to show her what he was referring to, he stated, "Miss Jones. For your punishment, I think that you should make all of this, wet." He then moved both of his hands behind his back and joined his fingers together.

As she nodded her agreement, her brain emptied of all thought but the desire to serve.

With great satisfaction, Marlowe watched as she obeyed his command.

Louise took great pride in covering all of the muscles in his chest and lower tummy area with her hot saliva, and she loved the power she got from pushing him to the brink of erotic pleasure and then pulling him back again.

Satisfying groans erupted from deep within Marlowe's throat, and it was meant to encourage Louise to keep going. His head was thrown back, his eyes were closed tight, and his knees were becoming weak, as he immersed himself in the joys of receiving an outstanding blow job.

She didn't know why, but Louise received a sick thrill from being his love slave, and she voluntarily denied her own pleasure until she gave him what he demanded.

His body was now radiating with raw, animal strength, and when he became consumed with unbelievable lust for her, Marlowe pushed her down on the bed. He spread her legs and began to explore every part of her body with his tongue.

She soon became a refuge for his roving hands and mouth, and Louise closed her eyes in order to experience every caress more deeply. Goose bumps appeared on her skin as his touch whispered over her body, and she was soon powerless to resist him.

He thought he would lose it when she raised her head and pressed her eager lips against his magnificent male flesh, so he ordered her to lay back and not move.

Louise did as she was asked, and playfully pinned her wrists and ankles to the bed. This excited her more than she wanted to admit, because she loved this part of their time together; it was what was missing from her own marriage.

Marlowe loved that she was stark naked and open to his cravings, and that she eagerly obeyed his every command. She was his perfect pet and her body belonged to him. Furthermore, he would use it any way he wanted, and he knew that she would let him.

They spent the next two hours completely overtaken by the deepest of pleasures, and then they said good-bye and went their separate ways.

It was almost 12:30 at the Broken Hill Prison, and the buzzer was about to ring loudly to announce lunch. While he was eating, Roger rehearsed what he was going to say to Marlowe.

On the outside, he would be pleasant and fake a warm forgotten friendship, but on the inside, he would be seething with utter anger.

Roger hated the thought that Marlowe had taken Molly's virginity, and that he had been able to lay with her every night since High School. He then became extremely amused with how dearly Marlowe would pay for what he had done.

When lunch was over, Roger made his way to the line-up to use the phone.

Jayla's body was exhausted, her tummy was empty, and her legs had cramped up from sitting in an awkward position for such a long time. She pushed a few books aside and stood up, and proceeded to stretch every one of her stiff muscles. She then headed to the kitchen to find something to eat.

While she enjoyed her lunch of a freshly-toasted, BLT sandwich and a hot coffee, she contemplated every theory which had been explained in her books on Circle Magic and Infusions. She then focused on her handbooks on magic spells and potions, her large hard cover books on witchery and incantations, and her assorted books pertaining to Wicca. Each had their own theories about knots and lies, and each talked about how to get to the bottom of her current grumble.

As for the person who wanted to harm her, Jayla couldn't help but determine that Roger was the only person who she had had any regular contact with lately.

But she had been with him last night. She knew that he wanted to break up with her yesterday, but she had been able to change his mind about that. 'Had she not?' This uncertainty made her stare off into space with enormous curiosity.

After Roger had dialed Marlowe's phone number, he became disturbingly surprised when Molly answered.

"Hello?"

As Roger's eyes grew wide, his throat closed up, and no words could pass over his dry lips. At the same time, his mind was fluttering with a million questions.

What if he spoke and she recognized his voice? What if Marlowe had turned her against him and she was so angry that she hung up? Roger would never be able to get hold of Marlowe then, and everything that he had planned to do on the outside, would never work.

The fear that he could lose everything was much too high, so Roger slammed the receiver into the cradle and walked away. While he moved his body towards the double doors which led into the large courtyard, he pushed a wayward strand of dark hair off the highest point of his forehead.

As he sat down on the nearest wooden bench, a cold shiver raced up his spine. And as if it was looped to play over and over again, he continued to remember the haunting echo of Molly's adult voice.

Roger was sure it was her, because she sounded exactly the same as he remembered. Under different circumstances, he would have loved to talk with her, but not today: the timing had to be perfect or it could ruin his future.

Roger was staring across the yard, while he reached into his front shirt pocket for a cigarette. After lighting it, he drew a deep mouthful of air into his lungs. While exhaling a thick cloud of smoke, he looked around at all the inmates who were out in the yard with him. It then dawned on him that he wouldn't be with them for very much longer, for he was getting out of jail the next day. It was a gloomy perspective, and it made him happy and sad all at the same time.

Jayla had finished her lunch and was walking back to the living room to look through her books, when someone beckoned her to listen.

"R-o-g-er", the voice whispered, in an odd but gentle tone. Time slowed down, and the energy in the air frolicked as if it had become thick with loving magic.

Jayla felt an immediate calmness all around her, for this was the voice of her dearly departed mother.

Petra May died a year ago, after being poisoned by a young and malicious, Eclectic Witch.

Astrid Highmore had been jealous of Petra May's beauty and power for quite a while, and because she really wanted the seat which Petra May held in the coven, she made sure to catch her alone and off-guard.

Hemlock, nine rusty bent nails, some old wool fibers, and a large handful of Devil's Weed, were some of the ingredients used in the spiteful brew which Astrid made especially for Petra May. Astrid presented this 'soup' as a gift, and it took mere minutes for Petra May to taste it and die.

Sadly, the older witch had been totally unprepared for what was happening, and she had passed away before anyone could help her.

At the inquest, Astrid played innocent, but she was eventually found guilty and was then punished for Petra May's murder.

She was immediately stripped of all of her powers and hair, and was given detention and house arrest for four years. Because she slowly went insane from the humiliation of being bald, and the loneliness from being locked in her home with nobody to talk to, she hung herself by the end of the fifth month.

"Be-ware", Petra May cautioned softly.

Petra May wished that she could be of more help to her daughter, but the great power that she had once possessed, had died when she drew her last breath.

With a halo of doom hanging over her head, Jayla quickly put two-and-two together. She had already known in her heart that it had to be Roger who was going to hurt her, but she didn't want to believe it, because she could feel that he was attracted to her. But sadly, it was becoming obvious that there was something else pushing him towards a wayward act.

With her mother's warning, there was no doubt in Jayla's mind that Roger was the reason for her knot. Without a moment to spare, Jayla raced to her cupboards to gather the last of her black candles. After lighting all but one, and placing them strategically around her home, she was still nervous, but she now felt a little safer.

All black protection candles are hand-poured once a year, and Jayla's were made on Sunday, October 31, 1999. She remembered that day well - the Moon and Sun were in Scorpio in the 8th House, and it was the day after a violent thunderstorm.

Before these candles were set, Jayla had taken rosemary, frankincense, & a few other traditional fragrances from her garden, and added them to the wax. After placing a wick in the centre and chanting a short incantation over each one, the candles were allowed to get firm.

Jayla positioned the largest black candle in her collection, in between her hands. With her eyes closed and while she was humming in a single note, she visualized Roger's face in her mind. A full minute later, she opened her eyes and chanted, "Protection is what I seek, a shield against one person in particular." She then placed the large candle on the window sill, so that it could share its light with the sun and the moon.

As is the custom, the black candle has to burn all the way to the bottom in order for the spell to work, and it cannot be moved until the flame has gone out.

Now that all the black candles were lit, Jayla needed to find the blue one.

This primary color helps to obtain calming wisdom, inner peace, and adept guidance in solving problems.

After lighting it, she stared into the flame, as if it was giving her all she needed in the way of vitality. With her hands gently fanning the smoke to come towards her, she began to chant.

> As blue as the water
> As dark as the night
> I need your help;
> I shiver with fright
> As bright as the stars
> As round as the moon
> I need your protection
> And I need it soon

As if a mighty storm had somehow gushed into the small room, all of the flames flickered with excitement, while trying to hold onto their wavering beacon of light.

As she looked around, Jayla could feel that the ambience had now changed and that the fear in her body was all but gone. Jayla closed her eyes and said thank you to her mom for helping her.

Her mother's loving and possessive hug, suddenly warmed the small space. It was easy to note that it stemmed from the deepest spot in Petra May's heart, and it instantly replaced the sadness which used to be in the room.

Now that she was protected, Jayla needed to find out how and why Roger wanted to hurt her.

She had performed a love spell on Roger, but she had not counted on him wanting to do her harm – emotional or physical.

As she calmed her spirit and closed her eyes, Jayla thought back to a passage in one of her books on malevolent souls.

> 'While the feeling of love is very strong, it seldom erases the need to destroy. Annihilation comes from the darkest part of an angry person's soul, and the only way to change that instinct, is through death.'

As Jayla opened her eyes, she knew that she would be killing Roger in order to take his soul, but now she wondered if she had to kill him before he broke her heart. It was a scary thought, but she needed to be prepared for whatever came forward.

She made herself comfortable, and then meditated for the next few hours.

Meanwhile, Roger went back inside the prison and went straight to the prison library. He looked for books on reforming criminals, and soon found, Makes Me Wanna Holler. As he flipped through the ominous pages that explained the journey of how a young black man went from being a criminal to an outstanding newscaster, he focused more on the parts where McCall was living on the streets in Urban America, and of his time inside the daunting prison walls.

By absorbing the descriptive words in the inspirational story, Roger could now see what he needed to do when he got out. This included filling his pockets with money, and making Marlowe pay for taking Molly away from him.

Marlowe had gone back to work with a smile on his face. He very much enjoyed spending an invigorating morning with Louise, and he didn't think he'd see her again until their next class. So when the phone rang and it was her, he was more than surprised.

"Marlowe?"

"Yes." He was suspicious and staring blankly, and his mouth hung open with awe.

"I have a delicate situation that I need your help with. Can we talk?" She kept her tone very businesslike. "I promise to make it worth your while."

Marlowe was intrigued, and since he had nowhere to go after work, he agreed to meet up with her. "Okay, but I can't stay long."

"Thank you." An icy cloud of relief hung in the air when she replied.

Louise was intentionally acting detached, as if he was a homeless man with nothing to offer, but because she wanted him to feel like he mattered, she knew she needed to change the attitude in her voice.

"You won't be sorry", she added kindly. And even though he couldn't see her, she smiled as if the warmth could carry across the phone lines.

Marlowe told her where and when they could meet, and then they hung up.

As the receiver was pressed against the solid base of the phone, Marlowe's face showed his utter annoyance of her call.

Louise was no more important to him than a chattering of baby birds in the nest, or a flock of geese sailing quietly on top of a bed of smooth water. To him, she was a distraction, and there was no openness to wedge any access to his heart. Still, she was as warm and loving as a Sunday afternoon, and she knew how to make him happy.

While an amused smile slid across his lips, Marlowe decided that it wouldn't hurt to see what she had to say.

They met a few hours later, and in case anyone might recognize them, there were no hugs or displays of affection in their greeting. They walked into the bar as if they were brother and sister, and were escorted to a corner booth in the back where no-one could hear what they were talking about.

Once they were alone, Marlowe studied her expression. "Tell me what's going on", he begged softly.

Louise took a long swig of her beer, and while locking her eyes with his, she asked Marlowe if he wanted to be with her as much as she wanted to be with him.

Marlowe's heart sank into his stomach, for he didn't want to have that kind of talk. But because he liked the sex and he needed her help with his homework, he decided to stay in her good graces. "Yes", he answered, without any emotion attached to the word. A black curtain of hate fell over his hooded eyes, and he was slowly disappearing into a bad mood.

Unbeknownst to Louise, Marlowe had a wife and he was not about to change anything in his life. He hated this line of questioning, and could feel a flush of red spreading across his cheeks.

Molly knew that Marlowe had fooled around, and that her husband had done so for many years. There was no love lost between them, so rather than fight about something that wasn't going to change, she preferred to turn a blind eye to Marlowe's embarrassing stupidity.

Because she was Catholic, Molly knew that he would be punished for all the deceitful and unkind things that he had done. As a woman, she hoped that his final moment would be filled with a great amount of pain.

Ophelia's Curse

"Oh, good", she sighed, and she instantly became giddy. Without coming right out and asking for his help, Louise calmly explained her situation.

Marlowe wasn't listening with full interest at first, but when she started talking about a ton of insurance money, he perked up right away. He had tuned out the part where Louise said that they could be together all the time, but he certainly heard her talk about the amount of money that was involved, if and when Jack was no longer in the picture.

Louise leaned across the acacia wood bar table and assured Marlowe, "That it would have to look like an accident." As she sat back, her spirits lifted, for it was quite clear that Marlowe had taken the bait.

As Marlowe lifted his glass and took a long swig of beer, his foul mood had suddenly changed to one of mild curiosity.

He decided that he would be a fool not to question her proposal, but Louise should not underestimate his skills and determination.

Marlowe's heart began beating wildly in his chest, and he was more than stunned over how nonchalant Louise was being while talking about murdering her husband. His throat suddenly went dry, so he lifted his glass and took another long swig of beer. As he looked off in the distance, he could envision all the ways in which this scheme might work. And while he was quite fond of receiving money for 'an accident', he was not interested in spending the rest of his life with Louise.

For the time being though, he would do whatever she needed in order to get his hands on what she had to offer.

Louise watched his ever-changing expression, and because he had been silent, she prayed that he wouldn't say no. "Marlowe?" she called softly.

He had been pulled out of his trance and turned to meet her eyes. He then decided to approach the task with typical cheerfulness, and gave her a cocky masculine grin. "I accept", he stated, with a tender gaze.

Marlowe's greed blinded him, and because he now had so much disdain and contempt for both her and Molly, he couldn't wait until he was free from both of them.

"Thank you", she sighed with relief. Louise smiled with great joy, for she could finally see a happy ending in her future.

As Marlowe sucked more of the cool, light brown liquid into the back of his throat, his mind was rushing around with one thought after another.

He had never been to jail before, and he had no intention of ever being locked up. He wanted the money, but he didn't want to share his life with Louise.

All of a sudden, two simple words flooded his brain. A fall-guy! He didn't know why, but Roger's face suddenly appeared before him. In that same second, a wide smile exploded across his unshaven face, and a brilliant plan began to unfold.

Marlowe and Louise said their good-byes 10 minutes later, and each left the bar with a new purpose in life.

While he was driving home, Marlowe started planning a stranger's demise. Behind that thought, was how he was going to get hold of Roger. As for splitting the money with him, that was like an illusion that twinkling stars could grant wishes – it wasn't going to happen.

Marlowe parked his car in the driveway and walked into his home, and one second later, the phone rang. "Hello?"

"Marlowe?"

"Yah, but if you're selling something, forget it!" He was about to hang the phone up when he heard a man's voice summoning him to listen.

"It's me, Roger! How the hell are ya?"

Marlowe couldn't believe his ears when he heard Roger's voice, and his lips parted with complete surprise. He had entertained real-life coincidences before, but this one was insane. "Roger? Is that really you?"

Relief at getting hold of the other, was what broke the gawd-awful tension. They both laughed from the awkwardness of the call, and feigned a fake and forgotten friendship for the next few minutes.

Both men harbored anger from their teenage years, but each one needed help now. Unbeknownst to the other, they vowed to stay in character until the job was done, and then they would go their separate ways.

Once the phoney pleasantries were finished, Roger told Marlowe why he was calling. "I'm getting out of jail tomorrow and I'm wondering if I could bribe you into picking me up?"

Marlowe didn't hesitate for a minute, as this was playing out even better than he could have imagined. "Of course! And I might even have a job for you, with great pay and no hard labor. Just give me the directions and the time you need me to be there."

"Thanks, Marlowe." Roger smiled, and this time it was genuine. He was getting out of jail, he hoped to see Molly again, and he was going to make all the wrongs right. "I'll call ya in the morning. And thanks, again!"

Marlowe hung up and smiled, for the perfect plan was unfolding right before his eyes. As he made his way to his little office in the basement, he was already making plans of how the day would go.

He would be at the Broken Hill Prison on time, and embrace his ex-friend as if he honestly liked him. As they drove away, he would tell Roger all about Jack and the money – Roger's share of it, anyway. After Jack was dead, Marlowe would walk away from Roger without so much as a thank you.

As Roger walked back to his cell, he could almost feel his new life beginning. He would be free from these cold and dingy prison walls, he'd make a bit of money without breaking out into a sweat, and he would find a way to get rid of Marlowe so that he could have a life with Molly.

Roger laid his head down on his pillow and guided his hands to rest beneath his head. He had intertwined his fingers and was looking up at the ceiling when he sighed, "Sometimes the story of my life writes itself."

It was almost midnight when Jayla had had enough of the day's bitter hours, and just as she was dragging her weary body to the bedroom, she felt another shift of change in the air. After tucking herself under the handmade, quilted comforter which Auntie Effie had made for her, she bid her cat good-night, and then tried to push her worries to the side. As she lay there, staring up at the ceiling, she could taste that the threat against her was no longer one-dimensional; it now seemed to be multi-layered, and there were more people involved.

She struggled with this for a long time, and must have drifted off to sleep, because a vision of a woman flashed into her brain. The image was not part of a dream, and it was so strong and clear that it woke her up.

Jayla had been startled, and was now sitting up in bed with a wild look on her weary face. Was this the woman who Roger wanted to be with? Why was she haunting her dreams?

Suddenly, a cold whoosh entered her dark room and a voice spat out a rather vague answer.

> In a tale as old as time
> In a life that doesn't rhyme
> Where men cheat and girls are sweet
> And hearts are broken on a dime

"Of course!" Jayla's mind was quick to decipher what that meant, and then it made sense; the woman was part of Roger's life. He wanted to be free so he could be with her.

Jayla was livid and felt like a fool, but before she could continue her thought, the voice interrupted.

> Look to the stars to find the light
> The answer is burning very bright

> You don't have much time,
> so make it quick
> You'll have to muster up your best trick

Jayla jumped out of bed and scurried to the living room. She was furious at the thought that Roger might leave before she took his soul, because she would have just wasted the last year of her life.

Without a moment to lose, Jayla spread her arms out to the sides, lifted her chin, and closed her eyes. In a pleading and desperate manner, she opened her mind and called out to everyone she knew.

> "To all who can help me, please do,
> for I am alone and I need you."

Jayla's mind quickly filled with voices who were asking her what she needed. Through mental telepathy, she let them all know what was happening, and it didn't take long before the answers hurried in.

The majority stated that the result was simple; Jayla needed to find this woman and switch places with her. The trouble was, the 'Crone Spell' was only good for a few hours. In that short bit of time, she needed to gain Roger's full trust before the time ran out. If they could kiss, that would clinch the deal. If not, she might have to think of another plan.

The whole thing was pretty risky, and because she had never done this spell before, Jayla hoped that she could pull it off.

Because Marlowe had been hiding himself away in the basement all evening, Molly had been entertained by the TV. At 10pm she called good-night to him and he grunted good-night back, and out of sheer boredom, she put herself to bed.

When Marlowe came into the bedroom at midnight, he got undressed, crawled into his side of the bed, and went to sleep. He didn't look in Molly's direction, or even seem to care if she was there or not. His mind was full of this plan that he would be executing with Roger, and in deciding which way that he would leave 'all of this', behind.

Without needing to open her eyes, Molly could feel him get under the covers. Once his body had gone still, Molly heaved an unhappy sigh and tried to go back to sleep.

Now that Jayla had a plan, she tore through her books until she found the spell that would work. When she had it in her hand, she needed to find the woman who held Roger's heart.

She stood up and placed herself in the middle of the room, and then took a deep breath. With her eyes closed and her index and middle fingers pressed tightly up against her temples, she called upon the powers that be, 'to light the way to the woman I see'.

Faster than it takes for a coin to drop to the floor, a powerful force channelled her to Marlowe's front door.

Jayla's mind had instantly transported her to the woman's home. She now not only had the address and the street name, she also knew what the house looked like from the outside. And as quickly as she had been taken there, that same power brought her back to her own home.

As she opened her eyes, Jayla could feel a strong sense of determination flowing throughout her body. She smiled because of the powerful motivation that had linked itself to her soul, and after turning a few lights off around her home, she marched herself into the bedroom. Before she fell into a deep sleep, she went over the details of the plan in her mind.

Jayla was well-aware that the crimson energy of a spell of this magnitude, would pull a lot of energy from her body. And because this was last-minute, she wished that she could have been better prepared to do it.

On a lighter note, she was grateful that she would not be doing this spell in a moonless time period, for she needed to have the four corners and all the essential forces helping her.

CHAPTER EIGHT

October 27, 2000

It was 8am, and Marlowe had called Louise to tell her that everything was being taken care of. It was in code, but he knew that she would understand what it meant.

Louise sighed with relief. "Thank you", she whispered in a loving tone. She was becoming happier by the second and couldn't wait to be in the arms of this man whom she professed to love so much.

There was an inherent strength on his face as the corners of his lips curled upwards. "You're welcome. Talk later, ok?"

"Yes, and thank you again." She had tears in her eyes as they hung up, because everything was going according to their plan. She smiled as she turned around and looked out the large front window, and as she wrapped her hands around the bottom part of her warm coffee cup, she could feel that things were going to be ok.

Marlowe placed the receiver back where it belonged and got himself ready to drive to the prison. He found himself humming as he made his way down the isolated, two-lane highway, and then noted why he was in such a good mood.

At the same time, Jack had just arrived at work. The store wouldn't be open for another two hours, but he wanted to catch up on the inventory and clear off the pile of paperwork on his desk.

Jack Chisolm was a nice guy in his mid-30s, and lately, he had been living in a difficult marriage.

Louise didn't want to work, and with Jack toiling away at the hardware store at all hours of the day and night, she was alone more than she wanted to be. TV and housework could only fill up so much time, and then the loneliness bounced off the walls.

Jack was grateful when his wife decided to take a course, but it also seemed to change her personality. She was more detached now, and not so talkative. Plus she wasn't making as many home-cooked meals as she used to.

To keep her from becoming bored, Jack invited her to have suppers with him on the nights when he needed to work late, but she refused. Because Jack owned the hardware store, and he only had one other person working with him, it was hard for him to get away. Still, he tried to close his store early at least two nights a week, and then he raced home to be with her. To his surprise, those seemed to be the same nights when Louise had a headache and went to bed early.

It's been 2 months since Jack tried to do things to ease the tension between them, but Louise hasn't softened. To him, his relationship has reluctantly come to a standstill, and he feels like he's run out of options.

Just outside of town, Roger was in his squared cell, preparing to be released from his 'home away from home'. He had put everything he owned into the prison's over-sized, elegant duffle bag, and was now waiting for a guard to take him to the shower area.

Two minutes after Marlowe had driven away, Jayla parked in front of his house. She stood on the well-manicured lawn and stared up at the quaint, two-story building, and envisioned herself meeting the woman who Roger was in love with. Jayla felt nervous and had to force herself to begin this daunting task, so she took a deep breath as she shook her hands from the wrists.

Eight steps forward and she was then touching the outside wood panelling on the cookie-cutter building. The first thing she did was peer into the large front window, and it didn't take long before she saw who she was looking for.

A chilling gasp left her throat, when she identified the features of the person who was tidying up; that was the face of the woman who had appeared in her dream. And as if she had been pulled into a trance, she suddenly couldn't move her eyes or body away from the clean glass.

It took a good, long moment, and then something within Jayla's soul snapped her back to reality. She immediately removed the possibility of getting caught, and stepped out of the beautiful flower garden. As she planted her feet on the cement front porch, she knew that she didn't have any time to waste. With the speed of a falcon, the gypsy-witch's fingers were curved and weaving purple patterns in the air around her. All the while, in a raspy voice, she slowly hissed the following incantation;

> Eye of newt and toe of spider
> I've found the girl with hair like cider
> Change me into a fragile old crone
> A kind woman with a creak and a moan

The earth rumbled, the wind rushed in all different directions, thunder clapped, and without anyone else knowing, Jayla had turned into a 99-year old, frumpy hag.

As she looked down and examined her clothing, Jayla's left eyebrow arched in relief that the spell had worked. With the steel nerves of a thief who pilfers while everyone is asleep, she reached a bony finger towards the buzzer and pressed it hard. When the door opened, Jayla looked Molly straight in the eye.

Jayla's mouth tightened when she saw the familiar face, while suspicious lines began to crease the corners of her mouth. She couldn't help but stare blankly at the woman who stole Roger's heart, but if she wanted to retrieve his soul, she needed to act accordingly.

"Hello, my dear", she stated through stiff lips. "I am looking for a lady named Shirley."

Molly smiled at the old woman and replied politely. "I'm sorry, but I don't know anyone in this neighbourhood by that name.

"Oh." Jayla gave her a twisted smile and then lowered her eyes. She hoped that she appeared rejected and lost, so that this stranger would want to help her.

As she looked at the small and frail woman, Molly suddenly felt very sorry for her. "Do you want to come inside so I could call someone for you?"

Jayla's newly wrinkled skin softened, and in an old lady's shaky voice she stated, "Thank you, but before I enter, may I know your name?"

"My name is Molly. I live here."

"Hello, Molly. My friend, Roger, told me to come and see Shirley..." Before she could finish her sentence, Jayla watched as Molly's face turned a bright shade of pink.

The mere mention of his name shocked her to the core. Her instincts were trying to convince her that it couldn't possibly be the same Roger who she had known when she was a child, but she had never met anyone since then, with that same name.

Molly was sad for how things had turned out between them; they used to be friends and she knew that she had hurt him. Because she had doubts that she would ever see him again, hearing his name brought up a lot of memories.

"Are you alright, dear?" Jayla was loving the reaction which Molly was displaying, for it proved that there was a definite connection between Roger and Molly.

As Jayla took a second to analyze this fancy bit of information, it would seem that the attraction was only from Roger's side. This gave her a huge reason to wonder why Roger thought he should dump her for Molly.

Molly's eyes widened as she reacted to the old woman's question. "Yes, I'm alright." As she looked into the stranger's eyes, her right hand raced up to her chest at the same time as a puff of air got caught in her throat. "Your friend's name is Roger?" she asked carefully.

"That's right." Jayla nodded. "He's like a grandson to me, and we've been friends for many years." And while Molly fell into a grey world, Jayla studied the stunning features of the younger woman before her.

Her white skin had a soft satiny glow to it, her subtle beauty was quite intoxicating, and her Gothic quality was comparable to the doomed heroines in history. And because of her kind nature, Jayla could now see why Roger was in love with her.

"Molly?" she called softly. Jayla just wanted to make sure that she had said that word correctly.

After hearing her name, Marlowe's wife snapped back to reality. "Oh, um, yes. I'm sorry", she apologized, but a part of her was still in a daze.

Flashes of memories were coming into Molly's mind, about her childhood and friendship with Roger. They had had a lot of fun together, but after she met Marlowe, she felt like a woman and regarded Roger as a playmate of her youth. It was stupid, and it didn't feel important back then. Now that she was an adult in a loveless marriage, she could see how cruel she had been.

They were standing two feet apart and Molly's guard was down, so Jayla decided that the time was right to perform another spell.

Jayla made sure to lock eyes with the troubled woman, by drawing her attention to whatever she did or said. And when Jayla was ready, she spat out the following words:

> On my mark, hear and see
> Switch us places, one, two, three
> I command you now, so let it be
> I am her and she is me

In a dramatic puff of billowing white smoke, and a little bit of theatrical flair, the two women switched bodies. And to make it even more frightening, the old crone, who was now the real Molly, was instantly relocated to the street, while Jayla stood in the front hallway of Marlowe's home.

Molly had no idea what was going on, and now she had no memory of her name or of her life before that very moment. She was immediately disoriented, and could actually feel her bones and muscles stiffening from old age. It was more than terrifying to her, and she wished that it was a dream so that she could wake up. And as she moved her frail arms and legs, her mouth whispered, "How did I get here?"

Jayla, who now looked like Molly, went inside the house without a care in the world about what she had done. As she touched this and that, she tried to imitate the person who she believed Molly to be.

Meanwhile, the real Molly was standing on the curb and looked like a lost old woman who had wandered far from home. She had a heavy, empty feeling in her stomach, and because she didn't know where she was, she wanted to cry.

A neighbour saw her and ran out, but because Molly had no I.D. and she was too stunned to speak, the police were called. Mere minutes later, one of the two uniformed men from Station 53, placed the confused woman into the back seat of the squad car and drove her to the nearest hospital.

Jayla had been looking at everything in the home as if she owned it but hadn't seen it for a while, and she ended her tour in the large master bedroom. As she looked at her reflection in the mirror over the dresser, she decided that she would have to make a few changes.

She immediately took the pins out of Molly's fine, dark blonde hair, and picked out some other clothes to wear. After adding a little make-up to her eyes and mouth, and spraying some perfume to her neck and cleavage, Jayla felt that she was ready to go and see Roger.

It was near noon when Roger and Marlowe said hello for the first time in decades, and even though the meeting started out awkward, both had reasons for being in the other man's company.

"It's really great to see you!" Roger shouted, as he slapped his friend on the shoulder. He then stared at the ground as the two men walked towards Marlowe's car.

Roger's statement was partially true, because he was getting a ride to his new life and Marlowe was going to supply him with a lot of money. That was way more than he had expected to have on his first day of freedom.

"You too", Marlowe declared in a patronizing manner. He got into the driver's seat and started the car, and then squeezed his hands tightly around the steering wheel as he turned his head away from his passenger.

Marlowe hoped that Roger's greed would be his downfall, and that after Jack was found murdered, Roger would go back to jail where he belonged. He knew that all he needed to do was pretend to be nice to Roger for a few days, but it was hard when the former inmate chatted constantly, like a bunch of angry baby birds who were looking to be fed. Still, he needed a fall guy and Roger was it.

"You said you have a job for me?" Roger asked, as the car moved forward. He was intrigued that it involved a lot of money and no hard labor.

Marlowe nodded, but kept his eyes focused on the road ahead. While he drove the car away from the Broken Hill Prison, he explained the plan to Roger. "There's this woman who is willing to give us a ton of money, and in exchange, she wants us to get rid of her husband."

Roger was surprised at first, but since it seemed simple enough, he was all in.

"So, what's the first step?" Roger asked lightly. He undid the seat belt and twisted himself around, in order to make himself more comfortable.

Marlowe was relieved that Roger didn't even flinch at the suggestion of murder. "I thought we'd case the joint, so we could see the kinds of alarms and locks they have on the doors and windows."

Roger was pleased with this suggestion, and nodded as he brought his hand up to stroke his hairless chin. "That's a great idea. Is the store very far from here?"

"Naw. About a mile or so inside of the city limits, I think." Marlowe suddenly saw himself acting cold and indifferent, so he put a smirk on his rugged face and began to talk more about what would happen once they were inside the store.

Roger continued to stare out the front window as he listened, while debating all the possibilities which this scheme would bring.

Jayla felt confident as she drove to the prison gates, but she was shocked to hear that Roger had just been released. "He wasn't supposed to get out for a few more months!" she insisted loudly.

She was clearly becoming hysterical and couldn't calm herself down, because according to what she knew, Roger should be in jail for another few months.

As if to intimidate the uniformed man at the gate, Jayla took a step closer to get her point across. "What happened?" she asked with anger pouring from every cell in her body.

The guard was astounded by what was going on, but tried to be polite. "I'm not at liberty to discuss that with you."

"That's not good enough!" she shouted, as she took another step closer to his body. She was on the verge of crying and was about to have a meltdown, but she couldn't help it; Roger leaving prison today was not part of the plan.

The guard felt certain that he wouldn't be able to satisfy the woman, so he displayed an icy boldness in his stance and ordered her to leave the premises. "You'll have to go, or I will have you arrested!" he stated loudly. He hoped that the shock of his command would awaken her senses. Otherwise, he would have to call for backup.

Jayla was confused and slightly intimidated by the new set of circumstances, and reluctantly shrank from the uniformed man's ice cold gaze. Because she was furious and felt that she had no other choice, she got into the car to regroup.

The guard was thankful that the woman had decided to leave, but as her tires kicked up the dust and gravel from the dirt road, he could still hear her screaming with frustration at the top of her lungs.

As Jayla cursed Roger's name, she pounded her fists against the steering wheel, over and over again. "I will make sure that you die a wicked death, you stupid man", she vowed with grim conviction. She pushed her foot against the gas pedal as if the speed would somehow lessen her pain.

Jayla had no idea that Roger would be getting out of prison early, and she hated that she didn't know where he was. She knew that she needed to find him as soon as possible, before her contempt for him crawled into her throat.

Minutes before they arrived at the hardware store, Marlowe turned to Roger to find out if he was still ok with the plan.

Roger nodded with assurance that he was.

"Good." Marlowe was suddenly feeling a little more relaxed.

They walked into the store and pretended that they were customers, but they made sure not to stand together.

Jack had never met either man before, so he greeted them in a very warm and friendly manner. "Hi!" he called. "Have a look around, and if you don't see what you're looking for, I will help you."

"Thanks", Marlowe replied nonchalantly.

Roger walked to the south end of the store, while Marlowe asked Jack about a specific product that was on sale. Once he was alone, Roger studied the doors, the locks, and the security cameras.

"Do you have this in another color?" Marlowe asked innocently enough.

Jack took the product from Marlowe's hand and inspected it slowly. "I think I do. Let me go check."

Jayla's hands were gripping the steering wheel with all her might, as her posture stayed stiff and her eyes didn't engage in anything but the road ahead of her. A churning heat began to stir in her belly, as she tried to figure out all that was going on.

The instant that Jack stepped behind the curtain and was now in the back of the store, Marlowe's mind began tumbling around with a million thoughts.

He had just been speaking to a man who would be dead in the next few days. That same man was married to Louise, the woman who Marlowe had been having an affair with. And off to his left, was a criminal who he was pretending to be friends with, but hoped would go back to jail when the police find Jack's dead body.

As he exhaled with major concern, Marlowe took a sideways glance at Roger, to see how he was doing.

In turn, Roger peeked at his friend from out of the corner of his eye. He had been totally aware of everything that had been happening a few feet away from where he stood, but he needed more time. Without speaking, he smoothed his hair with one hand and signalled for Marlowe to keep talking to Jack with the other.

The curtain swished open and brisk footsteps clicked against the hardwood floor. "Here you go!" Jack called, as he brought the product to Marlowe for inspection. "I think this might be what you're looking for."

Marlowe didn't even know what this was, but he rolled it over and over again in his large hands to show interest. To keep Jack's attention away from Roger, Marlowe asked the man a few more questions about the product. And while Jack explained the ins and outs of the oddly shaped item, Marlowe pretended to be fascinated, but he was more interested in what Roger was doing.

The instant Roger was finished inspecting the security of the property, he signalled to Marlowe that he was ready to go.

Marlowe was more than relieved, and inadvertently let out a thankful sigh. He reached a hand out and thanked Jack for his time, and then he placed the product down on the counter. "Let me think on it", Marlowe stated.

"No problem", Jack replied, as he picked up the product.

Marlowe caught up to Roger and they left the store together.

Jack smiled and waved as he watched them leave, and then he put the product on the shelf, next to the other one.

The two old friends had a lot on their minds, and walked back to the car in silence. As they drove away, Roger told Marlowe all that he knew about the layout of the store. When he was finished, they each gave suggestions on how they could proceed.

Jayla arrived back at Molly's home, a little over an hour after she left the prison. She rushed into the house, and slammed the door behind her as hard as she could. She then plopped herself on the couch and crossed her arms over her chest, making sure to tuck her hands tightly into her underarms.

She was livid and it showed; she had no idea where Roger was and time was running out. "I have less than 4 hours to go before the spell ends", she groaned wearily.

Before she could have another thought, she was violently jerked into a sitting position. Goose bumps appeared on her skin, and the air around her suddenly became thick and mysterious.

Because some things are too strange to be classified as coincidental, Jayla connected this anomaly to Roger. 'Was it possible that he was somewhere not too far away?' she wondered. This confusion and doubt caused adrenaline to course swiftly throughout her body.

Jayla couldn't get Roger out of her mind, but knew that she needed to find him. In order to calm down and to release some pent-up energy, she went into the kitchen to look for a cool drink.

Unbeknownst to Jayla, Marlowe and Roger were only a few minutes away.

Without asking his wife for permission, Marlowe had decided that Roger would stay with him and Molly until he found his own place to live. That way, he could keep Roger close and they could continue working on their plan.

Marlowe put the key in the lock of his home and opened the front door. "Hey Molly!" Marlowe

Ophelia's Curse

shouted, once he was inside. "Where the hell are you?"

When Marlowe called Molly's name, all the muscles in Roger's body contracted; he was about to see the woman who he had loved since childhood, and he wasn't sure how he should act.

Jayla was shocked when she heard the commotion at the front door, and then a man's stern voice calling out to her. For some strange reason, it gave her a funny feeling that things were about to take a turn for the better. "I'm here", she called, in a soft voice from the middle of the kitchen.

Roger's eyes went wide and his heart began to pound in his chest, at the thought that he would see her in less than a minute. He knew he needed to hide his emotions from Marlowe, and he hoped that he could also hide them from Molly.

The features on Marlowe's face contorted when he heard her voice. He then began to wave his hand in the air, as if he was shooing away a pestering fly which was buzzing around his head. "Bring me a beer."

Jayla's anxiety had now grown to its maximum capacity. She wiggled her shoulders and took a deep breath, and tried to remember how Molly had acted.

Marlowe showed Roger into the living room, and then offered him a drink and something to eat.

Roger reluctantly agreed to both. "But only if it's not too much trouble", he added.

"Hey, it's no trouble." Marlowe moved his head backwards and shouted into the air. "Can you grab a beer for my friend, and a plate of food from last night's supper?"

"Sure", she replied obediently. As Jayla flung the fridge door open, she could feel a great amount of excitement flow throughout her body. But it couldn't be, because that would mean that Roger was somewhere very close.

The possibility that he might be in the next room made her nervous, and she now had trouble containing her joy. After running her hands down the sides of her body, and checking her hair and make-up in the glossy toaster, she took another deep breath and wondered if her hunch was right. And after collecting everything that was asked of her, she brought it all into the living room and placed it in front of man who she didn't recognize.

Roger watched her as she entered the room, and he could feel himself moan under his breath at how beautiful she still was.

Because she had to stay in character, Jayla raised her voice and acted accordingly. "Here you go." She then turned to look at the other man in the room, and her heart almost exploded. "Roger?" she gasped with relief. She was surprised, confused, excited, and honestly didn't know what to say. "What are you doing here?" she asked.

The question could be taken with a grain of salt, but for Jayla, it was said with the purpose of learning the reason why he was no longer in jail. And before he could answer, she raced into his arms and hugged him tight to her body. She was filled with happiness, while relief gushed over her from head to toe.

Jayla was very pleased that Roger was in her arms, and she vowed to never lose sight of him again.

Roger was more than surprised by her reaction, but he embraced her and took a second to savour every part of her essence. He smelled her hair, he formed a memory of what it felt like to be in her arms, and he couldn't help but feel the warmth and curves of her body as it pressed up against his.

He had dreaded what would happen and what would be said, when and if they ever got together again, and he couldn't believe that he was now in that moment. He had had so many fears of being here, and now he knew that everything was ok; it was playing out so much better than he ever thought it would.

"I just got outta jail and need a place to rest", he said, as he grabbed her under the arms and lifted her high into the air. The happiness over seeing her again, filled him with a great amount of joy. "My, gosh!" he stated loudly, as he looked into her beautiful face. He suddenly felt an immediate closeness to her, as if they had never been apart for very long at all. "You still look as yummy as hell!"

Their eyes were locked and their smiles were genuine, and they each felt as if they were the only two people in the world.

"It's nice to see you, Molly." He swung her around one more time, and then he eased her body down until they were standing nose to nose. With his hands closed over her hips, he stared into her eyes.

While Jayla was happy to see him, she was suddenly crushed that he thought she was Molly. She was upset and tried not to make it obvious, but she became cold and wriggled out of his arms. She then moved aside and stood closer to where Marlowe was sitting. "Thank you." Her head was lowered and her eyes were looking towards the carpet. "It's nice to see you again", she stated kindly. Which was the truth, but only to get ownership of his soul.

As she moved away, Roger was stunned and tried to speak, but his lips remained soundless.

While the embrace between Roger and Molly was playing out, Marlowe watched those few minutes with curious interest. He knew his wife well enough to know that she was not a touchy-feely person. Or at least she hadn't been in years. And the fact that she was usually a lot shyer than she was being right now, raised a lot of suspicion in Marlowe's mind. "Alright!" he grunted loudly, as he waved his hand in the air. "That's enough of this mushy stuff."

While Roger was having his own confusing moment, he could see that Marlowe was getting pissed, so he decided to bring him back into the conversation. "When are you gonna leave this ugly guy and come take care of me?" he teased outwardly. He was speaking from his heart, for he was still lusting after a woman who he hadn't seen since high school.

Jayla, as Molly, looked over at Marlowe and laughed, "When I get a better offer."

Marlowe's face was turning red, which meant that his temper would soon spike.

Jayla wasn't afraid, and turned her attention back to Roger. "So you just got out of jail?"

"He already said that!" Marlowe barked. He then grimaced towards her in disgust.

Roger, who didn't want to get in between the married couple, nodded, and before he could say another word, Marlowe intervened.

"Gosh, Molly!" Marlowe shouted a little too loudly. He then turned to Roger and suggested that his friend eat the food that was laid in front of him.

Jayla's blood was starting to boil at the way in which Marlowe was speaking to her. But because she wanted to stay close to Roger, she tried to obey Marlowe's wishes.

Marlowe's gaze was burning through her with such intensity, that he hoped that her soul would shiver. "Sometimes..." he stated slowly.

Jayla lowered her eyes and decided that he would be the next one to die. It wasn't the truth, but it was fun for her to think about.

Roger was wide-eyed with surprise at how rough Marlowe spoke to his wife, but he was too paralyzed with fear to step in. He saw how timid Molly had become, and he hoped that Marlowe only hurt her emotionally. For now, Roger knew that he needed to bite his tongue until after the job was completed. But once he got the money in his hands, he would make sure that Marlowe paid for all the shitty things which he had done.

While she sat there fuming over the way that Marlowe was treating her, Jayla wondered how come Roger had gotten out of jail so early. Surely he would have told her if that was going to happen, or maybe that was one of the reasons why he wanted to talk with her the other night? She obviously couldn't ask him with Marlowe in the room, so she tried to be quiet, and waited for the right moment to approach the subject again.

From the outside, Jayla wore a poker-face, but on the inside, she was bubbling with excitement over the fact that Roger was within her reach. And as she looked at the clock, she could see that time was running out.

As Jayla contemplated all the ways in which she could get Roger alone, she could feel him staring at her.

Roger looked as if he hadn't eaten in days; he dropped crumbs and sauce on the floor and on his clothes, and continued shoveling the food into his mouth with great speed. And as he ate, he watched Molly out of the corner of his eye.

Curiosity filled his soul, while a wave of apprehension washed over him. He loved seeing Molly again, but he hated how she was living. While he appreciated what Marlowe was doing for him, he swore that if Marlowe made Molly cry while he was there, he would have to take matters into his own hands.

As Marlowe watched Roger enjoy the leftover food, he informed Molly that Roger would be staying with them for the next few days. "You should go up and fix the guest room for him," he stated coldly. He then used a hand motion to suggest that she leave.

Jayla was delighted that Roger was in the house, and ran upstairs to prepare things for his visit. Once she was alone, she allowed her true feelings to gush through every pour in her body.

She was thrilled that Roger was within her reach, and hated how Marlowe treated his wife. In a moment of great merriment, she laughed when she envisioned how she was going to kill them. Sadly, her body could only have one extra soul at a time, so she decided to destroy Marlowe in another way.

As her mind created different death scenes, Jayla gathered towels and face cloths from the linen closet and brought them into the guest room. She fixed the bed, pulled back the curtains, and opened the windows to make the room look and feel homier.

While dusting the pillow on the bed with the back of her hand, she envisioned this as the place where Roger would give up his soul. There was a hint of fire in her eyes as she pictured his last breath, and then she rearranged her thoughts and went back down the stairs.

She sat in her previous seat, and was quiet as she calculated how much time she had before the spell was over.

Roger was grateful that Molly had come back into the room, for he wanted to spend as much time as he could with her.

Unfortunately, Marlowe kept his guest so busy, that Jayla was unable to be alone with Roger for even a second. Meanwhile, the clock was ticking away.

By 5:30, Jayla was frantic, and felt that she had no other choice but to put Marlowe into a non-frozen state of stillness.

This particular spell applies more influence to the gravitational pull, which the tides and moon already have on all living creatures. By increasing its power, it forces your feet and hands downward so you can't move.

She stood up and was about to execute that spell, when an odd feeling of doom filled the room.

Roger looked up and he couldn't help but see a peculiar twinkle in Molly's eye. This made his body ache with an incredible amount of fear. He wasn't sure what Molly's intention was, but he was scared and his heart was racing.

Roger wanted to be with Molly in every way imaginable, and he now believed that she wanted that too. But he couldn't possibly wreck 'the plan' before it had even begun. If he did, he wouldn't have the money, and with Marlowe alive, he couldn't have Molly. He lowered his eyes and took a second to contemplate the complicated situation.

He was very quick to decide, that as hard as this was going to be, he needed Molly to back off until he was ready to bring her into his life.

So with a large breath for courage, and after gathering every ounce of strength in his body, he begged her not to end her marriage today. 'Stop whatever it is that you're about to do', he pleaded with his eyes and body language.

As Jayla locked eyes with Roger, she could feel him pulling away, but why? Anguish and confusion stabbed her like a knife. 'Didn't he want to be alone with Molly?'

Roger drew his brows together in an agonized expression, as his eyes begged her to leave things alone for the time being. He had too much to lose, and he vowed to fight her tooth and nail so that they could have a future together, but it just couldn't start right now. 'Wait!' he ordered in his mind, while passion breathed life into his heart.

Jayla didn't have much time left, and she needed him to comply with her wishes before the spell was broken. Whether he wanted to be with her or Molly, was beside the point. She had him right where she needed him to be, and she was going to take his soul from his body, today.

With a high level of confidence, Jayla stood up and was about to freeze Marlowe, but Roger stood up and stared her down.

In that same split second, Marlowe stood up and looked at both of them with complete confusion. He wasn't sure why *they* were on their feet, but he needed to step out of the room for a few seconds. Without looking over his shoulder, he walked down the short hallway, and he hoped that all would be back to normal when he returned.

As soon as Marlowe closed the bathroom door, Roger and Jayla turned to face each other. "No!" Roger said out loud, quietly but sternly. The lines of concentration deepened in his forehead, and he trusted that she would adhere to his sincere request.

To her surprise, his body had stiffened and became a little wider and taller, while his eyes had glared fiercely into hers.

Roger watched Molly's reaction to his impulsive display of command, and he hoped that he had made it clear that he would not allow anything to change between them in that moment.

Roger hadn't counted on her really wanting to be with him, and he was under the delusion that she was trying to end her marriage. He expected that they would be together soon, but it couldn't happen today, and he hoped that she would comply with his wishes.

Jayla noted the sternness in his face, the strength in his tightly closed mouth, and the determination in his fixed eyes, and it suddenly dawned on her that while Roger did want to be with Molly, he did not want to upset Marlowe.

Roger stood a mere two feet away from her body, and watched the changing appearance on her face. He could see dozens of thoughts brewing behind her eyes, but knew that they couldn't discuss any of them in that moment.

While the clock ticked loudly over her right shoulder, Jayla silently gave in to Roger's demand. A second later, her eyes clamped shut, for she suddenly felt helpless for losing control of the situation.

In that same instance, the muscles in both of their bodies relaxed, and the peculiar feeling in the room disappeared. In its place came an overwhelming calmness, and a respect from one strong individual to another.

Roger thanked her for backing down, and showed his appreciation with a soft nod and an irresistible grin.

Roger was pleased that Molly had awarded him the ability to manage those few moments, and silently promised that they would be together soon.

Jayla's knees weakened as she stared into his eyes. She needed his soul to be part of her body, and she prayed that if it couldn't happen today, that it would happen very soon – with or without his consent.

Thankfully, Marlowe had not been privy to the soundless bartering that had gone on between Roger and 'Molly'.

After Marlowe had come out of the bathroom, he had slipped into the kitchen to get two more cans of beer from the fridge. He walked back into the living room at the same time when things between the two other people in his home had been resolved. While he could feel the drawn-out tension in the air, it wasn't anything that he wanted to be part of.

Rather than be bored by their useless explanations, Marlowe shoved a beer into Roger's hand and sat down. "When you're ready, we should get down to business." Marlowe had directed that sentence to Roger, and he hoped that Molly would take the hint that they wanted to be alone.

In a shy and uneasy manner, Jayla looked at Marlowe, and then over at Roger. Not surprisingly, neither one had caught her eye. With a heavy heart, it was quite clear to her that she had been defeated, but she was convinced that she had not lost the war.

Jayla had been terribly crushed by both of these men, and as she moved herself to the kitchen, she vowed that they would pay. As she stood there, leaning up against the outdated fridge, she was dumbfounded, but would not allow herself to cry. Instead, she pushed all of her anger down to her toes and tried to come up with another plan.

At the stroke of 6, Jayla reluctantly prepared herself to switch back. When the clock said 6:03, she was standing outside the back door of Marlowe's home. After a giant POOF exploded from within a cloud of white smoke, both women were instantly transported back into their own bodies.

Molly was now standing at her back door, with no recollection of what had happened in the past few hours. Her mind was a mess and she couldn't help but wonder why she was outside.

Meanwhile, Jayla was in her car and was driving herself home. As she tried to make sense out of all that had happened, she still didn't understand how Roger had gotten out of jail so early. For now, she knew that he was with Marlowe, and she hoped that he would wake up in that house tomorrow.

Molly came in through the kitchen door and was shocked to find Roger in the house.

"W-what are you doing here?" she asked, in a childlike manner. Her eyes were wide and she thought she was dreaming.

Both men looked at each other in complete wonder, while Molly waited for an answer.

Marlowe was suddenly embarrassed, and gave her a quick berating. "What is wrong with you tonight?" he stated in a cold tone.

It was now Molly's turn to be embarrassed, while Roger was frozen with fear over what he should do while this was going on.

Molly felt stupid for forgetting that they had already said HI and that she had served him supper.

"Maybe you should go to bed", Marlowe ordered. It was clear that her disposition had changed over the past half an hour, but he wasn't sure what was going on. And because he wanted to have some time alone with Roger, he felt it best that she go upstairs.

Molly's skin was cool to the touch and she was feeling more than a little off-balance, so she didn't hesitate to obey him.

When Molly looked in the bathroom mirror, she saw her own reflection, but she didn't feel like herself at all. As her mind tried to remember where she was and what she had done in the afternoon, nothing came forward. It was all quite distressing and left her nerves in a shattered mess.

It took a while, but when she finally calmed down, Molly put herself to bed. And as she laid her head against her pillow, she hoped that a good night's sleep would put all of her jumbled pieces back into place again.

Meanwhile, before Jayla was able to go to bed, she spent an hour trying to find another way to retrieve Roger's soul from his body.

CHAPTER NINE

October 28, 2000

Molly was surprised to wake up feeling refreshed, and after serving breakfast, she announced that she was going shopping. She had her hand on the doorknob and was watching how Roger and Marlowe were acting, and she was suddenly hesitant to leave them alone.

The two men had been talking in whispers whenever she was around, and while she hadn't seen Roger in decades, she found it odd that he was purposely trying to keep his distance from her. What made it even more confusing, was that she couldn't remember him coming into the house. Marlowe, on the other hand, was his same old grumpy self, but she was used to that.

"Ok, I'm going", she stated loudly. "I'll be back soon."

"Stay as long as you like", they concurred. They had spoken at the same time and in the same tone of voice, and because it looked like it had been rehearsed, it seemed almost comical.

Molly rolled her eyes and shook her head at the lack of humor in their silly antics. As she walked through the doorway, she decided to agree to disagree, and would come back as soon as she was ready.

In the past hour, Marlowe and Roger had the whole living room in total disarray. They had acted out schemes, they had written things down on paper, and they had taken turns suggesting ideas on how Jack would die. They were in the midst of talking up a storm when she drove up, but stopped once they heard her slam the car door shut.

"Quick!" Marlowe ordered. He was suddenly filled with anxiety at the thought of getting caught planning a murder, and haphazardly gathered everything up with ferocious speed. Together he and Roger shoved all of their notes into a large box, and then they straightened their postures while trying to look as if nothing was going on.

She opened the door and immediately stopped moving her feet. "Are you guys ok?" Molly asked. She lowered her chin as her eyebrows pushed together, and looked at the men over the top of her sunglasses. She was full of suspicion, and it was obvious by how they were standing and the silly expressions on their faces, that they had something to hide.

The two men were perspiring, they seemed nervous, and their voices had changed in pitch and volume. And because it looked like they were forcing the features on their faces to appear normal, they both looked quite unnatural.

"Yah, yah. We're good", Roger claimed. He turned and looked at Marlowe, hoping that he approved of that statement.

Roger's his face was flushed and that his heart was racing, but he knew it was because he was in the same room as his beloved Molly. As he stood across from her, he gazed into her angelic face, and he hoped that she would forgive him for all that was happening right now.

Little did she know that he was going to kill her husband, and after Marlowe was found dead, Roger would then ask Molly to be with him for the rest of her life.

"Yah, we're good!" Marlowe agreed. And as he looked at Roger and then at Molly, his face was also turning a bright shade of red.

Marlowe's normal uncaring regard for his wife had vanished, and it was replaced with an awkward embarrassment. He wasn't sure why, but he suddenly felt as if he was standing on a stage with a hundred people watching, and he had been caught with his pants down at his ankles. He was wide-eyed and nodded weakly towards his bride, and he hoped that 'the plan' would not be found out until after he had the large amount of money in his greedy hands.

In order to take the magnitude off of the moment, Marlowe rushed to the door to help Molly with the bags of groceries. "Here, let me take that for you", he insisted kindly and with a smile.

Roger quickly followed suit. "I'll get the bags from your car!" he announced loudly, as he dashed out of the house.

Molly was more than amazed by her husband's gallant behavior, and was suddenly frozen to the spot with total disbelief. After Marlowe came back from dropping the bags on the kitchen counter, he informed Molly that he was taking Roger to check out an apartment. "Unless you have something else for me to do?"

Molly turned her attention towards Roger, who had just come into the house with the last of her groceries. "Oh, you found something?" Her eyebrows shot up and wrinkled her forehead as she waited for him to answer.

Roger, who had walked in on the last part of the conversation, shot a quizzical look in Marlowe's direction.

Marlowe became instantly animated, and was using his eyes, eyebrows, and chin as signals for him to say yes.

Roger turned back to Molly and replied. "I… yah…we did." He had no idea what was going on, but felt the need to agree with whatever Marlowe had said.

As she took the last bag from Roger's arm, Molly breathed a sigh of relief. "Well, good for you."

While it was nice to see him again, she wasn't sure that it was healthy to have Roger hanging around her husband – he was a bad influence and a habitual inmate. On the other hand, she had to admit that Marlowe certainly seemed to be happier – this was a side of him that she didn't see too often.

Marlowe kissed her cheek and then the two men left the house. "Bye!" they called over their shoulders.

As Molly made her way to the kitchen, she chuckled at their childlike behavior.

"That was close", Roger stated, after he shut the car door.

"I agree, but now I have to take you somewhere", Marlowe replied. A devious smile lifted the corners of his mouth, as he thought of the perfect place to go. "Hang on!" he ordered. He then pressed his foot all the way down on the gas pedal.

As the small vehicle sped through the moderate traffic, Roger's eyes grew large like two saucers of milk, while his heart began to thump to an off-beat rhythm.

Marlowe chuckled as he drove like the wind, because it looked like his companion was fearing for his life.

Roger was not used to being in a fast-moving car, and he didn't want to die in a pile of twisted burning metal. He held onto the dash board as if he was bracing himself for a horrific crash, and he could feel that his lungs were beginning to burn from him holding his breath. As his mouth took on an unpleasant twist, he silently wished for them to arrive somewhere soon, and safe.

Now that she knew where to find Roger, Jayla had no problem coming up with another scheme to collect his soul. After she weighed the options, she decided to create an incident where Molly would be in trouble and Roger would have to rescue her.

On paper, it was brilliant. In reality, there might be a few bugs to work out.

Jayla waited until after breakfast to get started, and then she employed all of her skills to ensure total precision of her plan.

Roger was Jayla's main focus – she couldn't have him draw his last breath without her knowledge. Because he was out of jail and anything could happen to make her lose sight of him, she knew she needed to work as quickly as possible.

When she was ready, she placed herself in the middle of her living room. She made sure that she was surrounded by her lit candles and the fresh scents from her garden, and then she called upon the spirits in her world to help her.

> God of Thunder and Lord of Zim
> If Roger dies without me near him,

Ophelia's Curse

Please place me in that
exact place and time
So I can claim what is rightfully mine.

There was an immediate feeling of calmness in the room following this simple but powerful spell; a proud feeling like she had just conquered something insurmountable. While Jayla saw no sign of any physical changes around her, she knew that she couldn't take the time to *worry if the spell had worked or not.

Jayla was relieved that this little snag was behind her, for now she could concentrate on Molly. As she made her way to the kitchen, it looked as if she was brushing the dust off of her hands. In reality, she was getting prepared for the next step in stealing Roger's soul.

A flash of humor crossed over Marlowe's face, as he and Roger arrived at their destination.

---

*When witches worry, it uses up a considerate amount of unnecessary energy. This in turn, can dilute the effectiveness of all incantations.

Roger was more than relieved that the car had finally stopped, but he couldn't believe where Marlowe had taken him. As the words on the neon sign flashed into his eyes and the idea slowly sunk into his brain, Roger's face began to radiate with ultimate happiness. "Al-ri-i-i-ght!" he shouted. He then sprang from the car with as much vigor as a child had when they were being taken into a candy store.

Without caring if Marlowe would follow him or not, Roger rushed inside the double front doors and was instantly captivated by all that was around him.

Marlowe chuckled at his friend's obvious amusement, and shadowed Roger into the loud and smoky strip club. Once inside the dark establishment, Marlowe tried to find where Roger had ended up.

Roger had been locked away for a long time, and other than the sporadic moments of pleasure with Jayla, he had had no physical contact with women in the last year.

He was drooling as he plopped himself down on a chair near the stage, and then sat doe-eyed and silent as he watched the ladies dance before him - not unlike an eager hunter who was pursuing his unsuspecting prey.

Marlowe went to the bartender and ordered them a few drinks, and then he made his way to the chair beside Roger. Once he was sure that his friend was happily engaged by the entertainment, he walked to the hallway beside the bathrooms to use the payphone.

Louise answered on the first ring. "Hello?"

"Well, hello", he replied in a slow and sultry voice. Marlow's loins had been activated and he now needed relief, so he told her exactly what he wanted and when.

"Tomorrow at noon sounds perfect", she giggled. Louise felt like a teenage girl and couldn't wait to see Marlowe again. And while she didn't want to spoil the moment, she did want to know what was going on with 'their plan'.

Marlowe's temper soared as he hushed her to silence. "I'll tell you tomorrow", he whispered in an angry tone. He then slammed the receiver into the cradle, without so much as a good-bye.

Marlowe was fond of Louise, but he did not like anyone pushing him or checking up on his every move. He told her that he would kill Jack, and he meant it. He didn't need or want her asking him about it every two seconds.

As Louise hung up the phone, she pushed Marlowe's sour mood aside and focused on being happy. As she turned around and leaned her body against the nearest wall, she chewed on the fingernail of her right index finger, while deciding on how to give Marlowe the best time of his life.

Marlowe lit a cigarette as he walked back to the stage, and tried to blur his bad mood with a long drag on his Rothman's King Size cigarette. After he sat down beside Roger, and after he had forced the double shot of whiskey to go down his throat in one gulp, he felt a little better.

Roger couldn't help but beam in Marlowe's direction, for he was having the time of his life. He didn't know why, but in all his days on this earth, he had never been to a place like this before. He was very grateful to Marlowe for bringing him there, and he vowed to drink up as much of this sexual energy as he could.

Marlowe smiled as he looked around for a server, and then signalled for another drink. When it arrived, he lingered in the sensual awareness that occurred when the skin of the waitress made contact with his. It was an immediate reaction that slithered between their bodies, and now he wanted more. Marlowe turned and glanced in Roger's direction, and really studied his face. Since he could see that his friend was having a good time, he took that opportunity to partner up with the naughty waitress.

Louise had high hopes of being a widow before the end of the week, and she loved the fact that she would soon have more money in her hands than she knew what to do with. She walked towards the couch and sat down, and her thoughts immediately turned to the next day's activities.

Marlowe was a nice guy, but there were plenty of nice guys in the world. Louise loved being with him and she loved how he made her feel, but after Jack was dead, she would have to move on.

Long before Louise met Marlowe, she had perfected a 'how to get rich quick scheme'. Once this current plan was executed, she was going to sail around the world. She would be single, she would have no use for Marlowe, and she would be long gone before he came looking for the money.

Louise was more clever than anyone gave her credit for, and it showed: Marlowe had been but a little pawn in her deceitful plan, only he didn't know it. She had used him for whatever she needed, and she had him thinking that he was in charge the whole time.

Louise smiled as she pushed her body into the over-sized, fluffy cushions. As she placed her hands on her tummy and rested her head on the back of the couch, she couldn't help but revel in how easy this particular adventure had been, or how quickly her plan was unfolding.

Meanwhile, Jayla had come up with a shrewd way to get closer to Molly.

Because Molly had already met the crone, Jayla decided to pretend that she was the old lady's granddaughter.

The pretense was that the older woman had disappeared and Jayla would be looking for her in Molly's neighbourhood.

Jayla giggled at how clever she was, while thinking of all the ways that this would work. She then toiled until she had achieved the perfect level of deception.

Marlowe had been able to enjoy a few sinful moments with the willing waitress, while Roger had kept his eyes on the naked girls who were showing him their goodies.

Since Roger had stepped inside of the loud bar with a hundred strobe lights flashing around him, all thoughts of any other girl had disappeared. He had a smorgasbord of women in front of him, and each one was more tantalizing than the next. He wasn't allowed to touch any of them, but while one stripper raked her long nails down the length of his chest, another had pressed her taut young body tightly up against his. Later on, an older, more skillful dancer framed his face with her hands, while bringing her brightly painted, pouting lips close enough for him to kiss. She then laughed as she playfully pulled away before their lips could touch, and all of this was making him very excited.

To Roger, every caress was a distinct promise of an orgasm in his future, and every movement of their swaying hips brought him closer to the edge. His body was now glistening in a light sweat, and his erection was strong and wanted to be touched. He wasn't mindful of Jayla or Molly in that moment, and he was having so much fun, that he didn't want this night to end.

Marlowe had come back without Roger's knowledge, and sat down to enjoy the rest of the show. Together they lifted their glasses, toasted the dancing women, and continued to drink to their heart's content.

Without Roger's knowing, Marlowe had let it slip to the bartenders and waitresses that his friend was looking for a new home. It didn't take too long after that, before someone announced that they had a place to rent.

Marlowe automatically beamed with pride, and they both shouted their great appreciation in total harmony. "Wow! Thank you so much!"

From what Roger and Marlowe had been told, it was a very small and dingy apartment upstairs from the bar. It was somewhat furnished, the rent was cheap, and it was available right now.

Roger, who was as drunk as could be, was elated to have a home of his own. "Thank you!" he shouted over the noise in the bar. He then stood up and hugged the man who had offered him a new place to live.

Marlowe was delighted for Roger, and after seeing the place firsthand, he agreed to help Roger with the first month's rent. He even paid a generous amount of money for a girl to entertain Roger for the night. "Consider it a house warming gift", he laughed. After they picked the girl and brought her upstairs, Marlowe shut the door and let the two of them get acquainted.

Jayla had decided to gain access to Molly, under the pretense of needing her help in finding her grandmother. As she looked over her notes, she could see how the events would unfold.

Jayla had seen firsthand the immense love that Roger had for Molly, so she hoped to lure Molly somewhere far away. After Roger found her, Jayla would provide the two of them with a special beverage, which would render them incapable of waking up for at least an hour. She would then leave Molly where she was, and whisk Roger away to the Schilling Forest.

After the long drive, she would reduce Roger to tears, and after she told him why, she would then take his dark soul as her own.

Ophelia's Curse

Jayla sat back and couldn't help but smile at her intelligence, for her shameful idea seemed quite brilliant. And yet, as proud as she was, there was a strange catch in the back of her brain that seemed to gnaw at a flaw. It bothered her to the point that she was no longer 100% happy, so she went over all the details again.

Marlowe had somehow stumbled home and made his way to his side of the bed. Without removing his clothing, he climbed under the covers and quickly passed out.

Molly hated how he smelled, but because she assumed that Roger was going to be sleeping in the guest room, she felt that she had no choice but to remain where she was.

After a heavy sigh, and a light sob of remorse for marrying the first man who had turned her head, she shuffled her body to the very edge of the bed and tried to go back to sleep.

Meanwhile, Jayla was wide awake and terribly confused. It was just past midnight, and although everything seemed to be okay on paper, there was something that just wasn't sitting right.

She didn't know what the problem was, but she knew that she would work at it until morning if necessary, because time was getting the best of her and she couldn't let this opportunity disappear again.

CHAPTER TEN

October 29, 2000

Jayla stayed up much longer than she had intended to, and as many times as she had gone over all the details in her plan, she couldn't see where it was going to fail. She had eventually fallen asleep on the living room floor, surrounded by her cat and a bunch of open books.

Roger woke up in his new surroundings, and he was terribly frightened. He was naked, the smell of stale perfume and alcohol were lingering heavily in the air, and while he vaguely remembered being with Marlowe, he had no idea where Marlowe was now.

As Roger swung his feet over the side of the bed, his head swam in a lazy manner while he looked around the room. As he tried to get his bearings, little pieces from the night before, trickled into his brain.

Roger remembered sparsely dressed women dancing on a stage, and him and Marlowe laughing and drinking. He remembered being shown into a small room, and then being left alone with a woman who he didn't know.

It seemed so surreal at the time, as if he was watching it happen to someone else, so he went along with whatever was going on.

Roger's mind suddenly popped when he recalled how flexible the woman had been, and how she was able to move in ways that only a Yoga student could master. He wanted to chuckle when he recalled her slim body, because it had probably been toned due to all the dancing she did, but he was in far too much pain to enjoy the vague memory.

Roger tried to picture her face, but all he could see was bouncy dark hair on an untamed Mediterranean beauty. He didn't remember much else, and hoped that Marlowe could help him fill in the blanks.

Marlowe couldn't wait to find out how Roger's evening had gone, so as soon as he was alone, he dialed the number.

Ri-i-i-i-ing

The loud shrill of the rotary phone startled the former inmate, and jolted him to near soberness. He picked it up immediately, if only to stop the loud noise from continuing. "Hello?" He was hunched over, his elbow was leaning on his thigh, and his aching head was being supported in the palm of his free hand.

"Roger, you old dog! How was your night?"

Roger's eyes sprung wide open as soon as he recognized the voice. "Marlowe?"

"Yah!" he laughed, and pressed his ear closer to the receiver so he wouldn't miss out on any juicy details.

Roger's tongue felt like it had fur on it, his head was banging, and his stomach was gurgling as if he had eaten a plate of rotten eggs. "What the hell happened last night?" he asked, as he massaged the side of his throbbing skull. "And where the hell am I?"

Roger had been in prison for a long time, and was not used to having a violent hangover. What made it worse, was that the dirty blinds were open and the sun seemed exceptionally bright and overly-warm.

Marlowe chuckled with great delight, as he began to fill his friend in on all that had happened.

As Roger listened to the interesting specifics of their evening, he put his hand up to shield the light from his eyes.

Jayla's cat was purring in her ear as it continually brushed up against her face.

"Thank you, precious. I'm up now", Jayla promised. As she reached out to stroke her furry companion's head and ears, she opened her eyes and was quite surprised to find that she was laying on the floor. Anxiety spread quickly throughout her body, as she turned to look at the clock.

"Listen", Marlowe stated, as he began another thread to their conversation. "I will be busy for about two hours this afternoon, but let's get together right after that.

Roger grunted his answer while trying to nod his head. That was all he could do in that moment, because he really wasn't feeling well at all.

"Good", Marlowe added. "We need to tie up all the loose ends regarding our plan as soon as possible."

"Ok", he mumbled. As he hung up the phone, Roger was relieved that he could go back under the covers again. While smothering a groan, he shifted unhappily until he found a good position. He then tried his best to ignore the pain and ugliness of the unforgiving hangover, and soon slipped into a deep sleep.

Marlowe met Louise at their usual place, and after a jaunty hour of exhilarating sex, they lingered in each other's arms and talked.

Her eyes were still glassy and in a sexual haze, as they followed the sleek line of his muscular jaw. And while the index finger of her right hand caressed the softness of his bottom lip, she asked, "Can you tell me what's happening with our plan?"

Their eyes met immediately, and in a voice that rang with command he stated, "Roger and I have got it all under control." He stroked her hair in a fatherly manner, to let her know that it's going to be alright. "Don't worry about that stuff", he scolded kindly. "You just get the paperwork ready for when the police find Jack's body."

Louise wondered who Roger was, but couldn't help but smile as she nodded. She was happier than she'd been in a long time and couldn't wait until all of this was over. "Ok, and thank you", she sighed in an obedient manner, and then she lovingly laid her head against his shoulder.

Nobody knew what a shrewd woman Louise was. If you really looked at her, you could see that both her voice and her behaviour echoed with the certainty of a woman who could never be satisfied with only one dream. She knew what she wanted and she knew how to get it, and she wasn't about to release Marlowe from his promise.

Marlowe was on the verge of melting, for she had no idea that her velvety voice sent ripples of awareness to every part of his body. "You're very welcome." As he spoke, he moved his naked and sweaty chest even closer to hers.

How he repositioned himself, caused her throat to let out a long, audible breath. As she gazed into his rugged face, her eyes brimmed with unexpected passion. She placed her hands around the back of his neck and locked her fingers together. She then kissed his nose, his eyes, each cheek, and then she captured his lips with her own.

Marlowe was about to explode, for he knew that a kiss like this could only have one conclusion.

Louise kept her lips locked with his, as if to swallow every moan that either of them might utter in the next few minutes.

Her kiss set off a sharp, wild need in his lower region - a need that he couldn't supress. And as her hands roamed eagerly over his moist flesh, he could feel his body becoming taut with anticipation.

Because she was anxious to have him one more time, Louise pushed the front of her body tightly up against his.

He immediately pushed her against the sheets, pinned her wrists to the mattress with a playful grin, and slid a strong thigh between hers.

Louise was now lost in another storm of sexual heat, and she couldn't wait for this new game to begin.

Marlowe's voice became thick with desire as he whispered her name. "Louise", he hummed, followed by a breathy sigh.

As tortured sounds squeezed past her lips, Louise couldn't wait to have him, so she decided to take control of the situation. She released the hold which he had on her left wrist, and wrapped her slender hand around his erection. She was not surprised when he grew even harder, or when the blunt head pressed urgently against her palm.

Marlowe had his eyes closed and was waiting to be destroyed by the pleasure which she was delivering. But as he moved his knee to the highpoint between her legs, she removed her hand and laid it softly against his chest.

They immediately locked eyes and kissed until their lips were burning and bruised. And as their tongues continued to fight a silent battle in the warmth of her mouth, he pushed himself into her inner passageway, and they enjoyed another fifteen minutes of uninhibited pleasure.

Jayla hopped into the shower and then took some extra time to make herself look presentable. As she drove to Molly's house, she rehearsed what she was going to say. As she stood on Molly's porch, she tried to give the impression that she was sad.

Knock, Knock, Knock

Molly was doing dishes when she heard someone at her front door.

"Hello", Jayla said, when she stood face-to-face with Molly. "I wonder if you could help me."

Molly stared at her with wide eyes and a kind smile. "I could try."

"My grandmother was seen in this neighbourhood yesterday, but I don't know where she is today." Jayla paused for dramatic effect. "Is it possible that you've seen her?"

In an alarming pace, Molly's right hand rushed up to the top of her chest. "Yes!" she said a little too loudly. Up until that very moment, the image which she had of an elderly woman, seemed like a dream. "I did see an older lady here yesterday! I'm just not sure where she is today, but we could call around. Do you want to come inside?"

Molly was overjoyed and suddenly felt as if a huge weight had been lifted from her shoulders. She had had faint flashes of an old woman throughout the last 24 hours, but nothing was specific. She couldn't even remember parts of the day herself, and now she wanted to cry from happiness because she wasn't going crazy.

As the adrenaline started to race through her body, Molly was becoming more and more alive with a renewed sense of normal.

Jayla smiled when she answered. "Yes, thank you."

"I'm Molly, by the way." She closed the door and guided her guest to the couch. "Can I offer you a tea or a coffee?"

"I'm Jayla, and a coffee would be great. Thank you." As she watched Molly dash away, her eyes scanned the room which she had been in the day before.

Roger was fast asleep in his new apartment, and he was dreaming of how he was going to spend the money that would soon flow into his greedy little hands.

Molly was enjoying a nice chat with a woman whose grandmother had come to her home, not 24 hours ago. "Shall we try calling the police department to see what they might know?" she asked with hope.

Jayla smiled and replied, "That's sounds like a good place to start."

Jayla knew full-well that the old crone was nowhere to be found, and she was delighted by the fact that Molly was about to begin her fictional pursuit of a ghost.

When Marlowe was finished with Louise, they said good-bye, and he headed to the nearest fast food, drive-through window. With a bag of greasy grub in his hand, he drove to Roger's building, walked up three flights of stairs, and banged on the door. "Are you up yet?" he called from the semi-dark and shabby hallway.

Roger had been able to sleep for another few hours before Marlowe had tapped on his door. He bolted out of bed when he heard the noise, and rushed his lanky body across the room while still being half-asleep. "Yah, I'm up", he insisted. He ran a hand through his unkempt hair, while his lips stretched wider than normal capacity, in order to accommodate a giant yawn.

Marlowe walked inside the small room and stared at his friend. "Look at you!" he teased. "What happened here last night?"

Roger's shoeless feet brought him back to the familiar twin size bed. After he sat down, he answered. "Nothing. I don't know. Why?" His thoughts were jumbled and his head was foggy, and it was clear that he didn't catch on that Marlowe was fishing for details about the sex he might have had, with the girl who Marlowe had paid for.

Marlowe was pissed that he wasn't going to get any juicy details, and his anger rushed to the surface. "Yah, whatever." He made a swift sweeping gesture with his left arm, his nostrils were now flaring, and he suddenly had a tightening look around his distant, caramel-colored eyes.

Marlowe took a seat on the worn out, two-seater couch, and tried to ignore all the mess that was around him. "Here", he said sternly, without making eye contact with the other man in the room. He passed the large paper bag forward and offered it to Roger. "I brought you some food."

"Thanks." Roger was extremely grateful that there was coffee, and he appreciated the deluxe cheese burger and fries.

As Roger ate, Marlowe tried to calm himself down. Minutes later, he talked about the plan and suggested that time was running out. "How about if we case the joint from the outside?"

Roger agreed and nodded, but his mind was more on satisfying his upset tummy.

Because it looked like this was going to take a while, Marlowe spotted a small TV sitting on a dresser on the other side of the room. After reaching for the remote, he searched for something to watch.

Molly hung up the phone, but had a pained look on her face as she gave Jayla the news. "The police confirmed that they had brought an old woman to the Regal Hospital yesterday, but she has since disappeared." Molly tried to phrase her words tenderly, so that Jayla wouldn't become upset. "They will need you to go down to the police station to give them a full description of your grandmother, and any other information which you could provide."

"Oh, wow." Jayla purposely lowered her chin to her chest, in order to give the illusion that she was sad and worried. She wanted to pull at Molly's heartstrings, and was pleased that her amazing acting skills had worked.

Molly's brow had wrinkled, and she suddenly felt like a mother hen. She sat down beside Jayla and patted her hand, and in a sympathetic tone she asked, "Do you want to go to the station now?"

After reaching for a tissue, Jayla replied. "I have family members who would be very interested in what's going on, so do you mind if we go later in the day? Or possibly tomorrow morning?" As she spoke, she wiped some invisible fluid from the underside of her nose.

"Of course not", Molly replied in a soothing tone. "And if you would like to have some company, I'd be glad to go with you. If you don't mind, I mean." She took one of Jayla's hands in between both of hers, and spoke from her heart.

While she presented the image of a disheartened granddaughter, Jayla felt as if she was giving the performance of a lifetime. "That would be great, thank you." She placed her free hand on top of Molly's and patted it twice.

While Molly saw a thankful expression on Jayla's face, she didn't see the shimmer of satisfaction behind her deceitful eyes.

To Jayla, step one was now complete, and step two would be to kidnap Molly so that Roger would have to come looking for her.

After their coffee cups were empty, the two women agreed to meet the next day.

Jayla left Molly's home smiling, she knew that she was that much closer to receiving Roger's soul.

In that same moment, Roger and Marlowe were heading towards Jack's store. After they arrived, they parked in the back to avoid being seen. Neither spoke as they got out of the car, and both went to the back door together. After covering the lens of the hidden security camera, they got down to business.

Roger ran the tips of his fingers all along the edges of the door frame, while Marlowe stood quiet and watched for anyone who might be approaching.

Roger used his experienced hands to feel his way around the two back windows. He then checked all around the doorknob and under the doormat, and when he was done, he nodded to Marlowe and walked back to the car.

Marlowe followed directly behind him, without saying a word.

Once the doors of the car had been closed and locked, Roger began his review.

"#1, they're using a cheap security system, and I think it can be passed quite easily.

#2, because of our great detective work, we know that Jack stays late to lock up, and he's usually alone.

#3, we have to wait until closing time before we can go in."

"Then what?" Marlowe asked, with greed and revenge on his simple mind.

Roger turned his head to the left and looked at the driver with absolute disbelief. "Then we kill him and make it look like an accident, of course!" he stated unkindly. Roger's beady eyes found their way to the back door of the hardware store, and then he slowly continued his thought. "He must have to empty the garbage before he goes home at night. That's when we get him."

"Of course", Marlowe agreed. "The front is all lit up and can be seen from every angle, but the back is private and it's not lit very well at all."

"Exactly!" Roger chimed.

The two fake friends smiled as they shook hands to seal the deal.

"Now we wait until tomorrow night."

"Until tomorrow", Roger repeated.

Jayla was excited and couldn't wait until tomorrow, for that's when she would take Roger's soul as her own. And now that she had made contact with Molly, she felt that the rest of the plan will be easy enough to pull off.

Jayla looked at the clock to see how much time she had left, and then laughed at the simplicity of this mission. As she reached her hands out to the sides and twirled her body around as if she was a dancer, she sang the following words: "Tomorrow night, your soul will be mine, and when you are dead, my eyes will shine." She laughed as she did a pirouette, and now she couldn't wait until the night turned into the day.

Jack locked up the hardware store and went to the bar across the street for a quick drink. To his delight, the Calgary Flames were playing against the New York Rangers, and an illegal body check had driven some of the players from both teams, into a nasty group fight.

Jack smiled as he ordered two large beers, and then sat at a small round table by himself. As he looked with great intent at the large TV on the wall, he began to feel all his stress melt away.

The game went into overtime, and by then Jack had consumed way more than he was used to drinking. But, as drunk as he was, he made it home safely, although he couldn't walk any further than his living room.

When everyone was sound asleep, they dreamed about their expectations for the next day. Unfortunately for some people, it would be their last day on this earth.

CHAPTER ELEVEN

October 30, 2000

It was sunrise on the day before Halloween, and Louise was ready to begin her new life as a single woman. She grabbed her large suitcase from the bedroom closet, and threw as much as she could into it. After she had a shower, she slid her favorite blue and white polka-dotted dress onto her body. She styled her hair, added a necklace and earrings, and then sprayed perfume to her neck. She liked how the dress hugged her curves, and felt quite confident that she looked beautiful overall.

When she was ready, Louise took one last look around the bedroom which she had so lovingly decorated, and then grabbed her suitcase and walked down the stairs. When she got to the last step, she was surprised and stood very still, because there before her, was Jack.

Her eyes went wide and her heart skipped a beat when she saw him on the couch, and now she wasn't sure if she could make it out of the house without getting caught.

He was lying on his tummy so she couldn't see his face, but she could tell that he was very relaxed. Louise didn't know if he was sound asleep or just resting, so she listened for the steady breathing one has when they're having a nap. When he snored, she knew the answer.

She used that as her cue to leave, and slowly tip-toed towards the door. With her hand on the door knob, she took one last look in his direction and bid him a silent good-bye. She held her breath as she opened and closed the door very quietly, and then made her way to her car.

It was a very sad and difficult 1-minute walk, because a lot of feelings and memories flooded her brain. And when she took that last look at the place she called home, she almost ran back inside.

Louise shed one single tear as she turned the motor over and began to drive to the motel, but in her heart, she knew that this was best. At least for her it would be.

After 15 minutes of driving, she arrived at her destination, and she asked for the same room which she and Marlowe had been in every Wednesday. Once she was settled and had finished her fancy coffee, she called Marlowe's work from the black phone in the provincially decorated room.

Marlowe was with a customer so the receptionist asked if she could take a message.

"Just tell him to call me back." Louise's voice was a little harsh as she gave the woman her name and phone number, and then she hung up the phone without saying good-bye. She was jealous that he was with someone else, but had no other choice but to wait. She turned on the TV to pass the time.

Marlowe got to work early that morning, and because of 'the plan', he knew it was going to be a long day. He kept himself busy and pushed all of the details of the evening to the back of his mind, but when it was quitting time, he knew it would all come tumbling out.

Roger didn't seem to have as much on his mind as Marlowe, and he had been able to sleep in until almost 10am. After he got cleaned up, he went to the nearest diner and ate a hearty breakfast. Minutes after paying the bill, he grabbed his list of items and went shopping.

Fifteen minutes after entering the thrift store, Roger left and made his way to the Raistlin Shopping Centre. They didn't have all of the items which he had been looking for, so he had to go someplace else.

Roger ended up in five different places before he got back home again. By that time, he was like a little kid on Halloween, and he couldn't wait to dump everything out of the bags and onto his bed.

Jack woke up with a splitting headache, and his body was extremely sore and tired. He stood up quickly, but sat right back down again when the room started spinning. He listened for any sign that Louise might be in the house, but sadly, there weren't any. "Louise?" He called her name as he tried to stand up again, and though he moved slowly, he was able to get himself up the stairs to the bedroom. As Jack shuffled his feet across the floor, he rubbed his forehead as if that would make the pain go away.

He looked everywhere, and after realizing that Louise was not in the house, Jack picked up the phone and called his work. When his employee answered, Jack asked how everything was going.

Adam assured Jack that all was okay. "It's the day before Halloween", he stated with a lilt in his voice. "It's always slow on this day."

Jack chuckled and agree. "You're right, but I'm coming in anyway."

"You're the boss", the young man laughed.

Jack hung up, and while he looked around the room, he noticed that some of Louise's clothes were missing. Upon closer inspection, he also noticed that her perfume bottle, her hair brush, and her toothbrush were gone.

He was terribly dismayed and now quite confused, for he couldn't figure out what was going on. They hadn't been fighting and there were no tell-tale signs that told him that she would be leaving, so he could only guess that there had been some sort of emergency.

He was now a lot calmer, and felt that he had no choice but to wait until she got back, so they could talk about what was going on. In the meantime, he decided to get ready for work. The trouble was, he was queasy and didn't want to move a muscle.

For many months now, Jack had been working 6 days a week, from sunrise to sunset. He was hoping to buy the space next door when it went up for sale in November, but he hadn't told his wife of his plans - Louise had always talked about opening up a dress shop, and this was going to be a surprise for her.

Jack's sullen mood sank even lower, for as he drank in the ugly emptiness of his home without his wife in it, his body grew cold and covered itself with goose bumps. As another awkward chill raced up his hairless back, he wondered if he should have told her about his idea sooner.

Jack got off the bed, removed his clothing, and hopped into the shower. Because the tiled cubicle was dotted with stale droplets of water, he figured that Louise must have been in there before she left. A warm smile grew across his face, for it gave him great comfort to know that he was standing in the same place as she had been standing, not that long ago.

Jack stood underneath the showerhead and relished how the warm water felt against his skin. He liked how it pounded the pain away from within his skull, and how it made his weary bones feel a bit better. And after many minutes of not moving, he finally reached for the soap. By the time he was rinsing the scented bubbles off of his body, he had recovered a bit more than he had expected.

Jack didn't want to go to work, but in his 15 years at the store, he had never called in sick.

He was sick today, though; his tummy was nauseous, he was no longer sweating, but he was still overly-tired. "I'll never drink again", he vowed, as he made himself something to eat. He then giggled at how many times he had heard that statement in his lifetime.

When he was done eating, he got into the car, and 5 minutes after he left his house, his thoughts went back to his wife.

Jack loved Louise and hoped that she was ok. He also hoped that she would reach out to him at some point during the day.

Louise was bored and pouting, and wondered why Marlowe had not called her back. She redialed his work number, but the receptionist said he was busy. Louise was livid and slammed the phone down with anger. After she cooled off, she decided to give him one more hour, and if he hadn't called her back by then, she would march herself down to his office.

Little did she know that Marlowe had told the receptionist not to put any calls from Louise through to him. He wanted to stay focused on work, and he somehow knew that she would be calling to check up on him. He also knew that he was going to be confused and tense as it was, and he didn't want to deal with her until after everything was done.

While Louise waited for Marlowe to call her back, she searched through the channels until she found a romantic movie.

It was well past lunchtime when Marlowe decided to call Molly, to tell her that he would be late for supper. When she didn't answer, he wondered where she could have gone.

Marlowe was anxious, and sometimes he found Molly's voice to be rather soothing. When he couldn't get hold of her, it made his anxiety swell, and now his mind was playing all sorts of tricks on him.

While Molly was vacuuming on the second floor, her home was filled with loud music which she could sing and dance to. After she had finished cleaning those rooms, she kept the music on and hopped into the shower.

Jayla was ready to leave the house at 1pm, and had promised to be at Molly's home by 2. She was happier than she'd been in a long time, for tonight was the night that she'd be getting Roger's soul – no matter what.

The beautiful gypsy-witch appeared quite giddy as she drove down the roads in Molly's neighbourhood. Her spirits were high, and she knew exactly what to do and where to go.

Molly was in the kitchen, making sure that everything had been tidied up before Jayla arrived. As she glanced at the clock, she hoped that they would be back by suppertime, because she had laid some food on the counter to thaw out.

Jayla rang the doorbell at precisely 2:01, and was thrilled to be able to play the broken-hearted granddaughter role again.

"Coming!" the voice inside the house called. Seconds later, Molly opened the door. "Hi Jayla! How are you doing?"

"Hi, Molly. I've been better, and when we find my grandmother, I'll be fine."

"I'm glad to hear that", Molly stated, while showing her new friend a sympathetic smile.

"Thanks. And thanks for going with me", Jayla said kindly. "As you can see, none of my relatives were able to be here, but they are all waiting for me to tell them what's happening."

"I don't mind, and if you can give me 5 minutes, I'll be ready to go."

"Good." Jayla's voice was patient and kind, and she was wearing a sincere smile on her sun-kissed face. However, behind the mask of happiness, was the cruel worm of jealousy which was burrowing itself under her skin.

Jayla was about to kidnap the woman who Roger loved, and while she wanted to believe that she was not in love with him herself, she truly thought that there was something going on between them.

Suddenly, all the things which she had done with him and to him, came rushing into her mind. This caused the logical part of Jayla's brain to become unpredictable, and all she could feel was the contempt of a scorned woman.

In the next second, she realized that while Molly had Roger's heart, she was going to have his soul. Because of this, a genuine smile began to adorn her full and pouty, painted lips.

After Molly grabbed her purse and put her shoes on, she was ready to go. "Shall we?" she asked, as she extended her hand towards the outside.

"Do you mind if we take my car?" Jayla asked in a sweet voice. "I don't know the city and I'd like to get the lay of the land", she lied.

Jayla's face suddenly took on a menacing appearance, for while it's true that she would be driving her own car, it was false that she didn't know the area. And they would certainly not be ending up at the police station.

Molly smiled with the look of an innocent child. "Of course", she replied.

Ophelia's Curse

The two ladies got into the car and Jayla started the motor.

Molly had tucked her purse in between the two bucket seats, and Jayla immediately grabbed it and moved it into the back. "It's in the way", she volunteered, even though she hadn't been asked why she felt that it needed to be relocated.

Molly was a little startled by this unexpected move, and while staring out of the front window, she wondered if she had the right to retrieve it. Her eyes were wide as she swallowed a mouthful of spit, and after deciding that it was nothing to get excited about, she calmed herself down.

The car continued to move forward, and when Jayla missed the first turn, it caused some major turmoil to erupt in the tiny two-seater car.

"No, no! You missed the turn!" Molly stated louder than she should have. She was still upset about the purse situation, and now there was more to deal with. "There's only one way to get there, so now you have to turn around!"

Jayla's lips eased into a calm smile, betraying nothing of the displeasure of her current passenger. "I just remembered something that my grama had said, and I want to check it out."

The expression on Molly's face showed an uneasiness that she hadn't felt in years. She didn't know this woman very well, but she wanted to help. She just hoped that they weren't going to be driving around all day long.

Jayla faced Molly and continued speaking. "Are you ok if we take a minute to see if she's at her friend's house?"

Molly was surprised at the mention of a friend, and reluctantly agreed. "Sure, of course." Because of the mounting drama, she reached a hand up and began to play with the beads on her fragile necklace. This had been a habit for whenever she was nervous, and she didn't even realize that she was doing it.

Roger had gone through all of the items which he had purchased in the morning, and was now ready to pull off this job and collect his reward. As he held a small gun in his hand, he thought of Marlowe. "This one is intended for you, my friend." Roger chuckled as he inserted a bullet into the gun and rotated the cylinder. He then looked down the barrel as he aimed the gun at an imaginary target, and with his thumb on the safety catch, he pretended to shoot. "Bang!" he called happily. He then blew across the top of the barrel with great pride.

Marlowe looked at the clock on the wall and wondered how early he could leave work. He was starting to get anxious about what would be happening later, but the money part egged him on.

As he watched the time tick away, Marlowe tried to convince himself that Roger would be doing most of the work, while he would stand back and make sure to do very little. That way, if they got caught, he could say that he had been coerced into doing this, and then Roger would be convicted on the more serious crime.

Marlowe didn't feel bad about this decision, because he felt that jail was like home to Roger. Marlowe even talked himself into believing that he was doing Roger a favor by sending him back to prison. And once Marlowe got the money which he'd been promised, he would also be gone - without Louise and without Molly. He would be keeping all of the money for himself, and he loved the idea of having a fresh start somewhere else.

The thought of a better life made Marlowe smile, and this was the push that he needed to keep going forward with 'the plan'.

After Jack parked the car, he found no-one in the store except a regular customer at the counter. He smiled to himself as he agreed, that Adam did indeed have everything under control.

Jack went into his office and sat down, and he looked at the pile of paperwork in front of him. As he sifted fearfully through each item, he saw bills, quotes, the payroll, messages that he would need to return, and a long list of new inventory items. His head was spinning as he realized that it would take him hours to complete everything on his desk, and he was in no mood to do even half of it.

When Adam was finished with his customer, he went into Jack's office. "You look terrible", he stated kindly and with respect. "Why don't you go back home? I can take care of things and then lock up for you, if you want."

Jack looked into Adam's kind eyes, and then looked at the amount of paperwork on his desk. After a half a minute of hesitation, he agreed with Adam. "Ok, you win!" he laughed, and then he stood up. He grabbed his keys and half-heartedly walked towards the front of the store. "Good luck!" he called over his shoulder.

"I don't need it, but thanks!" Adam walked back to the middle of the long counter and studied his surroundings. He had never locked up by himself before, but he felt confident that he would be ok. He knew exactly what he had to do before he closed the store, and he would make sure to get it all done by the time it got dark. Then, all he would have to do is lock the back door as he was leaving.

Jayla could feel the tension building in the car, but instead of addressing it, she kept her eyes glued to the road.

Because something about this situation didn't feel right, Molly's expression had now grown serious. She could tell that the color and temperature of her cheeks were changing, and she was becoming less eager to help the pretty stranger. "And if your grandmother is not there, we go to the police station, right?" she stated with fear in her voice. Molly held her breath until Jayla answered.

"Of course." Jayla's voice and facial features were now soft and nonthreatening, as if she was dealing with a temperamental child. "If I'm not mistaken, I think it's just around the next corner."

Molly's heart was beginning to race and she felt as if she was going to cry. Her face was flush and her wide eyes were darting here and there, and she hoped that someone would want to stop the car and see why she looked so scared.

Minutes later, when the car seemed like it was never going to stop, Molly couldn't help but cry out. "Maybe we should just go to the police station and let them help us!" Her voice was pleading and on the verge of quivering, but she was trying to keep calm.

"We're almost there", Jayla stated quietly. After turning her blinkers on and looking over her shoulder, she steered the car into the left lane.

Before they reached the next intersection, Molly wondered how Jayla knew her way around the city so well. It suddenly dawned on her that Jayla had said that she was a visitor to this area, but by the way she was moving along the roads without the use of a map, Molly sensed that she knew more than she had let on.

As Jayla weaved in and out of traffic, Molly took a minute to put all the pieces together. None of it made sense, and it didn't take too long before she felt danger claw its way up her spine.

She suddenly felt disconnected from the reality of the moment, and her heart was preparing for a nerve-wracking startle. Her vision seemed to alter, as if she was seeing things in one-dimension, and she felt like she was being controlled by motion sensors and touch pads.

'Was any of this actually happening?' Molly wondered out loud.

Because Jayla had picked up speed, Molly automatically reached out and braced herself against the dash board. She could feel the hair on her body lifting upwards, while her mind searched for a way to back out of her promise to help. She was well-passed the worry stage now, and hated that 'just around the corner', never seemed to happen.

Jayla hoped that she had made enough twists and turns during the route, to confuse Molly of where they were.

Molly was terrified and felt as if she was dreaming; she was in the moving car spiritually, but she was no longer there in mind and body.

Roger could see that he still had a couple of hours to go before Marlowe would come and get him, so he laid down on his bed and envisioned how tonight would play out.

Jack hadn't gotten too far when he left the store a little while ago. He had grabbed a coffee from the nearby coffee shop, and drove to the big lagoon at the end of Tooley Avenue. As he sat on the weathered bench at the water's edge, he watched the light of the sun dance across the top of the little waves. And as he contemplated parts of his life, he could see how much he had left Louise on her own. He lowered his chin to his chest and agreed that that needed to stop, and right away.

Jack soon thought about Adam, and decided that he needed to make a change at his work, too. As he sipped his freshly brewed coffee, Jack thought of ways which he could make everyone happy – including himself.

Jayla had driven the car for another few minutes, and there still didn't seem to be any clear indication of where they were heading.

Molly was beyond anxious and spoke again. "You know, maybe you could do this on your own?" She paused to collect her thoughts and then continued. "I just didn't realize how far away this was going to take us. And if we're lost, perhaps we could go to the police station in *this* area?"

"We're not lost!" Jayla replied in a harsh voice. She continued to drive through back roads and down unwelcoming back alleys, and she took turns that made it feel like they were going around in circles. And a minute before Molly was about to have a panic attack, Jayla slowed the car down and parked. "We're here!" she announced.

Molly was filled with frantic fear. She became more than a little relieved when the motor had turned off, but she was still horribly frightened from all that had happened since they had left her home. And with apprehension seeping through her veins, she felt that the drama was not over yet.

Her eyes took a moment to carefully scan the immediate area, and even though she had lived in that city all of her life, she had no idea where she was.

"Come on!" Jayla urged loudly. "Let's get out and see if my grama is here."

Jayla had scared Molly so bad, that the purse was now forgotten. Without the purse, there was no cell phone. Without the cell phone, there would be no way that Molly could communicate with the outside world.

Molly pushed the car door open and followed Jayla up to the old but quaint-looking little house. As she reluctantly moved her feet up the cemented path, she prayed that she would be back home within the hour.

With her hand on the door knob, Jayla looked behind her to make sure that Molly was following. "Come on!" Jayla called. There was a glint in her eye, but it was more evil than noble, for Jayla had no intention of letting Molly out, once she went in.

The door opened with an alarming squeal, as if it was warning you not to enter.

Molly's eyes widened and her body tensed, for she had just witnessed Jayla walk inside of the stranger's home as if she owned it. "The door wasn't locked?" Molly gasped quietly. It was more of a question than a statement, and the words stung in the back of her throat like hot sauce.

Jayla knew that she was playing a risky game. And with all that had happened and all that will happen shortly, Molly could certainly bolt. However, if Jayla played her cards right, everything would go according to plan.

"Hello?" Jayla shouted for effect, once her foot landed in the front entrance of the old house. The sound echoed throughout the empty space, while a shutter clanked rhythmically against the siding. Jayla turned around and glanced into Molly's restless eyes. "They must be in the family room and can't hear us."

When Molly heard the word 'family room', it formed a huge knot in her throat, for she knew that that couldn't be anywhere near the entrance. "No, no!" she insisted sharply, as she stepped from the weathered welcome rug with frayed edges, to just inside of the home. From what she could see of the surroundings, it was too dismal for her to want to go any further. "I'm good here!" she maintained happily. She waved her hands in the air as a clear sign that she did not want to move. More importantly, she was close to the front door in case she needed to run for her life.

"Come on!" Jayla ordered strongly. She was suddenly acting as if she was the aggressive older sister and would not take no for an answer. Jayla grabbed Molly's arm and held on tight, as she dragged her away from her comfort spot. "Let's go and see where they are."

The muscles under Molly's skin were jumping from fright and her soul was screaming for her to run. But because Jayla was insisting that she follow, Molly felt that she had better do as she was told.

The old hardwood floors creaked and moaned as the two women made their way to the back of the one story building. As their feet moved, millions of molecules of dust were kicked up and were now sparkling in the air. The ambience around them gave off a huge sense of not belonging, but perhaps that was because it was still light outside, and the darkness inside, made it feel gloomy.

Molly was in shock as she stepped through the house; there were deep wells of shadows and dark corners all around her, and it was far too quiet for her liking. The silence was actually straining Molly's ears, while her other senses found it hard to carry out their duties.

As she took another step, her eyes spotted a few withering plants. They were once there as a decorative presentation, but were now dried up and possibly dead. To her right, she spotted the dining room through the kitchen area. Silverware and elegant dishes had been prudently laid out, but were now layered with dust, as if they had not been touched in years.

There were cobwebs everywhere and she hoped that she wouldn't see the creatures who lived in them. There were sheets on some of the furniture, gaps in the floorboards, and the wallpaper was peeling in most of the corners.

There was a chandelier with broken strings of crystals hanging in the middle of the dining room, and shards of broken glass on the floor underneath it. Some of the curtains were ripped, or had rotted off the bar and were now laying crumpled on the ground. Off in the distance, she was sure that she could smell phantom perfume lingering in the air, and a strong scent of pipe smoke mixed with yeasty beer.

Molly, who was already dangerously close to running for her life, saw something flicker out of the corner of her eye. Her heart stopped and then pounded back to life, and she desperately wanted to scream out. Because Jayla was leading her and she didn't want to be alone, she reluctantly followed her abductor, just to stay close to another living person.

The 2nd movie was over, and after she had seen the time, Louise became frustrated that most of the day had gone by without hearing from

Marlowe. She picked up the receiver and tried calling his number again.

From her end of the line, she could hear the phone ringing and ringing. "Why don't you pick up?" she shouted. Her voice was loud and emotional, and it was clear that she had passed the point of being patient. As she slammed the receiver down, she wanted to know what had gone wrong.

All of a sudden, Louise's mind became still, and she began to conjure up all sorts of terrifying scenarios. She wondered if everything had gone according to plan, or if something had happened and Marlowe was the one who had been killed. And what about this Roger fellow? She didn't know him, so how could she possibly trust him?

As she became more and more concerned, Louise wondered if maybe they had all been taken to jail. 'What if Marlowe had blamed the whole thing on her? What if Roger had killed both Jack and Marlowe, and would now look for her to give him the money?' But Marlowe wouldn't be that stupid to actually tell anyone her name and address, would he?

Her eyes widened as she crossed her arms tightly over her chest, and she was starting to get sick to her stomach with worry. 'Naw, even he wouldn't be that stupid', she surmised. 'The worst scenario was that he would kill Roger and Jack, and keep all of the money for himself.'

While Molly was drawing in deep and desperate breaths, she could tell that her body was quickly filling with a great deal of anxiety. The strangeness of the house was closing around her like a straitjacket, and her acute awareness of everything near her, had spiked passed the breaking point. The only other person she could count on was Jayla, but because her personality had changed so drastically in the past hour, she seemed to be in charge, and Molly wasn't sure how to go against her.

"I guess they aren't here", Jayla stated nonchalantly, as she looked around the ominous room. "We could hang out until they show up, though." It sounded like a question, but it was definitely presented as more of a directive.

Jayla threw her keys onto the table as if it didn't matter where they landed, and then she looked into Molly's direction. "Have a seat", she ordered. She then watched as the terrified woman sunk into the cushions of the dirty old couch.

Jayla's smokescreen was disappearing, and she was now showing her true colors. As she leaned against the hard smoothness of the nearest wall and stared into Molly's face, she could see that Molly was hugging herself and that she was about ready to cry.

Molly did as she was told, but she desperately wanted to go home. Because she didn't know where home was from here, she didn't know if she could get there by foot.

As she looked around, she suddenly felt vulnerable, like an animal who had been separated from its herd. As her breathing became shallow, she ran the fingertips of one hand across the palm of the other. She was definitely nervous, but to avoid Jayla from getting upset, Molly opted to stay quiet and hoped that they would get to leave soon.

Jack had no idea why Louise had left, but after sitting in silence for what seemed like forever, his coffee cup was empty and his turbulent thoughts had rolled into a calmer state.

As he walked to his car, he realized that with Louise gone, he had nothing to go home for, so he decided to return to work. Jack arrived minutes later, and was greeted by his co-worker, Adam Ward. "Pretend I'm not here", he giggled, when the two men made eye contact.

Adam wasn't surprised to see his boss return, for he was a well-known workaholic. He was grateful, though, that Jack went into his office to take care of the small mountain of paperwork, because this would allow him to continue to take care of the customers.

Molly didn't want to remain in that house for another minute, but she wasn't sure how to speak up without getting into trouble. As she glanced into Jayla's puzzling face, she could feel an invisible force instructing her to remain seated. It was strong and unrelenting, and it felt as if she would be sorry if she didn't obey.

Molly was reduced to a robotic state, and in a home that she'd never been in before. The TV was on, but she wasn't watching the program. From where she sat, she could see Jayla from the corner of her eye, and because she wasn't doing anything out of the ordinary, Molly didn't feel that she needed to have as much concern as was flowing through her body. However, the house was alive with spirits of the past and she hated that they were all waiting for this mysterious grama to return.

Marlowe had watched the time go by for the past forty minutes, and he jumped out of his chair when 5:00 came. He had called his house three times since 2pm, and still hadn't been able to get hold of his wife. Because of this, he was going to go home rather than meet up with Roger.

It was so unlike Molly not to be there all day, so Marlowe felt a need to see what was going on. Had she been hurt? Had she left him? Those were two threats that plagued him on a daily basis. He would hate for either one of them to be true, but the only way to find out, was to go home.

The sun was sitting low in the sky and Molly couldn't stand it anymore. "Do you think it'd be ok if we came back tomorrow?" she asked politely, in a voice that was slightly louder than a whisper. Her eyes were wide with hope and her elbows were pressing into her sides, as she watched Jayla's reaction.

"No!" she stated firmly. "We're here now, and grama shouldn't be too much longer." Jayla's chest enlarged as she took a large breath, and then she turned and left the room to avoid answering anymore questions.

Molly was getting frustrated by this entire situation. She crossed her ankles, and then swept a hand across her forehead to get rid of the tiny beads of nervous sweat. She was clearly anxious and needed to pee, but she wasn't sure if she should ask. As she lowered her chin, tears spilled over her bottom lashes and were now rolling down her warm cheeks. She was tired and scared and wanted to go home, but she didn't know if she had enough courage or energy to run to the front door.

On a hunch, Molly turned to see where the windows were, and was dismayed when she found out that they were closed and painted over. There was a faint ash-grey light which outlined the panes of glass, but it provided no real illumination to the room. There were also no pictures on the walls, no household ornaments on the shelves, and nothing that said that people lived there now.

Her eyes searched for a phone, but she couldn't see one anywhere, and it occurred to her that this dismal setting was like being in a haunted house. Glancing around in a nervous manner, Molly could see somber portraits staring back at her. The glum eyes of the long-dead, seemed to penetrate her very being, and it was all getting too much for her.

Molly began to mindlessly pick the brightly-colored varnish off her nails, as her ears scouted the house to find out where Jayla was. A strange pressure seemed to be touching her arm, and she could feel herself wanting to scream out for help. But before she could fully inhale her next breath, she heard the hard soles of Jayla's shoes coming towards the back of the house.

When Jayla sauntered into the room, and she sat down in the ragged grey chair across from the couch, Molly's heart fell into her tummy. She desperately wanted to speak, but something told her not to. Instead, she studied the features on Jayla's face and it seemed like she was relaxed, but why? If that old lady was Jayla's grandmother, why wasn't Jayla worried or doing more to find her?

Molly's heart was pounding in her chest and her eyes appeared damp and overly bright. She tried not to stare, but she found herself examining the woman who was holding her captive. Molly suddenly noticed the brief flicker of amusement which had flashed in her eyes at the humor of something on TV. She also noticed no stress in Jayla's body language, which seemed rather unusual, because her elderly grama had been missing since yesterday afternoon.

Jayla turned to Molly, and in an unconcerned tone of voice, she asked her if she wanted something to eat.

Molly's body flinched in fear that she might have got caught staring. "Y-Yes, thank you." The color of her skin paled, as she waited to see if she would be reprimanded.

"Let me see what we have." She exhaled loudly as she placed her hands on the arms of the chair, and then pushed herself into a standing position. And as she went into the next room, she acted as if she did not want to be a maid to anyone.

Molly was tense as she watched Jayla leave, and she didn't make a sound as she listened to the fridge door open.

"There's some lasagna that looks like it was just made this morning. Want to try some?"

Molly was surprised when she heard that statement, and while she wanted to say no, she hadn't eaten since breakfast. "Sure. Thanks." She looked down, and when she realized that her hands had been roughly fidgeting on her lap, she forced them apart. She quickly shoved them under the thickest part of her thighs, and that's where they stayed until Jayla came back into the room.

"There's no microwave and I don't know how this stove works, so do you mind eating it cold?"

Molly was hungry and didn't care. "No, that's fine", she stated lightly.

Jayla cut two small squares of the pasta dinner and brought them into the family room. "Here you go", she said, as she pushed one of the pretty patterned, china plates toward Molly.

Molly accepted it with both hands. "Thank you." She inspected the food as discreetly as she could, and found that it looked ok. Because her stomach could sense that there was food nearby, a great deal of saliva rushed into her mouth. Her nasal passages could smell the aroma and she couldn't help but nibble on all the outer edges.

A few minutes later, Molly was passed out on the couch.

The witch had assumed that Molly would get anxious about being there for too long, and she was prepared.

Jayla had mixed a slumber tonic into the tomato sauce while making the lasagna, and had slipped the large dish into the house in the middle of the night. The plan was to wait until Molly's whining and worrying were driving her crazy, and then she would feed it to her. And by having Molly sleep for a while, Jayla could only assume that the babysitting would be far easier from then on.

Jayla had no idea that keeping Molly entertained would be so challenging. She actually found it to be worse than taking care of a brand new baby, while housetraining an 8-week old puppy.

With Molly now out of the way, Jayla could put her feet up and enjoy the rest of the TV show in silence.

Marlowe had rushed home to see what was going on with Molly. After searching for anything that might tell him where she had gone, he found nothing – everything looked quite normal. He went into the kitchen to get himself a beer and noticed a package of meat thawing on the counter. He was stunned and picked it up, and the hair on his skin began to rise. "She would never let this happen", he stated with absolute conviction. His heartbeat raced when he felt the warm temperature of the meat. "Now I know that something's wrong", he whispered into the air. He was terribly confused and could feel an odd fluttering developing in his chest.

Marlowe didn't know what else to do, so he went to the phone and called Roger.

"This is not like her", Marlowe stated wildly. His voice was trembling and his knees were weak, but he didn't care; Molly was his life, and whether it showed or not, he honestly loved her.

"Are you sure that she's not just out and will be back soon?" He was also curious as to what had happened to Molly.

Marlowe's body was hunched over and he was running his free hand through his black and silky straight hair. "Naw, she would've left a note", he said as he tried not to over-analyze everything that was happening.

"Ok, listen", Roger ordered, as he tried to calm his friend down.

It felt like his future was slowly slipping through his fingers, but he wasn't about to let that happen. And because Marlowe seemed to be struggling with his emotions, Roger felt like he had to make a quick decision.

Roger decided to get Marlowe out of the way, and then he would rush to Molly's arms with the sad news that her husband had died. He could see no other way around this.

"Let's do what we planned to do, and then we can spend the rest of the night looking for Molly", Roger continued. "How does that sound?"

Ophelia's Curse

"I guess so", Marlowe replied. His voice was sullen and quiet, while his eyes were searching the carpet for another answer.

"And it's more than likely that she'll be there when the job is done!" Roger stated. It was almost as if he was trying to convince himself that everything would be fine, at the same time as he was trying to encourage Marlowe to stay strong.

Marlowe was clearly not in the right frame of mind to form a solid opinion on his own, but because he hoped that Molly would be back before he was, he reluctantly agreed to Roger's suggestion. "I hope so."

"That's what I want to hear. Now, go get ready and I'll see you soon." Roger was pleased that the plan would move forward, just as he had intended. After he hung up the phone, he got himself ready, but he continued to wonder where Molly had gone.

Marlowe left a note on the coffee table, advising Molly that he would be late coming home.

He then finished his beer and headed over to Roger's apartment.

It was past suppertime and Jack's stomach was rumbling, so as a thank you to Adam, he decided to go and get them some food. "Anything greasy, right?" he laughed towards the younger man.

Adam chuckled and his cheeks began to blush. "You know me so well."

Marlowe arrived at Roger's building at the same time that Jack was leaving the store.

From a half a block away, Marlowe could see the figure of a man waiting by the curb. His head was down, he was smoking a cigarette, and he was dressed in loose, dark clothing. Beside him, on the ground, was a medium sized gym bag.

Roger was pleased that Marlowe had arrived quickly, and he vowed not to talk about Molly, because they needed to stay focused on 'the plan'. After throwing the bag into the back seat, Roger closed the door and sat down in the front passenger side. Seconds later, they were heading towards the hardware store on Leiland Avenue.

"Have you got everything?" Marlowe inquired. He wasn't trying to be flippant; he was trying to start a lazy conversation.

Roger whipped his head to the side and glared at Marlowe's profile. "That was my job to get everything, so yah. It's all in the bag."

Marlowe blushed with anger as his eyes became cold and hard. He kept his focus out the front window, but could feel himself pushing his foot a little harder on the gas pedal. Because he didn't want Roger to be aware of how much rage he had towards him, he immediately eased up and drove at a more sensible speed.

If it wasn't for the money dangling in front of his face, Marlowe would not have involved Roger in this caper. The money was going to be his ticket to freedom, and he was not going to pass this up because of an ingrate little mouse of a person like Roger.

Marlowe bravely sucked up every stitch of awkward emotion that he had in his body, and tried to ride out the rest of the night pretending to be civil with Roger. But after all of this was done, Marlowe never wanted to see or hear from that miserable inmate again.

CHAPTER TWELVE

October 30, 2000

Louise was pissed that Marlowe had not answered his phone, and that he had not called her back anytime during the day. She was now worried and pacing as she questioned what had happened to him. 'Had he encountered any problems?' she wondered. Her forehead had wrinkled as her gaze flitted around the room, and she was not able to settle on anything for more than a split second. As she clasped her hands tightly together, she prayed that she would hear from Marlowe soon.

With quiet regret gnawing at her insides for what she may have done to Marlowe and Jack, Louise grabbed her purse and strolled down to the nearest restaurant to get some food.

Jack was in the Arby's buying burgers and fries, at the same time as Marlowe and Roger were arriving in the parking lot of the hardware store.

The sun was pushing its last bit of light towards the earth, and in ten minutes or so, the ground would be covered in the dusk of twilight.

Marlowe drove his car slow enough to allow them to have a good look through the large front windows, and they were relieved to find that there were no customers walking around inside.

"Nice!" Roger stated, in a sinister voice. Using hand motions, he signalled for Marlowe to drive to the back of the building. Once the car was parked, the motor was turned off but the keys were left in the ignition. Both men exited the vehicle, but closed the doors quietly.

"We stick to the plan, and go in and get out in five minutes!" Roger insisted sharply, but in a mere whisper.

Marlowe nodded his head, but showed no great interest in what was about to happen. Sadly, all of his thoughts were on his wife. He hoped that she was ok, and that she would be at home before he got there.

Roger glared into the face of his accomplice and stressed the following words: "This is very important, so stay focused!"

Marlowe nodded his head again, if only to show his obedience, but now he wasn't sure how much of this he wanted to do.

Roger was looking at him straight in the eye, and hoping that everything was going to be okay. "Are we good?"

Marlowe nodded half-heartedly.

Now that they were both on the same page, the two men walked to the opposite ends of the building.

Marlowe was fuming with anger as he marched the forty-three feet from the car to the front door, and in that time, he vowed to make Roger pay for the bitterness which was burning in his gut. Just before he grabbed the handle to go inside the store, Marlowe knew enough to shake off his current mood and get into a better headspace.

Meanwhile, Roger had disarmed the reasonably priced security system with very little effort.

Marlowe cleared his throat, and shivered his shoulders to get rid of any uneasiness. He then walked straight to the counter with his chin up, and a fake smile on his handsome face.

The tiny chimes rang loudly when the front door opened, and it alerted the clerk that someone was there. "Just a minute!" came the voice from in between the rows of shelves.

Roger was grateful that the flush steel, commercial back door had been left unlocked, as this made his job that much easier. With slow and exact precision, he turned the knob and cracked the door open. His heart immediately skipped a beat when he could now hear and see everything that was going on inside.

Marlowe had placed his hands flat on the long laminated counter, and from where he stood, he could see a tall sliver of light shining into the building from the back of the store.

"I'm coming!" Adam called.

"No hurry", Marlowe replied. He picked up a small object which was laying on the counter, and rolled it over and over again, as a way to pass the time. And as he studied the writing and shape and color of the thing he was holding, Roger was watching and listening.

Once Roger knew that the back area was clear, he made his steps light and quiet as he entered the building. When the two cohorts made eye contact, Roger twirled his hand in the air as if to give Marlowe a signal that the clock was ticking.

Marlowe nodded and aimed his question at 'Jack'. "Are you almost done?"

It was his job to lure Jack to stand at the counter and get him into the line of fire. The attack would then be a total surprise, and he wouldn't be able to press the alarm or grab a weapon to defend himself.

"I am, and I'm sorry that I'm taking so long", Adam confessed. "I'll be right there, though."

Tina Griffith

Adam wanted to take another minute to finish unloading the rest of the box of batteries. By doing that, he was sure that he could start a new project when he was finished with this customer.

"It's just that I've changed my mind and I am kinda in a hurry now", Marlowe stated to the man's voice. And that was the truth; they were only going to be in the store for five minutes at best.

Roger got a line on the voice and crept over to where 'Jack' was standing. He wanted to be close but not too close, and he kept his body in a crouched position to avoid being seen.

Adam was finally finished putting the batteries on the shelf, and then walked out from between the tall rows of products.

As the clerk walked towards the counter, Roger moved slow and quiet until he was directly behind him.

"Hi", Marlowe said a little too loud, as if to keep the man's focus forward.

Without anyone's knowledge, Roger had cocked the gun and was aiming it towards 'Jack's' back.

"Sorry to keep you waiting. How can I help you?" Adam stated happily.

As soon as 'Jack' was standing face-to-face with Marlowe, Roger made his move. He stood tall, spread his legs apart, stretched his arms out in front of him, and made sure that his balance was perfect. "Hey!" he shouted loud and sharp.

Adam was more than surprised that someone had been behind him, and he couldn't help but turn around. While wearing the wide eyes of total shock, his body began pumping an overload of adrenaline through his veins. "Wh-hat's going on?" he asked in complete disbelief.

As soon as he saw the clerk's face, Roger pulled the trigger.

BANG

Adam sunk to the floor like a bag of wet noodles.

Without wasting any time, Roger placed the gun on the counter and quickly retrieved two plastic bags from his carryall.

Louise had been patiently waiting behind a few other people who were wanting to get Chinese Food for supper, and she was finally up at the counter. Because of the large assortment of instruments which were woven into the Asian music, and all of the talking from the patrons inside the delightfully decorated restaurant, Louise did not hear the gun shot.

"I'd like to order the dinner for one, plus a small won ton soup", Louise stated kindly. As she was paying she added, "And it's to go."

The small lady at the counter nodded. "It will take a few minutes, but you can have a seat and wait."

Louise gave the woman a friendly smile, and moved herself to the line-up of chairs where the lady was pointing.

The bang was loud and resonated off all the walls in the tiny building, and it left Marlowe in total disbelief. The whole idea of shooting someone was something which they had talked about at great length, but the absolute reality of it was completely different.

Marlowe felt as if he had been transported into a horror movie and there was no way out. And as the taste of acid was burning up his throat, he wasn't sure what he had been thinking about when he had agreed to do this. Now that the situation was real, he was frozen to the spot - unable to move or breathe.

With 'Jack' dead on the floor, Roger went into a familiar criminal role. After putting rubber gloves on his hands, Roger took all of the money out of the cash registers and put it into a white plastic bag. "Come on! Help me!" Roger ordered, and he turned and looked into Marlowe's direction with absolute hatred. "We have to make it look like a robbery!" He then filled another white bag with some of the products from the shelves.

Meanwhile, Marlowe stood motionless with a terrified look on his face.

Tina Griffith

The loud explosion from the gun caused Marlowe's brain to overreact. He didn't want to go to prison, and he didn't actually want anyone to die. Because of what had just happened in the last few seconds, Marlowe wanted to leave. But when he tried to move, it felt like both of his feet were stuck to the floor.

Marlowe was not a nice guy, but he was also not a criminal. As he stared into Roger's angry face, he could feel misery rain down all around him. And as much as he wanted to go home, Marlowe suddenly felt like he had no choice but to stay right where he was.

Roger could see that Marlowe was in shock, and more importantly, that he wasn't nearly as tough as he acted or had claimed to be. It was clear that Marlowe was panicking, and it looked like he was about to run out of the store and into the arms of anyone who would comfort him. If that happened, Roger knew that Marlowe would gladly spew forth all the details of their well-thought-out plan.

Roger now had to think fast, or the whole deal could blow up in his face.

Marlowe's heart was pounding in his chest, and his head was exploding with crazy ideas of what would happen if they got caught. As he looked down at the bloody mess on the floor, Marlowe wondered if Roger had actually killed Jack. 'Oh, my God!' his mind screamed. 'Is this really real?'

This was all happening much too fast for his mind to process, and now Marlowe was freaking out and couldn't breathe.

As Roger looked into Marlowe's face, he knew that he had to do something drastic. He grabbed the gun off the counter, and with both hands, he aimed it in Marlowe's direction.

"Hey! Hey!" Marlowe was completely stunned, and with his open hands waving for Roger to stop what he was about to do, he tried to move himself out of the direct line of fire.

"Sorry pal, but you've suddenly become a huge liability." Without an ounce of remorse, Roger pulled the trigger and shot his former friend in the face.

BANG

At the same exact time as the sun had disappeared behind the crest of the earth, Marlowe's body dropped to the floor with a wet thud.

Without missing a beat, Roger put the gun on the counter and went back to grabbing as much loot as he could.

Because of the distinct sound of the two gun shots, each about a minute apart, the owner of the restaurant across the street, called the police. He explained that there were no cars parked outside in front of the store, and from where he stood, there didn't seem to be any commotion inside. "I just heard two loud bangs coming from that direction, and yes, I would describe them as gun shots", he told the officer on the phone.

"Ok, thank you. We'll send someone over to check it out."

While Roger was inspecting the cash box in the office, he found another gun, and this gave him a great idea. He placed the smaller one in 'Jack's' hand, and then cleaned his own gun and placed it in Marlowe's hand. After grabbing his heavy bags, he took one last look around the store and then headed for the back door.

In his haste, Roger didn't realize that the gun which he had placed in 'Jack's hand', had never been loaded. While the larger one in Marlowe's hand had gone off twice, the other gun had not fired a single bullet in years.

Unbeknownst to Roger, this small thread of evidence was going to be the key item which would destroy his otherwise, perfect plan.

The officer, who had been writing the address down on a piece of paper, signaled for his partner to come to his desk. At the same time, another call came in reporting that two gun shots were heard in that same block. After the addresses were compared and confirmed, the information was shouted into the air.

The whole room suddenly exploded with loud and overexcited commotion, while in another room, dispatch was frantically ordering all units to respond to the hardware store on Leiland Avenue.

All officers in the entire building were now jumping out of their desks, grabbing what they needed, and running to their assigned squad cars. Sirens could now be heard rushing to the store from all directions, and they were not stopping for red lights or pedestrians who were using crosswalks.

In that same moment, Jack had started his car and was about to drive back to the hardware store.

Roger had arrived at Marlowe's car, and he was grateful to find that the door was unlocked and that they keys were still in the ignition. He removed the gloves and stuffed them into one of the two large bags of loot, and then threw them both into the back seat. After starting the motor, he sped away as quickly as possible.

Roger had been able to duck into the nearest back alley, just as the police were pulling into the front parking lot of the store.

All units except for two, parked facing the double front doors, and all officers – front and back – were armed as they stayed low and hidden.

The senior officer was the one who announced their arrival, and he did it through a portable loudspeaker. Because it had a modified built-in microphone and amplifier, the officer's voice could be heard over a two-block radius.

"This is the police!" he shouted. "We've got the place surrounded! Come out with your hands up!"

Before he had gotten too far away, Roger could hear sirens singing somewhere off in the distance. He chuckled at what the police would find, but he wasn't worried that they could trace it back to him.

The senior officer had given the culprits a good minute to come out, and because there was no movement inside the premises, he gave the official order for everyone to go in. Eight policemen charged through the front door with their pistols cocked, while two stayed with their vehicles. After the back door was opened, four police officers rushed inside the store, while two stayed behind with their vehicles.

By this time, Roger had been able to make his way down a side street, across a bridge, and was now entering into regular traffic. He was long gone, and he would never know how close he had come to getting caught.

Her dinner-for-one, take-out order was ready, and after Louise stepped out of the restaurant, she could hear sirens driving towards her. Terror rushed through her veins and guilt gripped her throat, and she suddenly had trouble taking a breath. When the city vehicles stopped at the hardware store, not too far from where she was standing, her first instinct was to go over and see what was going on. Her second was to figure out how to act nonchalantly, while knowing full-well that she was behind this circus of mayhem.

After taking a huge amount of air into her lungs, she went over to join the rest of the people who were gathered in the north end of the parking lot.

Louise was paying Marlowe to kill Jack, but she didn't know when or how it was going to happen. To be at the hardware store in this very moment and know that Jack might have been murdered, was an ugly feeling that she couldn't describe.

Louise had placed herself into the group of about twenty-five people, in such a way that she would not stand out.

As Jack was nearing his store, he heard the sirens nearby. When he was about a block away, he saw the commotion in the parking lot and he immediately sped into the area. He was greatly confused and becoming scared, and parked his car haphazardly beside the large fire truck. He burst through the crowd and ran towards the entrance of the store, but was instantly detained by two large police officers.

"Hold it, buddy!" an officer shouted, as he kept a strong hold on Jack's coat.

"But I'm the owner!" he shouted, with a wild look on his face. "Let me show you!" he pleaded.

Because of the sound of the car who had screeched to a halt mere feet away from her, Louise got onto her tippy toes to see what was going on.

After Jack had been given permission to prove who he was, he took his wallet out of his pants pocket and showed his I.D. to the older of the two officers.

'Jack was alive?' her mind questioned. 'No, it couldn't be!' As her senses heightened and the adrenaline level in her body raced out of control, Louise wanted to run away, but she couldn't take her eyes off of her husband.

After Officer Daniel Nykulak checked the I.D., he grabbed the attention of the policemen guarding the door. "Let him through!" His strong request was followed by a familiar hand gesture.

Jack mumbled his thanks and dashed away.

Her heels were touching the ground now, and she couldn't believe what she was seeing. She had watched the whole scenario with cruel doubt, and she desperately wanted to faint or become invisible. She was suddenly struck with a strong current of paranoia, as the reality of the situation ricocheted through her skull. 'He was supposed to be dead, and yet, here he was, walking around.'

With sheer anxiety guiding her next move, Louise looked up towards the skies and prayed. "If this is a dream, please let me wake up." But as she opened her eyes and listened to all that was around her, it was inevitable that all of this was real.

Her knees were weak and her skin went pale, as Louise tried to make sense of what was happening. She lowered her head with the dreadful thought that something had gone awfully wrong. 'If Jack was alive, did Marlowe get shot?' As she pondered all the ways in which that could have happened, her mind suddenly snapped. It caused her to panic, but before she could react, her attention was immediately drawn to another area.

Louise watched in horror, as yellow tape was being placed around the entire parking lot of the small strip mall. To her left, three cops with outstretched arms, were trying to keep everyone at bay. And then, an officer poked his head out of the front door and aimed his statement to the paramedics. "We've got one dead body and one injured man in here!" he called loudly. He then disappeared inside the building.

Louise was confused to the max and was now running on automatic pilot. Her expression was blank as she wondered who the dead man was, and she couldn't decide if she should stay or go.

Jack bolted inside the store, and he was surprised by the number of uniformed personnel who were walking around. They were touching everything, and checking all the doors and windows for any sign of entry. Some had clipboards while others were taking pictures, but everyone was poking around while looking for evidence.

In the midst of all this confusion, Jack only had one thought on his mind. "Adam!" he shouted, hoping that his friend had not been hurt.

"Jack?" a weak voice called out.

When he heard Adam's voice, Jack's heart stopped and he couldn't think. "I'm here!" he called, and he let his listening skills guide him to where he needed to go.

Jack was trying to keep himself calm, as he made his way through this unbelievable bit of chaos. He budged in front of the police photographer who was taking pictures of the crime scene, and stood beside the two paramedics who were giving medical attention to another man who was lying on the floor.

Jack was becoming nauseous and didn't want to focus on anything in particular, but he couldn't help looking at the size of the puddle of blood by his feet. Every fibre in his body was now shaking, and his legs had gone weak like jelly. He wasn't sure that he wanted to be there anymore, and then he thought about Adam.

Jack took a deep breath, in order to increase his encouragement. He then steadied himself by holding onto the counter, and tried to talk to the nearest police officer. "Excuse me. I wonder if you can help me."

The officer had his hands full and wasn't able to give Jack the attention he was needing.

Jack bent down to meet the cop's eyes, and continued with his request. "I'm looking for my co-worker. His name is Adam."

"Yah, I heard you, and I'll get to you when I can." The uniformed man was busy helping someone to stand up and didn't have time for anything else.

Relief zipped through Jack's body when he looked into the injured man's face. "Adam?" Jack rushed over to give him a hug. "Are you okay?"

Jack was writhing in total disbelief at all that was happening around him. He had only been gone a few minutes, but it looked like a war had broken out since he left. And the amount of guilt he had for leaving Adam to fight this battle alone, was overwhelming.

"I've been better", Adam replied, trying to make light of the situation.

"Here! Let me help!" Jack assisted the officer in whatever way he could.

He was very thankful that Adam was alive, and vowed to spend the rest of his life making this up to his friend.

When Adam was up on his feet, he locked eyes with Jack. "I don't know what to say; it all happened too fast."

"It doesn't matter; I'm so glad that you're okay." Jack moved closer and let Adam hang onto his shoulder, while the officer encouraged Adam to also lean on him.

"Me too", Adam whispered. He reached his arms out and let the two men carry his weight. Although he was in a daze, Adam was quite relieved that he was alive, and that Jack was now there with him.

Jack was full of questions, just as much as Adam was full of curiosity and pain. They each had a hundred things which they wanted to ask and talk about, but the police and detectives wanted answers to the crime, and they were pressing everyone for any tidbit of information.

More and more people were gathering in the roped off parking lot of the hardware store, and anytime anything new happened, the whispers and gossip spread like wildfire.

As soon as she heard that people were coming out, Louise hopped up on her tippy toes. Her eyes grew wide and she inhaled sharply, when she saw an injured man being escorted outside by Jack and a police officer. 'Is that Roger?' she wondered. She knew the name but had never met him, and she was now full of the same curiosity that a dog has when it's hot on a trail of fresh food.

When Louise saw that the injured man was being walked over to the ambulance, she made her way over to that same area.

The instant that Adam was in the hands of a paramedic, the officer went back to the store while Jack took a step to the side.

Louise was mere feet from where the injured man was being examined, and she listened like crazy in hopes of hearing his name.

Because of the commotion that was going on around him, Jack's vacant eyes scanned the immediate area in total amazement. He was looking at the destruction that had been caused, and he had trouble drinking it all in. "I was only gone for a few minutes!" he chanted, with enormous regret in his heart. He then turned his attention back to Adam. "I am so sorry that I left." Tears were welling in his eyes, and it was obvious that he was having trouble staying in control of his emotions.

"It's ok", Adam sighed bravely. "Neither of us expected this to happen."

A detective, who had been standing close by, wrote something down in his notebook. *'The crime happened when the owner left his associate alone in the store.'* He marked the name of the man who had made that statement, along with the date and time. He then looked into Adam's face and asked him what he was doing a minute before he got shot.

Adam took a deep breath, and then he recounted things as best as he could remember them. "I was putting stock away when someone came into the store. I knew that there was a man at my counter, but I guess another one must have come in through the back door."

Shock exploded across his face. "What does that mean?" Jack asked with total surprise. "Someone came in the back way?" He brought a shaky hand up to his forehead, and then he paced like a wild animal within a 5' square area. "I thought that I locked that door!" Jack's tummy muscles tightened, his legs were about to give out, and he desperately wanted to sit down.

"The guy who shot me was standing right behind me." Adam began to whimper at the image that he wanted to forget. "He said something which made me turn around, and that's when I got shot."

"So, you saw a gun pointing in your direction?" the detective asked. His eyebrows were raised with an incredible amount of interest, while his pen was ready to write.

Adam nodded, and with a pained look in his eyes, he turned and spoke to Jack. "I didn't hear him, and it all happened so fast." His chin was quivering and he was choking down a sob.

The detective took his time to write down all that Adam was saying.

"It's ok", Jack cooed, as he tried to get Adam to calm down. Jack was light-headed and trying not to become hysterical, and he didn't know how he was going to make things right for Adam. "I'm so sorry."

Louise had heard pretty much everything up until that moment, but she was angry that she hadn't been able to confirm if the injured man's name was Roger.

"Sir, we need you to step back", the attending paramedic stated coldly. "We can't suture the wound properly, and you're upsetting the key witness."

"Of course." Jack lowered his head and stepped away, but he didn't go too far. He was grateful that Adam had swerved when the gun went off, because otherwise, he would have been shot in the heart.

Louise was stunned by all that she had heard, and while she tried to blend in with the rest of the crowd, she stayed well within ear shot.

Jack's thoughts were spinning and he was dredging up recent history, hoping to understand how he got to this moment. As he turned his focus towards the front of his store, he felt broken inside. Not a moment later, everything changed.

Jack watched the police going in and out of the front doors, and he suddenly remembered that someone had mentioned that there were three men inside the store at the time of the shooting. If Adam was one of the men, and the other one was laying on the floor, then the third man must have gotten away.

Louise was watching Jack's every move, and she felt awful; she couldn't believe that she had been behind this whole mess.

Jack was becoming more and more livid, and his mind flashed with a hundred different images and thoughts.

"Excuse me, sir?" the attendant called.

When Jack turned around, the paramedic was able to explain his findings. "Your friend's shoulder has been badly grazed by a bullet, but more than anything, he's pretty shaken up."

Jack was relieved and nodded, as if he understood. "But he's going to be ok, right?"

"We're going to take him to the hospital, but I think he'll be alright in a day or two."

"Thank you." Jack was more than relieved, and he let out a loud and long sigh. He smiled as he shook hands with the paramedic, and then he turned his attention to Adam. "They say that you're going to be okay."

"Yah, I heard." The young man was pleased that he hadn't been hurt worse than he was. "I'm just happy to be alive."

"Me, too." Jack smiled. "I'll check in on you later, ok?"

Adam reached out and held onto Jack's arm as if his life depended on it. "Can you call my folks for me? If they see this on the news, I just know that they will worry."

"Will do", Jack promised. He locked eyes with his friend, in hopes of giving him some emotional strength.

"Thanks." Adam let go of Jack's arm, and the paramedics got him prepared to be transported.

Jack tapped Adam's leg as the stretcher was being lifted into the ambulance. "I'll see you soon", he promised.

Before the back doors were closed, the same detective who had been jotting down notes, jumped into the back of the city vehicle.

"I'm Detective Andrew Katts, and I'd like to ask you a few questions." He stared into Adam's face as he introduced himself. "Shall we begin?"

At the same time as the flashing lights turned on and the siren began to warble, Adam nodded. And while the ambulance drove to the Regal Hospital, the detective continued his line of questioning.

As Jack moved himself to the front of his store, Louise walked into the middle of the large crowd of people. She was in shock and didn't know what to do. She wanted to run away, but because there were a lot of people milling around the congested area, she didn't think that Jack could see her, so she stayed put. However, Jack was still in her direct line of sight.

Jack felt as if he had been sucked into an emotional tornado. With a confused look on his face, he raked an open hand through his hair as he tried to process all that was happening.

He then viciously rubbed the back of his neck, as if that would erase the last few hours. With a quick turn of his head, Jack began gazing at everyone around him, but he was not able to focus on any faces in particular.

He heard a heavy jingling noise from behind his left shoulder, and turned to see a second stretcher being sent inside the store. Because he was guilty, tired, and terribly inquisitive, Jack walked towards a cop at the front door, and asked if the police department had any new information on what had happened here tonight.

The cop was polite and shook his head no. "We need time to check everything out, but maybe you could help us identify the other victim?"

"Me?" Jack could feel a great deal of apprehension building in his body as he answered. He decided that he might be willing to try, but his stomach didn't know how he was going to look at the man's torn-up face without throwing up. "I-I guess so", he stated solemnly.

"Good. Stand over there and wait until the stretcher comes out." The police officer pointed to a spot about four feet away and off to the side, and then he went back to his post.

Jack did as he was asked, but his mind did not want to obey. He was now standing where he was supposed to, and looking blindly down at his feet. He began to kick invisible stones on the ground, while he made sure to avoid having eye contact with anyone around him. He was nervous and began clearing his throat, and he was going over any questions that he could imagine the police asking him.

Jack suddenly felt overheated, his eyes grew very wide, and whatever had been fermenting in his stomach, was now trying to come up and into his throat.

When the crowd whispered that there was a second victim, Louise became filled with great fright. A part of her wanted to leave, but another part needed to see who the victim was.

Louise was deathly afraid that it was Marlowe – a thought she couldn't bear. She had forced him to kill Jack, and now he might be the person who was dead. And while she was trying to breathe normally, she was actually beside herself with great worry.

As she stood still and waited along with everyone else, her body took her through a long range of unbelievably perplexing emotions. At the same time, her hollow eyes showed the tortured dullness of disbelief for all that was happening around her.

"The stretcher's coming out!" someone from the crowd shouted.

All eyes turned to watch the gruesome sight, and most of the spectators stood tall while they held their breath.

When the double doors opened, Louise got up on her tippy toes in order to see things better.

The stretcher was wheeled outside, but to everyone's horror, the body was covered from head to toe, with a red-dotted white sheet.

The same officer who told Jack to stand to the side, now asked him to come forward.

While the rest of the crowd gasped in unison at the sight of the yet-unseen bloody corpse, Louise's eyes widened.

As the officer pulled the sheet away from the upper part of the victim's body, someone in the crowd screamed.

Her heart dropped when she recognized Marlowe as the man on the stretcher, and from somewhere deep in the core of her soul, her body released a blood curdling shriek without her knowledge or permission. Louise desperately wanted to cry, because that was him. The features on his handsome face were mangled, but she could recognize his ears and hair and mouth, anywhere.

Everyone who had come to spy on the goings-on, quickly gathered into smaller groups to whisper their thoughts and feelings, but Louise stood alone.

Marlowe was dead, and her face bore witness to her misery and concern over the horrid situation. In that same moment, her body went into a fight and flight mode and she became totally overwhelmed. Louise wanted to run, but instead, she flattened her feet against the solid ground and tried to duck out of sight. As she stood there crying and shaking, she wished that she could become invisible.

Jack did not hear her scream, for his mind had been filled with exaggerated torment. It had taken him a minute or two to gather up all of his courage, and now he was staring into the butchered face of the man under the soiled cloth.

A kind woman reached out and patted Louise on the back. When Louise turned around to look into her kind eyes, they shared a sympathetic smile. Louise turned around again and faced forward, and it was like she received the answer to another prayer:

A loud and unruly commotion broke out in front of her, and it demanded more attention than her self-centered concern.

The police were suddenly waving their arms and blowing their whistles, while ordering everyone to move even further away from the

Ophelia's Curse

crime scene. "The show's over, folks! Let's move along! You can all go home now!"

There were four officers taking turns calling these orders, and each one was more persistent than the other. "Let's go!" they shouted.

The large group of lookie loos were reluctant to leave, but they did as they were told, and stayed in small units as they headed for the nearest bar.

Louise was thrilled to be able to back away, and tried to stay as close to the middle of the crowd as possible. She kept her face hidden as she walked towards the motel, and moved her feet at a quick pace.

As Jack looked at the bloodied mess on the stretcher, it was clear to everyone around him that he recognized the dead man. "I think I've seen him, but I don't know him", he confided.

"What does that mean?" an officer asked. He was taking notes, but wasn't sure how to write Jack's statement down.

"He and his friend came into the store a day or two ago." Jack pointed to the dead man and continued. "This one asked me about a product that was on sale, and the two of them left minutes later without purchasing anything."

"What was the other man doing while you were busy?" another cop asked.

"I didn't get a good enough look at him because I was deep in a conversation with this guy, but I think he was standing by the door."

The two police officers shared a knowing glance, and then they placed their attention back on Jack. "Could you identify that man if we gave you a few minutes with a sketch artist?"

Jack looked towards the ground and shrugged his shoulders. "I could try", he replied, but he really just wanted to go home.

The day was already way too long for his liking, and now, with all that had happened, he just wanted to crawl under the covers of his bed and make it all disappear.

The officer could read Jack's mood and added, "We know that you're tired, but we still have a few questions to ask you.

Jack nodded his compliance, but his head was swimming with uncertainty. He was exhausted, and he wanted to go and see how Adam was doing. All of a sudden, the thought of Louise popped into his mind. He wished that she was at home, and he wondered why he hadn't heard from her.

Most of the uniformed personnel could see that Jack was having a hard time, so they decided to end their interrogation. "I think that'll be all for now, but we'd like you to come down to the police station in the morning." An officer thrust a business card into Jack's hand and continued. "That's the address, in case you don't know where we're located."

Jack's head was lowered as he took the tiny card. He was relieved that he was free to go, and he couldn't wait to get home.

"We'll see you tomorrow!" the officer stated, as he pointed his finger into Jack's face. It was clearly an order, to which Jack reluctantly agreed.

Jack put the stiff card into his pocket and walked to his car. From there he watched the second ambulance leave the area and drive to the hospital, while the police wrapped yellow caution tape around the rest of the parking lot.

Louise arrived at the motel room in a frantic state. She collected her things in a hurry, and then drove aimlessly around the city. Tears were streaming down her reddened face as a million thoughts swam through her mind. She had no idea where she would end up, but after contemplating her options, she felt that she had no other choice but to go home.

As she drove in the direction of her neighbourhood, she could see the image of the mangled face of her former lover before her. She hated that Marlowe was gone, and it was intimidating to think that she might have caused his death.

It was growing dark, Louise was baffled by all that had happened, and she began to cry from her own sorrow and fear.

As Jack sat in his shabby car, his mind began to wander. 'If he had not gone to the store for food, that would have been him going to the hospital tonight. Or, with the two of them in the store, maybe nothing would have happened at all.'

He slammed both of his hands against the steering wheel, while frustration seeped from his pours. And as he tried to calm himself down, Jack's mind focused on Louise. He wondered where she was and if she was ok. He then realized that if she saw the news report on TV, she might be trying to call the store. With a rush of adrenaline guiding him, he turned the key and began to drive.

Many minutes later, the ambulance pulled up outside the emergency doors of the Regal Hospital. Their precious cargo was an exhausted gunshot victim and a rambling investigator. When the large double doors to the city vehicle opened, Detective Katts jumped out first. He then waited while the paramedics removed the stretcher.

To ensure the safety of the patient, the driver of the ambulance had radioed in ahead of time. He told the Unit Clerk of the special circumstances pertaining to the injured man, in hopes that a medical team would be on hand to help Adam get inside of the hospital. Otherwise, the media might find him and it could take a lot longer to get him to the emergency area.

"Sir, you'll have to step aside." The stern request was given to the large man who was asking a lot of questions to the man on the stretcher.

Detective Katts had been with the police department since he was 22 years old, and had always done his job to the best of his ability. He had been decorated quite a few times, and was proud of every one of his achievements.

Today the 46-year old man's job was to get to the bottom of whoever was behind the shooting. He hoped that once Adam had been examined and placed in a regular room, that he could finish his interrogation. Not surprisingly, security had been called before Adam had been assessed, and they told the detective to back away.

"I'm only doing my job", Detective Katts replied. He took a step backwards as his eyes went hard and distant.

A nurse heard the commotion and rushed out of the small curtained space where Adam was laying. Because of how disruptive everyone was being, she found it necessary to add her two cents into the troubling conversation. "He needs to rest for at least 24 hours, and then someone from the hospital administration office will give the police an update", she stated sternly. She immediately turned her attention to the left and ordered the guard to secure the area. After he nodded, she wedged her way back behind the closed curtains.

Detective Katts understood the situation, and because he was not one to cause a scene, he apologized and scurried away. As he placed his pad of paper into his coat pocket, he smiled as if he knew something that they didn't.

Tina Griffith

The aging but handsome detective had his eyes and ears open for the past few hours, and he had been writing down everything that he had seen or heard. He was quite certain that he had enough to go on for now, so he took his notes and headed to the police station to get them typed up.

CHAPTER THIRTEEN

October 30, 2000

Jack had been quite distraught when he left the store, so when he turned left onto Tooley Avenue, he felt a strong need to stop at the 2-acre lagoon to collect his thoughts.

In the daytime hours, or at night when the park was lit up by old fashioned street lamps, this was his trouble-free place. It was surrounded by large areas of green grass, lots of trees, a huge children's playground structure, and plenty of small wildlife.

Jack released a soft sigh as he parked his car and looked around. He suddenly felt peace cover his body, for this was his second home. He felt safe there, and he had worked out many a problem while sitting on the wooden bench by the water's edge.

As he walked over and made himself comfortable in his favorite spot, Jack was quite aware that this was his second time there today. He had struggled emotionally during the first visit, and as the dark of night covered him with its cool blanket of air, he knew that these next few minutes were going to be a lot harder.

Louise was on her way home, but because she was near Marlowe's neighbourhood, she decided to drive by his place before going anywhere else.

Marlowe had never told her where he lived or that he was married, but Louise had accidently peeked at his student card, the week after they had had their first coffee date. She automatically recognized the name of the area of his address, but had never gone to his place, out of respect for his privacy.

After she had fallen in love with him, she hoped that she would be invited over for drinks, but that never happened. Instead, they continued to meet in the same hotel room week-after-week, and they declared their love on a 10-year old, queen-sized, used bed.

She was confident about their relationship, and often envisioned that the two of them would be sharing his home, sometime down the road. Because he was now dead, that was no longer possible.

When Louise turned onto S. Esford Avenue, her heart beat a little faster. She had been stunned by Marlowe's sudden death, and out of curiosity, she wanted to see what he was leaving behind.

With Marlowe's demise, Roger decided that it was better if he left town. He had enough money and stolen products from the hardware store to tide him over for a few months, and if he needed to, he could find out the name of the woman who hired Marlowe to murder Jack. But for now, the thing he wanted to do most in this world, was to see Molly one more time.

Roger couldn't help but remember that Molly had been missing all day. He was worried about her and wondered where she had gone. And with him being so close to her neighbourhood, he couldn't see any harm in going to her home to see if she was okay.

Roger was stressed out; he was driving a dead man's car, and he was trying to avoid being seen by the cops. He was not sure if it was too early for the car to have been reported as stolen, but he didn't want to take any chances.

Louise arrived first, and reduced her speed so that she could get a good look at the outside of the house. Because the sun had gone down and everything around her was growing dark, she stopped the small car and decided to get out.

She approached the 2-storey home and peered into the large living room window. Because the house looked so quiet and lonely, she wondered if she had the right to go inside. In a brave move, she went to the front door to see if it was locked.

Even though Roger was quite agitated, he became elated when he turned onto Molly's street. He was hungry, he felt very alone, and with Marlowe gone, he worried about his immediate future.

He wanted to believe that he would not get arrested for the murders, but something in the back of his mind gnawed at the truth, that nothing was 100% undisputable.

Roger's attention was solely on picking out which house was Molly's, but he wondered if his mind was playing tricks on him. 'Had he missed the house? Was he travelling down the wrong road?' These concerns were real and it was making him anxious.

Roger had always been the passenger in Marlowe's car, and this made it more difficult to distinguish where he was.

He was stooped forward like an old man, and gripping the steering wheel with both hands. His eyebrows were drawn together and his eyes had narrowed, as if he could see the front of the house better that way. His neck muscles were tightening as he looked on each side of the street, and something told him not to give up.

But while he kept the car at a low speed by lightly applying the brake pedal, every second that ticked by, gave him more reason to worry.

Not surprisingly, the door was locked, and Louise was frustrated that there was no key in the mailbox or under the black mat on the porch. Because she didn't want to force her way inside the house in the dark, she decided to come back in the morning.

Roger was about a block away, when he saw a woman walking towards a car that was parked in front of Molly's home. His heart began to flutter with excitement and he made his car move a little faster.

He was delighted that Molly was there and seemed to be ok, and now he couldn't wait to be in her arms.

When Louise arrived at the driver's door of her car, she became blinded by the glaring headlights which were shining directly into her eyes. She raised her hand to shield herself from some of the intense light, but couldn't recognize the car or the person driving it.

Roger pulled up behind her white Honda Civic, and jumped out of his car while screaming Molly's name.

Louise froze. It was dark, they were alone in the street, and all of her breath was trapped in her lungs. She was quite frightened by this unnerving display of attention, and her first instinct was to run. As she fumbled to find the correct key to the car door, she cursed herself for locking the vehicle in the first place.

"Molly! It's Roger!" he shouted, as he ran towards her. His arms were waving back and forth like crazy, in hopes that she would recognize him and not be too eager to leave.

"Roger?" she whispered so low, that only her soul could hear it. Her body cringed at the mention of the name, and suddenly time was moving in slow motion. Her mind automatically clicked through her memories until she recalled when Marlowe had used it. Her eyes widened and her heart beat stronger, when she remembered the details of how and when it was said. "Roger and I have got it all under control."

Air got sucked into the back of her throat from immense fear, and now that man was rushing towards her. It was chilling. But perhaps this was just a simple fact of mistaken identity – something which could be cleared up right away.

She took a deep breath and decided to face him head-on, but the closer he got, the more traumatized she became. Her mind took over, and with fierce reasoning, it told her not to look weak or he could over power her. Louise straightened her posture and tried to appear strong and unafraid.

Roger was now standing face-to-face with the woman who he thought was Molly, and because it was so dark outside and his body was running on pure adrenaline, he couldn't tell that it wasn't her. "Molly", he stated nervously. He bent his body all the way forward, and laid his hands against his knees as he tried to catch his breath. "Listen", he said. "I have something to tell you."

Louise was terrified, but before she could explain that she wasn't who he thought she was, he interrupted her thought pattern.

"There's been an accident", he stated, as he stood up. "Marlowe got shot." He paused again and then continued. "He died, Molly." With a mountain of compassion radiating from his heart to hers, he stared into her eyes and waited for her to respond.

As his words stung in her ears, her body fought against every survival instinct that she had. Even though this was not new information to her, she was puzzled that he felt the need to deliver it. 'Had he been there? Why did he think this Molly woman would care?' These and other questions caught her like a deer in headlights, and she wasn't sure if she should stay here with this deranged man, or leave and not look back.

Roger grabbed her shoulders and shook her as if she was in shock. "But I'm here, and I'll take care of you for as long as you need."

Louise was sickened by his touch and her body recoiled. And as she looked into his eyes, it suddenly dawned on her that Marlowe's death might not have been an accident.

Her pulse ramped up as she struggled with all that had happened since lunchtime, but now she was motivated by a large bundle of curiosity. "How did he die?" she asked shamelessly. She continued to stare into Roger's eyes while she waited for the answer.

"He was shot, straight in the face." As he watched her reaction, he became jittery and began bouncing from one foot to the other. "But I'm here and I can help you get through this", he repeated, as if he didn't know that he had just said those same words a few seconds ago. He still had a strong hold on her with one hand, and it was quite obvious that he wasn't about to let go anytime soon.

The mental explosion of clarity behind her eyes was unbelievable. 'No-one could have known how Marlowe had gotten killed', she surmised with great concern. 'It hadn't been announced out loud, and unless he was inside the store or he was a cop, he couldn't possibly have that information.'

According to what Louise and most of the crowd had heard while they were witnessing the aftermath of the crime, there must have been three people in the store - one was taken to the hospital and another one was dead. That left a third man, and by all accounts, he had been able to get away.

Louise looked dead straight into Roger's vacant eyes, and as she held her breath and stood motionless before him, a dozen thoughts invaded her mind. 'Did Roger know that she was going to pay Marlowe to kill Jack? If he killed Marlowe, would he kill her too? Or was this Molly woman who he was really after?' It was a lot to drink in, but Louise needed to know.

She was dumbstruck and starting to hyperventilate, and this stranger was holding onto her upper arm. 'Was he ever going to let me go?' she wondered. 'If not, I need to find a way to escape.' Before the fears in her mind could build up into something more, her attitude changed when the promise of a brilliant idea came into her head.

She was grateful that Roger did not seem to know who she was, and if she could persuade him to keep believing that she was Molly, then she might be able to talk her way into leaving.

As she took a deep breath and tried to find some courage, she began to wiggle herself out of his strong grip. Louise leaned herself into Roger's body and began to act weepy and sad.

Roger's heart was breaking at her sorrow, and he released the hold he had on her arm.

"I can't bear to go into that house now that Marlowe is dead. You understand that, right?" she cried. She made sure that soulful tears were braided into her voice, while she dug her nails into the emotional side of his heart.

"Ah, Molly." He wrapped his arms around her back and held on gently.

Louise felt naked and exposed, but didn't dare liberate herself from the awkward embrace. She forced water to come out of her eye ducts, and she tried to sound deeply drained. "And I don't want to talk to anyone about this tonight, so maybe I should go to my friend's house until morning."

As a woman, she was crafty and knew all the deceitful ways to get to a man's heart. Though she didn't know Roger or the desires that stirred his passion, she would drop down to a level that caused panic in everyone's life – helplessness: the powerless inability to defend oneself against an emotional hurricane.

For dramatic effect, Louise pressed herself even harder into the front of Roger's body. And as she wrapped her arms lovingly around his neck, she pretended to become even more distraught. "I just can't believe what has happened, and I don't think I can stay here right now", she insisted. She spoke over her frightened soul, in a voice that was as reasonable as she could manage. "And with Marlowe gone, I just don't know how I will ever cope." She lowered her eyes to give her sadness more believability.

Roger felt something exciting and familiar when their lower bodies touched. Was it the casualness from their childhood that was coming forward, or the anticipation of the beginning of a romantic relationship? He wasn't sure, but there was a different tenderness between them now, and it wasn't there when they were inside of Marlowe's home a day ago.

Because of the velvety darkness that was surrounding them, and all that had happened in the hours leading up to this moment, Roger decided to forgive his silly mind for conjuring up these pointless notions.

As Roger pulled her even closer, he gazed into her eyes as he continued to enjoy this warm bit of intimacy. He loved how her shapely body was molding with his, and he saw this moment as the beginning of their future together. "Of course", he whispered, as he moved his open hands lower. He was now gripping her hips and pulling them towards his groin, as if he was giving her something to look forward to.

Louise felt the stranger's hands on her lower back, and while it frightened her, she knew that she couldn't do anything to make him feel ill at ease.

Roger's heart had softened when he realized that she didn't pull away, and he could now see that she wanted to be with him as much as he wanted to be with her.

Roger needed her to know that he loved her, but her mental safety was his first concern. And before he could let her know what was in his heart, his mind began a whole new battle.

Because Roger had a huge deficiency of trust, something inside him was trying to fight against the uneasiness which his mind was creating. 'But what if she left and never came back?' To him this was real, and it was something he dreaded.

Louise could feel his arms loosen and then tighten against her skin, and it spoke volumes about how he was feeling. Did he have a false confidence that she would return if he let her go? Or was he scared that she would disappear into the night?

She knew that she was taking a huge risk, but she desperately wanted to get away from him.

With tremendous fear in her heart, she leaned her face into his shoulder and sincerely began to cry. She hated the fabric of his clothing and she detested the smell of his body, but these were only two reasons that she hoped that she would not be trapped in his arms for too much longer.

Roger loved having her so close, and he took great pleasure in cradling her body against his.

An idea suddenly flashed in her head, and it quickly lightened her mood. To make him feel like she was not about to run away, Louise nuzzled his neck. This simple gesture was supposed portray 'love and protect me' and 'I am scared', and it took no time at all before he responded.

Up until now, his body had been engulfed in tremendous tides of exhaustion and confusion, but because 'Molly' had placed her moist lips against his skin, he was compelled to obey. "I understand, and I will let you go", he stated tenderly. His promise was laced with absolute truth, and was delivered with undying love.

It was late and he'd had a very long and difficult day, but he felt that they were experiencing an eagerness to be together. Were they not? His mind was still a bit confused.

Louise was grateful that he was letting her go, and smiled from ear-to-ear with enormous relief. But just in case he had an inkling to change his mind before she could drive away, she made sure to keep her lower body tightly up against his.

"Thank you, Roger", she breathed one inch away from his mouth. As she pulled her entire body away from him, she batted her eyes and added, "I could be back around 9:00 in the morning. So, in case you are still in the area, perhaps we could have breakfast together?"

"Of course", he stated happily.

Roger's heart swelled, for he had just heard her say that she was coming back. He looked into her face and he could feel himself beaming. As a smile worked its way across his thinning lips, it lit up every awkward feature on his rugged face. He was now more relaxed than he'd been in a very long time, and it showed.

Roger checked the time on his watch, and knew he would be counting the hours until she stood in front of him again.

Louise took one last look at the house which Marlowe used to live in, and she let out a heavy sigh.

Roger looked towards the same house and a thought occurred to him. "Would it be ok if I stayed here tonight? I mean, to make sure that everything is perfect for when you come back." He then waited to see how that would make her feel.

Louise was stunned by his question, but in reality, she didn't care where he slept. "Of course." She wasn't sure how he was going to get inside the house, but she nodded her approval of him staying there.

This was Marlowe's home, and he was now dead. She didn't want to be caught breaking in, and she desperately wanted to escape from this man before her. If Roger could get in, she knew that she would be able to get in in the morning.

Plus, if he stole anything, how would she know?

"Thank you", he sighed. He was wearing the look of a man in love.

Louise gave him a smile and then took a step away from him. She was quite thankful that she had been able to convince him that she was Molly, and she was very happy to be given the chance to escape.

On the outside, she was wiping a few sad, invisible tears away from under her eyes, but on the inside, she was celebrating a huge victory.

While still playing the part of Molly, she leaned in and kissed his cheek. "See you tomorrow." Without waiting for him to reply, she walked away, got into her car, and started the motor. As she shifted into 'Drive', she was extremely grateful that she was getting away from this unbelievably odd man who was terrorizing her, and she hoped to never see him again.

"See you tomorrow", he echoed, but she never heard his words.

Louise was shaking and her heart was pounding, as her small car began to drive down the street. Her mind was swirling with a million unstable thoughts, while her eyes were glued to the reflection of Roger in the rear-view mirror.

"I did it!" she cheered. "I escaped!" She was actually smiling as she turned off of Picasso Drive and made a right hand turn onto Harvest Gold Heights. Her own home was two neighbourhoods away, but she opted not to go there right now.

There was a second or two where Louise thought that Roger might change his mind and make her stay, but lucky for her, that didn't happen. She was safe now, and all she could think of was to drive as far away from Marlowe's house as possible.

Roger waved as 'Molly' drove out of sight, and then he made his way up to the house. Because he had Marlowe's keys, it was easy for him to use the one which opened the door. After turning on some lights and grabbing a beer from the fridge, he made himself comfortable in front of the TV.

Jayla was finishing up her second movie of the day, and was getting quite bored from just sitting and doing nothing. When the credits rolled, she made a point to get up and stretch.

Ophelia's Curse

Molly had been drugged and sleeping for approximately 4 hours. Not once did she snore or roll from side to side, and because Jayla checked on her as often as possible, she could tell that Molly was fine and still breathing.

Jayla had enjoyed her short freedom from Molly's continual whining, but she was now becoming restless. After doing a few trivial moments of exercises, she walked to the front door for a change of scenery.

With the sudden movement of blood in her veins, Jayla's mind began to work overtime. 'Did I kidnap Molly too early?' she wondered with a bit of concern. She quickly decided that she had indeed jumped the gun, for she wasn't going to take Roger into the forest until closer to midnight.

Jayla lowered her face and involuntarily giggled, and then shook her head because of her own stupidity. About a minute later, Jayla checked her watch again, and calculated how much longer she would have to wait before she could call Roger. When she realized that she still had another couple of hours to go, Jayla sighed with emotional agony, and went back to the family room to search for another movie.

Louise had a lot of questions floating around in her mind because of Roger. 'Had he heard the name Louise before? Did Marlowe give Roger any information about how to get hold of her, if something happened to him? Surely Marlowe must had said that there was someone else involved, and whether it was a man or a woman?'

Her head was swimming with insurmountable scenarios, and Louise didn't know what she should do or where she should go. She realized that she was probably worrying for nothing, but everything inside of her was running on a phobia of being thrown into jail.

Instead of stopping and making another mistake, Louise decided to grab a coffee from a drive-through window. Once she had the hot drink and a chocolate glazed donut in her hand, she drove aimlessly around the city.

Ophelia's Curse

Jack had been at the lagoon for far too long, and now he was cold. After taking a last look around, he silently agreed that enough was enough. He walked back to his car to warm up, and then he tried to talk himself into going home. As he lowered his head, he thought about Louise and the fact that she might not be there. It tore his heart out and he hoped that he would hear from her soon.

Jack started his car and drove away from the beautiful park, but before he got too far, he decided to stop at the hospital to see how Adam was doing.

Now that Roger knew that Molly was fine, he was floating on cloud nine. He had seen her in person and was convinced that she would be okay until the morning, so he decided to ditch the money and the products from his car before the police arrived.

Roger was not new to the world of criminals. He understood that once the police learned of Marlowe's name and address, that they would come there to look for evidence. He certainly would not be in Marlowe's home in the morning when they showed up, but it was a good place to crash for now.

Everything was in plastic bags and it was quite easy to transport, but he wondered where he could exchange the stolen items for cash.

With much delight, Roger sprang to his feet when he realized where he could go. He grabbed the keys to Marlowe's car and drove to his dealer on the other side of town. Twenty-three minutes later, he pressed a buzzer and asked his old buddy to come downstairs.

Greg Hines lived upstairs from his 15-year old pawn shop, and he had a healthy appetite for Ghost Train Haze marijuana. He had been enjoying a night off by celebrating alone, but because he hadn't seen his friend in years, he pushed his plans aside and raced down the rickety back stairs.

They hugged when they saw each other, and quickly chatted about old times and what was new. A few minutes later, Roger took two bags of items out of the trunk of Marlowe's car, and opened them so that Greg could see the contents.

Greg was sleep deprived and a little spaced out, but even he could see that these items were brand new. And because they all had price tags, he could only assume that they were stolen.

Greg knew that the stickers would come off with very little trouble, but he would not be able to sell any of these items anywhere in town. Because of those two factors, plus the hardware genre of what these items were, Greg had to come to a decision about the price.

"Well? What do ya think?" Roger asked. He was getting cold and very much wanted to be back in Molly's house, but because he needed the money, he vowed to stay right where he was, and for as long as it took.

Greg smiled and reached out to shake hands with Roger. "I think I can move these items for you."

"Thanks", Roger sighed with relief. He now waited to hear how much he could get.

Greg pulled a nice-sized doobie from behind his right ear and lit it up. As he inhaled the extensive notes of citrus, he smiled as if he had a secret.

He had not only made a nice profit from Roger, but he would get these items to a friend of his by morning. This friend lived close to 800 miles away, so that pretty much guaranteed that no-one would be able to trace all that he was moving.

To Greg, this was a win-win situation – he got to see Roger again, and he was about to make a lot of money.

After he exhaled the floral tasting, smokey air, he handed the soft stick of cannabis to Roger.

Roger was shocked at first, but mostly because he seldom indulged in such pleasures. Since he didn't want to offend his friend, he took the doobie in between his thumb and index finger, and then inserted the wet end in between his lips like a pro.

Ophelia's Curse

Roger was pleased that the inhale was earthy and smooth, and that it had touched his lungs in a gentle manner. He was also relieved that there was no urgency for him to cough or appear to be choking, because that would embarrass him in front of someone who he had known for over 20 years.

Greg watched with great interest, because while Roger wanted to look cool and experienced, he actually looked like a guy who was smoking weed for the first time in his life.

Roger was surprised when the taste of the exhale seemed to linger in his mouth, and it continued to do so, long after the thick smoke had left. Not surprisingly, was that the feeling of euphoria hit him right away, and all the stress and confusion about the last few hours were gone within minutes.

Rather than reach to have the magical stick back, Greg chose to continue observing the effects which the marijuana was having on his friend. It was amusing to watch the calmness take hold of Roger's face, and that his stance and mood was also changing. And because of the difference he saw in Roger from when they said HI a few minutes ago to now, Greg wondered why Roger didn't smoke more often.

Roger was having a wonderful out-of-body experience, and was about to take another drag when he was stopped.

"No, no!" Greg stated firmly. "A little of this goes a long way, plus you haven't done it in a while and you're driving." Greg could see that his friend was having a nice buzz, and while he didn't want to ruin the experience, he gladly took the weed from Roger's hand. "You can always come back for more", he added, as he gave his friend's shoulder a friendly pat.

Roger didn't care that Greg took the doobie back, because he was now in a really good mood. "I'll make sure to come back soon", he promised.

"You do that!" Greg stated, while playfully pointing his index finger towards Roger's face.

The two men laughed and shook hands, and after Roger tucked the money he had gotten for the stolen products safely into his pocket, they said good-bye.

Greg went back upstairs to finish the dope by himself, and Roger drove back to Molly's empty home. Both of the men had music playing all around them, and both were happily swimming in the sweet smog of a brilliant high.

Her cardboard coffee cup was empty and she had had enough of driving in the dark without any direction, so Louise decided to go home. She even hoped that Jack was there, so that she could wrap her arms around his soft figure and generous waist.

With all that had happened since she woke up, she decided that she wanted to have her husband near her. He hadn't been home very much lately, but he had always been a great source of comfort to her. Even when she was in the throes of having an affair with Marlowe, Jack was always kind to her.

It was in that revelation when she inhaled with great fear. She had hired Marlowe to kill Jack, and tonight he had come *this* close to being dead. Louise shivered from the thought of being without him, and tears soon followed.

The movie was half-way done and Jayla was bored, so she checked her watch again. She was excited to see that she would get to call Roger soon, but to her unhappy surprise, Molly was stretching and making small noises.

Jayla hated this part, because she knew that the questions would no doubt begin. Nonetheless, Jayla was very interested in reuniting Molly with Roger, so she decided that she would do whatever was needed in order to keep Molly in a good mood.

Molly felt like a train had hit her; her head hurt, her chest felt heavy, she had no energy, and she ached all over. She forced herself into a sitting position while she opened her eyes, but that didn't make her feel better. Because of the empty feeling in her tummy and the full feeling in her bladder, she looked at Jayla for comfort.

Without saying a word, Jayla went over and helped Molly to stand up.

On her first real breath of air, Molly felt like vomiting. And before she took a second wobbly step away from the couch, she thought she felt a rodent scurry across the floor near her feet. "Ah-h-h-h!" she yelped, and she wanted to jump on a chair.

Jayla ignored her worries and continued to guide her half-way down the hall. Once Molly was inside the bathroom, Jayla crossed her arms over her chest and stood guard outside the door. When Molly came out, Jayla walked her back to the couch, and as soon as Molly was sitting in her spot again, Jayla went into the kitchen and made them a plate of food.

Before she did anything else, Molly scanned all the corners of the room for anything small and furry. Noting that nothing was scurrying about, she turned her attention to other elements of the room.

Molly was scared and completely unaware of what had happened before a few minutes ago, and she was amazed that she had been able to fall asleep.

The ragged curtains were drawn, but Molly could see that dusk was giving way to the night. As she tried to guess what time it was, she wondered what had happened to the grama. And because there was absolutely no noise other than what Jayla was doing in the kitchen, she believed that the grama had not returned.

As her heart dropped into her stomach, Molly's worry had now turned into panic. She was living in a moment where her palms were sweaty, her heart was racing, and the air around her was terribly thick. She wanted to go home, and she wasn't sure why they couldn't leave.

Tears were forming in her eyes and she desperately wanted to get out of this strange house. 'It just didn't seem right to stay, when there was no real need to.'

Jayla entered the family room and handed one of the plates of food to Molly.

Ophelia's Curse

As Molly accepted it, she decided to eat and be quiet, and after she had gathered some courage, she would then ask if they could leave.

Minutes after Jack left the lagoon, he was turning from Coventry Blvd onto Bridgeland Drive. His eyes caught the powerful display of the well-lit, Police Station sign on his right, and he was suddenly conflicted to do one of two options.

Jack wrinkled his face and automatically groaned with a loud sound, and then forced himself to pull the car over.

Jack had absolutely no interest in climbing out of bed in the morning to answer questions, so he decided to go into the office right now. He then hoped to put all of this behind him and concentrate on building his business back up again.

Detective Katts was one of the police officers from the crime scene who was still at the station, so they got paired together.

"Thanks for coming in, Jack. Have a seat." The detective had pages of notes already typed up and prepared to submit, and he now glowed with happiness over the fact that he'd have even more to present to his boss in the morning. "Can I offer you a coffee before we begin?"

Jack was tired and still confused by all that had happened, and he kindly accepted the offer. "Two cream and two sugar", he stated kindly. As soon as the large porcelain mug had been placed in front of him, Jack reached out and allowed the hot cup to warm his hands. "Thanks", he muttered under his breath.

"Shall we start?" Detective Katts put a clean sheet of paper into his typewriter and lined it up. He then launched his lengthy interrogation. "What was your association with Mr. Marlowe Perkins? How did you come to know him? In your opinion, do you think that your associate was involved in the robbery?"

The questions were being fired at Jack, one right after the other, and he was having a hard time staying focused. He answered each one as best he could, and wished for the time to go faster.

Meanwhile, Roger had stopped at a fast-food restaurant to grab something to eat. While he waited for it to be ready, he ordered a beer. As he walked to a table, he thought about Molly.

It was good to be in her company without Marlowe around, and now he couldn't wait to see her again in the morning.

Because the murders had not been announced on the news, Roger was under the impression that the police were still doing their investigation. But with each victim having a gun in their hand, he concluded that this should be an open and shut case.

Roger chuckled because he believed that he had the gift to be a great lawyer, but also because the lingering effects of the weed was mixing with the alcohol in the beer. Without realizing it, the combination was making him quite giddy.

In a moment of merriment, he raised his glass and made a toast to himself. "With reasonable doubt, I decide that I am in the clear!" he announced quietly. As he leaned the tall glass towards his lips, he accidently spilled a little of the clear brown liquid down the front of his shirt. "Oooooops!" This made him giggle even more.

Over the last twenty minutes, Jack had answered each and every question with complete honesty. Once he was done, the detective allowed him to leave. "But don't go too far; we might have a few more questions to ask you", Detective Katts added.

Jack shrugged his shoulders and shook his head, and then made his way out of the building. As he walked to his car, he tried to calm himself down.

It had been an exasperating day, from beginning to end, and all he wanted to do was go home – but to what? He hadn't heard from Louise, and he promised Adam that he would go and check on him.

As Jack started his car, he decided to keep his word and go to the hospital.

Louise had been home for about 30 minutes. She had changed into her pink nighty, unpacked her suitcase and overnight bag, and had made herself something simple to eat. She suspected that Jack was probably busy with the police, and decided to stay up and wait for him to come home.

Roger was chuckling at how this day had gone. He was clearly drunk, and under the delusion that he was going to get away with killing both Marlowe and Jack. More importantly, he couldn't believe that he was going to live the rest of his life with Molly.

But in that very moment, he was in a festive environment with lots of happy strangers around him. And as he looked into their unfamiliar faces, he decided to eat at the restaurant instead of taking his food back to Molly's home. Because the unhealthy cuisine would take ten more minutes to come to the table, he ordered himself another beer.

Jack arrived at the hospital at 9:40pm, and was happy to see how much progress Adam had made since he'd last seen him. The younger man was sitting up, but his eyes were closed and he had a cast on his upper left arm and shoulder area.

"Hi, hero", Jack said when he saw his friend. He walked closer to the bed and tried not to bump the shiny steel frame.

Adam opened his eyes when he heard Jack's voice. He then smiled brightly when he saw his boss standing near the foot of his bed. "Hi, Jack. What a crazy day, eh?"

Adam had been given two tablets of Percocet and some codeine, to calm him down and to ease his discomfort. The combination of drugs was new to him, and he was suddenly floating around in his own head. There was no more pain, emotional or physical, and he was loving the blurry feeling that had enveloped his entire body.

Jack nodded. "Yah, it was quite the day. But not one that I'd like to relive again."

"I guess I won't be at work tomorrow, but they say I could come back in a couple of weeks." Adam wiggled his fingers to show his boss the reason why he'd be off.

Jack laughed, for he knew very well what Adam was trying to say. "I'll have to think about that", he teased playfully.

Adam chuckled. "Good, because I could get you a note, if you needed one."

Detective Katts tapped on the door to Adam's hospital room, using the knuckle on his left hand. "Can I come in for a second?"

Jack was surprised by the visit, and turned towards Adam. "I don't think he's up to answering any questions right now", he stated with some authority. "I think he's pretty doped up, but you could try again tomorrow."

The detective wasn't about to take no for an answer. He took a step inside, made himself appear to be bigger than he usually was, and walked into the room as if he owned it. As he made eye contact with Jack, he delivered the following statement: "Don't worry; this won't take long."

Jack wasn't worried, but he was confused. He had just left this man at the police station, and now he was here. Was this a coincidence? Or did the detective hope to learn something that Jack forgot to reveal.

While Detective Katts was in the hospital room with Jack and Adam, two squad cars and four policemen were at Marlowe's home, looking for clues to his murder.

They broke in through the back door, touched everything that they could see, and browsed through the belongings of the dead man and his wife. One officer checked the phone display while another checked the drawers for pieces of paper that spoke about any criminal activity. Another cop flung things around in the bedrooms and bathroom, while yet another overturned every piece of furniture in the home.

Nothing was ignored, and what was deemed important, was seized by the senior officer.

Jack wanted to be more protective of his employee, but the detective seemed to have the upper hand. Thank goodness a nurse was walking by and saw two visitors in Adam's room.

Nurse Jersey was bringing some paperwork to Nurse Jasper, who was standing at the other end of the hall. When she saw the commotion in Adam's room, she immediately stopped what she was doing, in order to address her concern. "Our visiting hours are long over, so you will both have to leave!" she stated firmly.

In his day, Detective Katts was quite the ladies' man; charming and thinner, and he had the luscious lips and full head of slightly-curly hair that all the girls liked to touch. Today, however, he was older and heavier, but he still maintained enough charm to influence the ladies into doing what he wanted.

As Detective Katts walked towards Nurse Jersey, he made sure to lock eyes with the middle-aged blonde beauty. He reached into his pocket and pulled out his business card, and when he got within two feet of her body, he extended it towards her in a sultry manner. "I'm with the police department", he professed, as he tilted his head to the left. "I realize that it's after visiting hours, but I'll only be a minute." He let his eyes linger on her face, and then he bathed the rest of her body with admiration.

As he listened to the hard, uneven rhythm of her breathing, he took another step towards her. "And if you ever need me after I leave, you can reach me at this number." He winked as if he was suggesting that her phone call didn't have to be about work.

Nurse Jersey took the small card and felt like she had somehow been dragged into a trance. Her heart was hammering foolishly in her chest, and she was looking at him with the smile of a 14-year old girl. The force in which she had asked both men to leave, had all but disappeared now. In its place was an unspoiled version of her former self, when she was young and in love for the very first time.

Nurse Jersey wasn't sure what had come over her, but maybe it was that the detective's gorgeous blue eyes reminded her of her former boyfriend.

James Sperry was her first love, and when he ran off with someone else, she cried herself to sleep for over a year. Arlene, as she's known to her friends, has never been in love since then, but she has often fantasized that James would come back to her open and eager arms, and never leave.

"Hey! Hello?" Adam called from across the room. He was going in and out of sleep, and desperately needed someone to help him use the bathroom.

The nurse was reluctant to pull herself away, but took a minute to help her patient. All the while, she watched the detective out of the corner of her eye.

When Adam was taken care of, she fluffed his pillows and smoothed out the blankets which lay over his body. She then walked across the room and took another long look into the detective's handsome face. "I have to go now, but you can stay for another five minutes and then you have to leave." Without looking in Jack's direction, she scurried out of the room to find Nurse Jasper.

The detective couldn't help but smile, because he felt an invisible web of attraction between himself and the pretty nurse. He waited until his quickened pulse had quieted down, and then he made his way across the room to Adam's bed.

"I better go, too", Jack suggested. He could see that there was a lot going on now, and he felt that he would be much happier by himself.

Jack desperately wanted to be away from all the troubles of the day, and at home where he could find out what had happened to Louise.

Detective Katts smiled and shook hands with Jack. "If I have any other questions for you, or if you have anything more that you'd like to volunteer to me, we can talk."

Jack nodded his agreement and looked over at Adam. Because his friend was passed out, he turned his attention back to the detective. "You probably won't get too much from him tonight."

"That's fine", he replied. The detective lowered his gaze with confidence and grinned. "I have all the time in the world to ask him questions."

Andrew Katts felt that he had gotten everything he could from Jack, and was now intent on finding out how much more he could get from Adam. Anything, even a small tidbit would be appreciated, and from all that he could uncover, he knew that he would be greatly rewarded.

As Jack left, he shrugged his shoulders and walked to his car.

In the meantime, the detective made himself comfortable in the only chair in the room. It was in the corner, across from Adam's bed, and out of sight of the hallway and everyone's prying eyes.

At first, the intensity of his patience blazed as dutiful as a microwave oven. But as the minutes ticked away, a premonition festered into his thoughts.

Andrew Katts was thrilled about all that he had discovered so far, and he hoped to learn even more when Adam woke up. In the back of his mind, he could see himself receiving another sash - an honourable mark of distinction to add to his esteemed collection. But he could also sense that something might get in the way. He didn't know what, but there was a disturbance looming over his head that advised him to be cautious. Because he knew enough to heed any and all warnings, the detective closed his eyes and let his body go into a resting mode.

Detective Katts knew better than to truly fall asleep, for he had done that very early on in his career, and he was rudely awakened by a black hand-gun pointing to his forehead. That same foreboding feeling was sinking into his thoughts now, and it made him wonder what misfortune destiny had in store for him.

On the other side of town, the police had left Molly's house with an envelope that was addressed to the dead man and his wife, along with a framed picture of the two of them together.

Once the officers got back to the station, they put an all-points bulletin out for Molly Perkins.

Molly had finished her food, and while she handed the empty plate to Jayla, she wondered why they were still there. "Did your grama ever come home?" she asked kindly.

Since she'd come back from the bathroom, she had been listening for sounds that someone else might be in the house. Sadly, she hadn't heard any.

Jayla made a disgruntled noise, rolled her eyes, and walked away in anger. She knew that the grumbling and constant questions would come out sooner or later, and she was ready.

Once she was alone in the kitchen, she placed the dirty dishes in the sink and then raised her hands towards the ceiling.

> You may have sight, but
> you'll not have sound
> From this moment on, your
> lips will be bound

> They will be released when I leave
> So you can cry and you can grieve
> But you will speak no more, now

The entire house shook as if there was a gigantic earthquake, while the lights blinked on and off for several seconds. During that time, the house moaned and creaked as if it was angry from all the uninvited commotion.

Molly held onto the decrepit old couch with great fear, and was extremely alarmed that she couldn't scream out for Jayla. With a hand against her throat and salty tears welling in her eyes, she was greatly aware that there was so much to be frightened for.

Molly chalked her lack of energy, her aches and pains, and losing her voice to the immense fear that was running through her body. She had never been so scared before in her entire life, and more than anything, she just wanted to go home.

Jayla entered the room and was smiling from ear to ear. Molly's anxiety brought her a lot of joy,

Ophelia's Curse

but she knew that torturing Roger would bring her so much more. The thought of him begging her not to kill him, pleased her, and while she continued to stare in Molly's direction, she laughed in a very cruel manner.

Molly's eyes grew even wider from the strange woman's bone chilling cackle, but because the house had stopped moving and the lights were no longer blinking, she tried to calm herself down.

While she sat in her warm spot on the old, worn-out couch, Molly hugged herself as she continued to wonder what was going on. And as a cold shiver inched its way up her spine, her inner voice was taunting her for opening the door for Jayla, yesterday afternoon.

CHAPTER FOURTEEN

October 30, 2000

It was 10:30pm when Jack pulled into his driveway, and he had never been so happy to be home. The first thing he noticed when he came through the door, was that Louise was sound asleep on the couch. He moved his feet as if he was walking on egg shells, and stopped when he was a few feet away from the quietness of her body. As he watched her sleep, he thanked God that she was at home and seemed to be ok.

His heart was melting as he looked down at her, and he could almost feel the burden of worry leave his tense shoulders. He suddenly felt as if he hadn't held his wife in years, and he wished that he could reach out and give her a hug right there and then.

As Jack looked upon Louise in the dimly-lit room, she seemed more delicate and lovely than ever.

The lace trim at the low-cut neck of her nightie was unhooked, and he could see the moist satin skin of her full but firm breasts. Her figure was sprawled in a seductive manner, and it was evident that there were generous curves beneath the shiny, light-weight material. Her serene face glowed with pale pink undertones, and while her lips were full and round, they had parted ever-so-slightly. Small bunches of loose tendrils of hair had tumbled carelessly all over the pillow beneath her head, and it made her look angelic.

As Jack stared at his bride of many years, he realized that she was truly a beautiful sight to behold. He suddenly remembered their first year of marriage, when Louise could be as playful as a school girl or as composed as an intelligent business woman, and all in the same day.

A few minutes had past, and he let out a sigh from the happy memories. In that same breath, he also wished that things could be as good now as they were back then.

Jack lowered his head, as he brought a hand up to brush the abrasive beginnings of a beard on his chin. There were now touches of humor around the edges of his mouth and the corner of his eyes, as he found himself falling in love with Louise all over again. He had always loved her, but he knew that he hadn't always shown his devotion to her. At least not in a way that had made her feel secure.

As he stared down at the calm look on her face - a look that reminded him of a child deep in slumber - he decided not to disturb her. Instead, he snuck away as quietly as he could.

While Jack took the stairs, one step at a time, he noted that she had placed two full glasses of wine on the coffee table. And was that her perfume which lingered in the air? He couldn't help but chuckle, for she must have sprayed it all over the house.

As he got himself undressed, he could see that all of Louise's personal items were back where they belonged. 'She was home', he sighed, and this made him extremely thankful.

Before Jack turned the bedroom light off, he flicked the hall light on; he hoped that Louise would wake up on her own before morning, and that the light would guide her up the stairs.

When he was ready, Jack climbed into bed and rolled onto his right side. As he closed his eyes, he could feel a happiness that he hadn't felt in years, and this allowed him to fall asleep with great ease.

Roger arrived at Molly's house in a drunken stupor, but he began to sober up when he noticed that Molly had been robbed; drawers were pulled out, cupboards had been opened, tables had been flipped over, and paperwork was strewn everywhere.

"Hello?" he called, with trepidation in his voice. His eyes were wide and blinking rapidly, his nerves were on edge, and his heart was pumping so hard, it felt like it was slamming against his ribs. "Is anyone here?" His senses were acute as he listened for an answer.

Roger developed a rolling, uneasy feeling in the pit of his stomach, and his first thought was that Molly had changed her mind and had come home. But after a quick look around, he decided that she wouldn't have damaged her own possessions.

Roger's body quickly developed an unnatural stillness, his breathing had become laboured, and he walked around the house as quietly as he could. When he made his way to the kitchen, he could see that the window in the back door had been smashed.

Nervous sweat dotted his forehead as he moved himself closer to the sharp edges of the shattered glass. As his eyes and hands inspected the area, it was easy to figure out that this was the way the burglar had gotten inside the home.

Suddenly, not far from where he was standing, the house wept and howled as if it was testing the limits of his bravery. Roger whipped himself around, and felt as if someone was about to jump out from the vindictive darkness of the eerie shadows. "Show yourself, or I'm calling the police!" he shouted into the air. His voice was quivering and his legs felt like jelly, and as a cold wash swept down his back, the little hairs on his body began to stand on end.

He was scared and becoming jittery, and it felt like time had stopped. His vision was quite sharp now, and he purposely strained his ears to pay attention to any kind of noise.

Roger hated this dreaded feeling of impending doom, and wondered if it was going to come down to a choice between his life or someone else's. He had watched enough horror movies to know how they turned out, but living in one was totally different; the spiteful torture of not knowing who was there with him, was eating him up alive.

Before he left the kitchen, Roger grabbed a thick broom handle with his ice-cold fingers, and in a semi-crouching position, he slowly made his way from room to room. "When I find you, you're going to be sorry!" he promised loudly, to anyone who was hiding nearby.

While intense fear made him slow his steps, he honestly hoped that he wouldn't come face-to-face with anyone. At the same time, he felt he needed to prove to himself that he was somewhat courageous.

He was riding the last wave of alcohol and he still had a small bit of marijuana in his system, and with this huge amount of anxiety and confusion racing through his veins, his body was filled with more adrenaline than it was used to.

Shoving each door against the wall so he could tell if someone was hiding behind it, was brutal, and looking underneath the beds and whipping the curtains aside, was complete agony. But thinking you are hearing things that aren't there, was cruel beyond all measure.

"Come out, come out, wherever you are!" he sang in a taunting manner. Sweat was drizzling down his face and his heart was pounding in his ears, but he continued to put one foot in front of the other.

Several minutes later, Roger stood in the middle of the living room and was relieved to find that no-one was in the house. As he tried to calm himself down, his mind was spinning from all of the day's surprising events.

Roger looked at the clock on the wall and saw that it was close to 11pm. He lowered his head in surrender and trusted that there would be no more disturbances tonight; he was exhausted and desperately wanted this day to end on a high note.

He grabbed a beer from the fridge and made himself comfortable on the fancy leather couch. With the remote control in his left hand, he sailed through the channels while looking for something interesting to watch. When he found a trivial but amusing game show, he dropped the remote control on the couch beside him, and he could actually feel the muscles in his body begin to relax.

With everything that had happened in the last three hours, the shooting at the hardware store had completely skipped out of his head. And the fact that the police might come there in the near future to gather evidence, deluded him on every level. His only thought in that moment was of Molly, and the start of their new life together.

Roger threw a few gulps of beer into the back of his mouth, and he loved how the cold liquid tickled as it went down his throat. When he could breathe again, he took a minute to listen to his surroundings. Thankfully, all he could hear was the small motor of a car driving by the house and an alley cat screaming for a mate.

Roger took another swig of beer as his sceptical eyes moved lazily around the room. He surveyed the damage as if he was looking for a needle in a hay stack, and he wondered what had been stolen. As he removed the edge of the steel can from his damp mouth, he became angry that someone had dared to break into Molly's beautiful home.

Because he hoped that she wouldn't think that he had done this, he pledged to get up early and clean it up. For now though, he was going to get some sleep.

The police were combing the city, desperately searching for Molly Perkins. They didn't find a wallet or purse in her house, and could only assume that she had those items with her. They did find some pictures of Marlowe and his wife, and the sketch artist at the police department, cropped their faces out of the photos.

Marlowe's face was used to show everyone what he looked like before the shooting, and Molly's was pasted onto a Wanted Poster. Both items were then sent to every police station for miles around. The crime would be broadcast on the TV in minutes, along with an account of all that had happened so far. By morning, all of this would be seen in the newspapers around the country.

Before the next 24 hours were up, the police hoped to find the person who they were looking for, and they prayed that she was still alive.

Molly was pretending to watch a program on TV, while continually stealing quick glances at Jayla.

She was scared, restless, and hungry for her own food. She felt unclean and couldn't wait to have a shower, and she desperately wanted to be in her own surroundings again. Unfortunately, Jayla held the key to Molly's freedom, and by studying the odd woman's calm and collective manner, Molly could see that going home was not in her immediate future.

The palms of Molly's hands were sweaty, so she wiped them down the full length of her thighs. She then closed her eyes and took a deep breath, while the question, 'where was the grama', rolled through her mind. She then wondered if there even was a grama. And if not, what was this all about?

Roger had finished his beer and he could feel himself smiling because of a silly moment on the game show. In his calm new state, he was convinced that everything was going to be alright from here on out; whoever had been in the house was gone, and they must have found what they were looking for, otherwise they would still be there.

He hated that Molly wasn't in her home with him, but she said that she would be back in the morning. He was going to hold her to her promise, because he couldn't wait to see her again.

Roger leaned his dog-tired body into the back of the couch, and this made him feel even more relaxed. As he closed his eyes and slowly drifted off to sleep, Roger had a feeling that the good part of his life would begin in the morning. He could then put the rest of it behind him, once and for all.

Molly was not happy that she was still sitting in a cheerless house that she didn't know, and with a strange woman who she had only met the day before. None of this felt right, and because it was now pitch dark outside, the two small table lamps which Jayla had turned on, gave the room an eerie glow.

It was 11:05 when Jayla decided that it was time to call Roger, but first things first. Jayla needed Molly to understand how important it was for her not to move or speak, so she commanded the spell of submissiveness.

Their eyes made a strange connection when Jayla stood up, almost as if there were strings of electronic messages that silently flowed between them.

The beautiful gypsy-witch raised herself tall and straight, and after drawing from the power of the four corners and her inner self, she bent her upper body forward and stared directly into Molly's soul.

Molly was instantly captivated by the invisible veil of authority that filled the room. She felt a tugging feeling in her chest, and a sense of being pulled towards Jayla with invisible hands against her back. There was also a tingling sensation in the forehead area between her eyebrows, and it warned her that she better not look away...or else.

Before Jayla spoke, soft strange music began to play all around her. A light breeze began to swirl gently, and as the witch moved her hands in the air, she recited the following words via mental telepathy:

> Into the threads of time I cast
> A spell of obedience at full mast

> Without your knowledge you will obey
> To everything I think or say

Molly heard the words as if they had been said out loud, and she immediately felt the immense need to conform to all that Jayla wanted her to do. It was as if she was in another body; the skin was hers, but the feel of her essence was different.

Molly shifted her eyes and turned her head, and this confirmed that she could see and think. She was terrified when she tried to make a sound and nothing came out of her throat. This made her panic and she tried to get up, but she found that she couldn't leave the spot where she was sitting. It was a very odd and frightening sensation, and she soon reasoned that nothing about the last 24 hours had been normal.

Jayla looked towards Molly with a great deal of enjoyment. She was quite satisfied with all that she had been able to accomplish in the past three days, and after ensuring herself that Molly would be okay on her own for a few minutes,

Jayla grabbed her phone and went into the kitchen.

Once her captor was out of sight, Molly took that time to speculate about her current situation. 'How can I escape when I can't even move? Was the grama finally making an appearance? Were they able to leave once she arrived?' These and other questions filled her head, while her body unwillingly stay glued to the cushion.

Jayla was standing in the kitchen, and with a sparkle in her eye and a wicked smile on her face, she dialed Molly's home number.

From where she was sitting, Molly could hear the discreet sound of musical buttons. She knew it was from a cell phone, and now listened intently to the one-sided conversation.

Jayla had pushed the last number, and was almost giddy as she waited for Roger to answer.

She had waited for over a year for this moment to arrive, and because she would be getting his soul before the actual due date, it felt like Halloween – her favorite night of the year.

Ophelia's Curse

The thought made Jayla giggle, because Halloween was less than an hour away.

Roger had only been passed out for a few minutes when the phone rang, and his head and thoughts were still quite clouded. He could hear the ringing off in the distance, but he didn't know where it was coming from. When he realized that it wasn't part of his dream, he reached out and picked up the receiver.

"Hello?" His heart began to pound with happiness over the idea that it might be Molly. 'Had she called so that they could say goodnight to each other?' he wondered. He pressed the receiver closer to his ear and listened.

Hearing his voice, brought both pleasure and anger to Jayla's body. Her first instinct was to be alluring and clever, but she became angry when she remembered that he was in love with someone else.

It bothered her a great deal that he didn't want her, and it ultimately left her feeling emotionally wounded. Until now, the pain of his dishonesty had cooked the juices of her hate, but no more.

"Well, well", Jayla cooed into the phone. "Hello, Roger." Her tone was stern but playful, and held no trace of sympathy.

"Uh...Hi?" Roger's blood-shot eyes suddenly sprang open very wide. And even with how confused he was, he didn't think that the female voice on the phone was Molly.

"How are you?" Jayla could hear herself talking, but it didn't seem like her - she was usually as tough as a broom's twigs. In contrast, the tone in her voice sounded almost frisky and daring.

She immediately removed the phone from her ear and nestled it against her shoulder. She then took a much-needed minute to clear her head.

"Who is this?" he asked with concern. Roger was hoping that it was Molly, but now he wasn't sure.

As Jayla contemplated what was going on, she decided that Roger had somehow touched the soft side of her heart. She let out a sigh at the idea that he had this way of making her feel like a voluptuous woman, but was ashamed of how much she liked it.

As she stood in a dream-like state, Jayla closed her eyes and lowered her chin to her chest. In that silence, she envisioned the two of them together.

'No, no!' her spirit shouted. The words were full of contempt, and seemed to emerge from a bitter pool of resentment. 'That idea needs to stop, and it needs to stop right now! He only has one purpose in this life, and that is to give you more life!'

Jayla heard the harsh reprimand and was suddenly jerked back to reality. She understood those sentiments, and reluctantly agreed that she needed to change her attitude.

After taking a huge breath, she tightened her fists with anger, and stomped her foot on the ground as she flaunted an erratic, child-like temper tantrum.

Once she had cooled down, she used every ounce of energy in her body to reverse her point of view. "I am not in love with him. I am not going soft. He is nothing but a donor to me", she chanted softly.

She really tried to convince herself to believe what she was saying, and after forcefully pushing all of her feelings away, she placed her focus on doing the job which she had to do, in order to survive.

After inhaling another large gulp of air into her lungs, she adopted a refreshing new outlook on life. And when she was ready, she positioned the phone back at her ear. "You're a fool, Roger!" she hissed into the mouth piece. "You should have been more honest with me!"

Jayla smiled as soon as she heard the familiar flash of cruelty in her voice. "I'm back!" her heart sang. Now to get on with the business at hand.

Roger's eyebrows shot up high on his forehead, as a look of utter curiosity covered his entire face. He desperately wanted the person on the phone to be Molly, but it sounded more like

Jayla. But how could that be? And how would Jayla have this number?

"Molly?" he asked. He was confused and concerned, and wasn't even sure if he was awake.

"Don't…talk!" the woman ordered sharply. She had purposely spaced the last two words out, in order to make him afraid.

As Jayla was preparing herself for the next step, the muscles and veins in her neck were straining to leap through the skin. Her eyes had narrowed and her shoulders were becoming tight, as if she was about to engage in battle.

Molly was sitting silent in the other room, and was stunned by all that she could hear. Her hands were in her lap, and her fingers had been squirming and intertwining until they were almost raw. Tiny droplets of tears were glistening in her eyes, and while one drop in particular was begging to be released, she didn't cry. Instead, she stayed perfectly still, so that she could hear every word with total clarity.

Roger bolted into a sitting up position, and as a small amount of air sucked into the back of his throat, the hostility of this alarming situation, was causing him to become more and more sober. "Jayla?" he asked in a whisper, as if it was a secret. "How did you know that I was here?"

"That's not important!" she screamed. "I have Molly with me, and she wants to see you! That's what you should think about!"

Roger was in utter shock. 'Jayla had Molly? But why?'

Jayla now had a mad desire for revenge, and she could taste that the moment of payback was just out of her reach.

"If you want to see her alive, listen carefully to the words which I am about to say!" Her voice was guttural as she spoke, and rang with a tone of absolute finality.

"I'm listening." And as if he was going into a trance, Roger's back straightened up, his eyes faced forward, and he couldn't help but pay attention.

When Jayla narrated the spell of command, it was as if the reality of death was dangling over his head.

> Filsom Folsom and spirits that fly
> Let me give this another try
> As the oceans curl and the clouds swirl
> Whisk him to me, so the end can unfurl

The spell was cast, and as she pressed the ear piece even tighter to her head, she waited to hear Roger's reaction on the other end of the phone.

Roger suddenly had the mannerisms of a robot, and responded to Jayla's demand without any hesitation. After finding the keys to Marlowe's car on the left corner of the coffee table, he sped to the house where Molly was being held captive.

Molly was stunned to hear the words and the manner in which Jayla had said them, and she was now more afraid of Jayla than before. She wondered who the person on the other end of the phone was, but before she could gather another thought, her body stiffened as Jayla came back into the family room. She immediately focused on the faint smile which Jayla's crooked lips were displaying, and she made sure that the two women didn't make eye contact.

Jayla was quite pleased with how the phone call went, and now all she had to do was wait.

Molly inhaled a little too sharply when Jayla took a seat next to her on the couch, and she hoped that Jayla didn't notice.

"It won't be long now", Jayla teased, as she turned to face her hostage. She was looking into Molly's face with both hatred and joy, and she was acting like a killer cat – cunning and totally unpredictable.

Molly was nervous with Jayla being so close; she was already fearful from all that had happened so far, and she wondered what else Jayla was capable of doing.

As if she could read Molly's thoughts, Jayla smiled. And as she turned her head, she got up from the couch and answered the unspoken question. "Don't worry, my pet. You won't have to be in my company for too much longer." Jayla walked out of the room without looking behind her.

Molly wasn't sure what Jayla meant by that last comment, but she desperately wanted it to mean that she would be going home in the very near future.

Roger held no thoughts in his head as he let the car guide him to where he needed to go. His hands were on the steering wheel and his right foot was bouncing between the gas pedal and the brake, but he didn't seem to have control over anything. At the same time, he didn't think it mattered; the end result was that he would soon be with Molly.

Jayla could feel that Roger was on his way, so she guided the car to turn right and left accordingly.

Roger watched out the front window with the sense of an android; he could speak and walk and talk, but not much of that was of his own free will.

As he watched the road ahead of Marlowe's car, he found that the route was much too complicated to follow on his own. There were even a few confusing moments where it felt like he was going around in circles, but then the car drove straight for another few miles.

Because he knew that he couldn't do anything to change his course, Roger decided to calm his nerves and do whatever it took to reach Molly.

Molly was back to watching unimportant nonsense on TV, while Jayla took a minute to use the bathroom. All of a sudden, a news flash trickled across the bottom of the screen, complete with a picture.

> **Missing Person – Mrs. Molly Perkins**
> **5'7", light brown hair,**
> **last seen in her Shelton**
> **neighbourhood home,**
> **at noon today.**
> **Contact the police if you**
> **have seen this woman.**

Molly's eyes zoomed wide open with complete surprise at this astonishing announcement. 'She

Ophelia's Curse

hadn't been gone that long, so why had she been classified as missing? Was Marlowe looking for her? Why was Jayla holding her captive?'

So many questions rushed through her mind, but for the first time since she had gotten into the car with Jayla, she actually felt like she would be going home again.

The announcement was now over, but Molly happily recited the words a few more times in her mind. The shock of the story on the news was euphoric and scary all at the same time, for while people were now searching for her, nobody knew where she was.

When the toilet flushed, she immediately leaned herself back into the couch and tried to look like nothing had changed.

Jayla came out of the bathroom and checked the clock on the wall. Because of her inherent talent to see things that other people couldn't, she was able to envision where Roger was in that very moment. She estimated how long it was going to take him to find the house, and the answer made her beady eyes light up with excitement.

Meanwhile, Marlowe's car was going a little faster than the speed limit allowed. Because Roger couldn't control how the car was maneuvering through the traffic, there was nothing he could do to lessen the pace.

A police cruiser was parked on the shoulder of the road, and he was calmly watching for violations of any kind. When Marlowe's car sped past him, he threw his paper to the side, shifted his vehicle into drive, and began to chase after the car with full acceleration.

Jayla could feel that Roger was getting close, and this made her perfectly content. All of a sudden, an edgy sense of danger prickled up her back. She turned and faced east, and could sense that something was terribly wrong. Because it was imperative that Roger arrive as quickly as possible, Jayla decided to redirect the composition of Marlowe's car.

As the skilled cop got closer to the back of the speeding vehicle, he turned his flashing lights and siren on. With the fingers of his right hand, he typed the numbers and letters of the license plate into his dash computer. He couldn't believe his eyes when the display read, 'Owned by Marlowe and Molly Perkins'.

"What?!" he rejoiced. The officer's emotions were now running high, and he couldn't wait to gush the information to anyone who would listen. With a ton of enthusiasm, he lifted the round handset and placed it near his mouth.

"Six twenty-one to dispatch"

"Dispatch, go ahead"

"I am driving behind a car that belongs to our missing person."

The feeling of danger was coming in incredibly strong, and this caused Jayla to become annoyed. Because Roger was getting so close to the house, she didn't want anything to disrupt her plan.

Without giving a thought to what Molly was doing, Jayla rushed into the kitchen and raised her arms out to the sides. "Block the hostility and obstruct the problem", she began, as a sheen of light sweat began to appear on her cheeks and forehead. "Spirits rise and don't waver from what I request."

She continued her mighty plea to the four corners, while she hoped that she was able to articulate her thoughts without stumbling. In that same second, Jayla flinched, for it was as if someone had touched the back of her neck with something cold.

The stiffening hair sent tingles to her sensitive skin, while the corners of her mouth lifted. And as her left eyebrow rose in amusement, she somehow knew that 'this problem' was being fixed.

The communication between the cop and dispatch had ended with an abrupt dial tone, but not before he had given out his exact location. After a few seconds of fiddling with the handset, his front right tire exploded. This made his squad car swerve, and he eventually lost control.

Roger was thunderstruck as he watched the whole thing unfold in the rear-view mirror. But while he was relieved that he was no longer being chased, he was overjoyed that he was about to see Molly again.

The cop car had been able to stop in the outside lane, so no other traffic was going to be affected. The officer got out to inspect the damage, and from sheer exasperation, he flew into a huge rage.

There was no real damage done to the squad car, other than it needed a new tire, but his ego had been badly bruised. The police officer was greatly annoyed that he would not be a hero, for he was 'this close' to capturing the person who was driving Marlowe's vehicle, and now that person was gone.

From the outline of the head and shoulders, the officer could tell that it was a man who was driving. Was Molly hidden in the back? He didn't know. And because he could no longer continue the chase or speak with anyone at the police station, he was now at a loss.

In his mind, he saw himself getting a medal for the capture of whoever had stolen Molly's car.

In reality, he would be forever known as the police officer who tried, but failed.

Dispatch had been surprised when the call had been cut off, so Officer Dytania Johnson reported it to his superior.

The superior was unusually loud when he alerted everyone in the building to hear what he had to say. "You have all been given the coordinates of the speeding vehicle, and now I order you to find it!"

Detective Katts had been asked to leave Adam's hospital room when the doctor came in at 11pm, and he was dismayed that he had learned nothing new about the case. After grabbing a coffee and a plain bagel with cream cheese from a popular drive-through window, he drove back to the station, but ate his snack in his car.

He happened to have his police scanner on, and he had heard this new bit of information. After wolfing down the last bite of his bagel, he started his car and looked forward to putting the final pieces of this puzzle together.

Ophelia's Curse

When Jayla lowered her arms and opened her eyes, she felt an enchanting sense of peace spray around the room. She smiled with confidence, and allowed herself to become immersed in the proud moment. She quickly thanked all the spirits for their help, and then placed her focus back on Roger.

Unbeknownst to Roger, he had just pulled into the neighbourhood where Molly was being held captive. He was getting angry at how long this was taking, and raised an untamed eyebrow as the car made another right-hand turn.

Since he left Molly's home, Roger had been travelling with excessive speed. He had not been able to guide the car as he would have liked, and he was going around corners at an uncomfortably sharp angle. He was more than ready to be on solid ground again, but he just didn't know when that moment would come.

Roger doubted that this nightmarish ride could last too much longer, and he held his breath while he hoped for the best.

Jayla could feel that Roger was five minutes away, and her eyes turned as black as coal from sheer joy. She cackled as she looked at the time, and was aware that she had to begin preparing the potion.

When Jayla's image flashed in his mind, Roger became paralyzed with fear. The blood drained from his face as he wondered how Jayla and Molly had come to be in the same place at the same time, because he would never have predicted that that could happen.

The fear of what Jayla might do to Molly, ate away at his sanity. 'Would she actually harm her?' he wondered. 'Or would this develop into a ghastly show-down, where Jayla would insist he pick her over Molly?'

Roger once heard that a woman scorned would do anything to protect what was hers. He then remembered a man who he had once been in jail with.

Simon had been caught cheating and received a brutal beating by his then-girlfriend, Lydia. He was arrested when he tried to defend himself, but the stabbing and other ruthless marks on his body, proved that the 'scorned woman theory' was true on all counts.

In the end, Lydia had been sent home to rest, while Simon was charged with domestic violence. Every day that grew closer to his being released, he cowered in fear, until that day, when a guard found him hanging in his cell...stiff as a board.

As he recalled the gruesome details, Roger began to tremble, for that time period would forever remain in his brain. And as he thought about his own situation, Roger was afraid that he would be up against this same kind of misunderstood scenario.

The car was moving forward without his assistance, and as he swallowed hard, Roger was suddenly being torn apart by incredible trepidation of what lay ahead of him.

From where she stood in the kitchen, Jayla could peer into the family room. She could see that Molly was losing hope, so Jayla engaged her in a conversation. "I think we've waited long enough for my grama to arrive. It might be best if we go. What do you think?"

Molly's eyes popped wide open because she couldn't believe her ears. Was Jayla actually saying that they could leave? She had no power of speech but she was filled with a great amount of excitement, so she nodded her head with complete agreement.

The two tears which had escaped from her eyes in that moment, were from sheer happiness, and she now had a great amount of difficulty sitting still.

Because Jayla wanted to hear her thoughts, she removed the simple spells of silence and stillness. "I asked you what you thought about going home." Jayla used a hand motion to encourage Molly to try speaking.

Molly opened her mouth and replied, "I'd love that." It was an odd feeling to use her throat again, and because she hadn't heard her voice in an hour or so, her entire body and soul rejoiced.

As she moved her feet, Molly's eyes began to dance with genuine happiness. She wanted to throw her arms up and spin in a wide circle, but she didn't, because of her enormous fear of her captor. She did smile though, for she was very appreciative of getting her freedom back.

Jayla loved how obedient Molly was, and she was glad that she had rewarded her. But once Roger came into the house, everything was going to change again.

While Molly's heart sang with the idea that she'd be going home soon, Jayla went back to stirring her strange mixture.

Jayla had just washed and quartered a 6" piece of Valerian Root. She then plopped a handful of it into the rapidly boiling water, along with some green herbs from her garden.

Because some of the ingredients which she was using were rare, and possibly poisonous if not handled correctly, Jayla stirred the nasty-smelling brew counter clockwise, in order to reduce everything down to the right potency. And depending on the strength of the potion, it would either force someone to sleep solid for a few hours, or it would kill them in minutes.

This is called the process of making a decoction, and Jayla had been practicing this since she was 13 years old. And because she wanted to take Roger to the Schilling Forest before she took his soul, she would really need to pay attention to what she was doing, in order to make the potion correctly.

Roger took a few minutes to think, and he realized how much he hated that he had not been in control of this situation. But because he was so determined to be with Molly, he vowed to do whatever it took to make that happen - even if it meant cowering to Jayla.

Something in his gut knotted and his body recoiled, at the thought of standing face-to-face with the woman who had entertained him during his last stint in prison. He was never going to stay with her after he was released, but he hadn't counted on her finding out about Molly.

Behind Roger's lined and troubled face, his sad eyes reflected what was in his heart. And as a halo of doom hovered over his head, he wished for Molly to remain unharmed.

All the officers who were driving around, kept their eyes open for Marlowe's car. The entire police department was surprised that it hadn't been seen since the tire exploded on their fellow officer's vehicle, but every rank of policeman or policewoman, was hopeful that they would find it before the night was over.

Marlowe's car was slowing down, and it eventually parked in front of a rickety old house, on the right side of the road. To his surprise, the car unlocked itself and he was able to get out.

Jayla heard a large motor rumble to a stop, and her heart jumped for joy with the anticipation of Roger's arrival. Though her potion was not fully ready, she raced to the front door to greet him.

Even though she looked slightly different, Roger recognized her the moment he saw her. "Jayla?" His heart leaped into his throat, for while there was some sensual tension between them, there was also a weird sense of danger.

"Hi!" she called. Her face was lit up, and she was waving to him like a silly school girl.

Roger nodded in a casual manner, and with each step that he took towards the porch, he could feel the threat of death growing stronger.

His heart was pounding and he wanted to run away, but because he was told that Molly was inside, leaving was not an option.

"Well, well. If it isn't my boyfriend." Her words were as cool as ice water, and Jayla took great pride in being aggressive towards him.

Roger tilted his head downwards as if he should be ashamed, and continued to take his last few steps towards the house.

He didn't know how Jayla had found out about Molly, and he wasn't about to tell her anything more than she already knew. As far as he was concerned, he was there for one reason and one reason only – to bring Molly home.

Jayla decided to remove the spell of obedience, which allowed Roger to become as she had always seen him in jail.

As the hex was being lifted, the air swirled and something popped, but there were no other significant signs to say that anything was going on.

Roger could feel the difference in his movements immediately, but he wasn't sure how that had happened. He suddenly felt emotionally unchained, and he loved this new sense of independence.

As she gazed into the rugged features on his tired face, Jayla wished that she could hear him laugh or see him smile. Sadly, she knew that that familiar part of their lives was now in the past.

"It's good to see you", he lied. A shiver curled itself through the tiny hairs on the back of his neck, and then cascaded down the bumps on his backbone as he spoke.

They had been together just a few days ago, but everything seemed very different between them today. It was odd, because their last visit was exceptional on every level imaginable. But standing before her now, was painfully awkward.

Molly was in the back room, and she thought she could hear a man's voice. 'Was it Marlowe?' she wondered. Her heart pounded to awareness as she walked over to the edge of the couch. She could then see the entire hallway from beginning to end. An incredulous dazed look had splashed upon her face, and she now waited to find out who was going to take her home.

When Roger leaned in to give Jayla a hug, he felt like he was about to be the victim in a deadly ambush. It was so odd to hold her now, as opposed to a few days ago, and he secretly vowed to never be in her company after today.

As he looked over her shoulder at the inside of the tiny home, he had an intense feeling that he was being watched. It was spooky, and he decided right there and then to be in and out of this mess as soon as possible, and then he could begin his new life with Molly.

"Welcome", Jayla stated kindly. She had her arms wrapped around Roger's body, and was remembering the warmth which they had experienced, only a few days ago. She closed her eyes and took a second to smell his aroma, and this created a wonderful memory for later.

Roger accepted the hug, but he wanted it to be over quickly.

He hoped that Jayla knew that he was only there to bring Molly home, and not to renew his relationship with her. And if not, he was scared that he'd be drawn into Jayla's indescribable sense of grimness, and he would somehow be persuaded to pick her over Molly.

Jayla could feel the lack of love between them now, and it was just as well, because he would be dead by morning. "It's nice to see you", she stated kindly. She allowed the hug to end gracefully, and then guided him into the home.

He stepped over the threshold and saw the remains of old furniture laying disorderly around the room. He took another step forward and the floorboards creaked under his foot.

"Come in!" she insisted. Because she couldn't wait to get this party started, Jayla grabbed his arm to drag him further into the house.

Roger's eyes were wide with worry as he walked through the ominous entranceway. He could immediately sense that someone had died, and was still lurking around to see who would be living amongst these old treasures.

As he took another step, a cold shiver raced up his back. His mind was running amuck and he thought he could hear the whispers of people who were long-dead, echoing through the dark rooms. It brought a strangeness to his soul that he hadn't felt before, and he frantically wished for the awful feeling to go away.

"We need to go down here", Jayla stated, as she pointed to the left. With each step they took, she was becoming more and more playful, and it showed on her face and in her mannerisms.

Ophelia's Curse

Roger turned the corner and was about to begin the long trek down the black and murky corridor.

When Molly saw him, her eyes widened and her body braced itself. An icy chill passed over her as she watched Roger come towards her, and it made her terribly confused.

When Roger saw Molly, his heart skipped a beat, and a sincere smile splashed across his face. He thought of nothing else but her as he began to run, while a flush of adrenaline tingled throughout his body. "Molly!" he cried. His arms were reaching forward as he let out a happy yelp.

Molly couldn't believe that the man from the front door was Roger; she honestly thought it would be Marlowe who had come to rescue her. But because Roger was better than nobody, she raised her arms in appreciation that he was going to bring her home. "Roger!" she cried, as she plastered a smile on her tear-stained face.

Jayla watched, and tried to be patient while they clung to each other. Inside, it stung that he was more excited to see Molly than he had been to see her, but she would make him pay for that.

Jayla was loathing him now, and she knew that she would find great delight in all that would happen in the forest at midnight.

"I'm so happy to see you", Molly whispered into his ear, and it was true. For if it couldn't be Marlowe who was saving her, then she was happy that it was Roger – her childhood friend.

As he stared into her eyes, Roger spoke with an underlying sensuality in his words. "Are you ok?"

He was under the impression that he had seen her at her home, just a few hours ago. She said that she was going to stay with a friend until morning, but he had no idea that the friend was Jayla. And because the house was creepy and dark and there was a huge sense of danger all around them, he was going to convince her to leave as quickly as possible.

Sadly, Roger had no idea that if and when they leave, was not up to him.

Their hug was close, and a great sense of relief had propelled them into a warm state of bliss. They shifted their bodies until they were standing less than a foot apart, and were holding hands while smiling from ear to ear.

"I am now." She looked at him as if he was her favorite movie star in the whole world.

"Please!" Jayla interrupted sharply. "Have a seat!"

It was torture for her to watch Roger wooing Molly, but she knew that she would soon get her revenge on both of them.

Jayla placed a fake smile on her sensuous lips, and extended her hand to encourage them to sit down. "Get reacquainted while I prepare a celebratory drink. One for the road!" she laughed, a little too loudly. She then left the room and made her way into the kitchen.

Roger and Molly also wanted to leave, but there was something in the air which warned them that they didn't have that option. While making facial expressions using mostly their eyes, each apprised the other, that to listen to Jayla was better than to disobey.

They were sad but both agreed, and then sat back and waited for the perfect opportunity to escape.

Jayla returned to the family room with drinks, and was wearing a smile that had forced the corners of her mouth to lift unnaturally high. "Voila! Look at what I have!" She lowered the tray to make it easier for them to reach.

Roger took one of the glasses, but only because he thought it would get him out of the house faster.

Molly also took one, because at this point, she would do anything to keep Jayla happy.

Jayla took the last glass, and then placed the tray down on the nearest solid surface. She had an evil gleam in her eye and a strange inner light that shone all around her, and as she looked directly into the confused faces of her victims, she wanted them to be happy.

Jayla had her plan down to a science: one minute for the poison to work, three minutes to get Roger into the car, and about 20 minutes to drive to the Schilling Forest. Once she got there, she would reduce him to tears and then happily obtain his soul.

She was suddenly reminded that it was almost Halloween, and it gave her even more reason to rejoice. With the full moon shining down upon the world tonight, Jayla couldn't think of a more perfect moment to perform the spell of transference.

With a new sense of happiness warming her heart, Jayla raised her glass in the air and made a toast. "To my friends, new and old. Let this be the beginning of something wonderful."

"Cheers!" they all shouted to each other, in one unassuming voice.

Behind the smiling faces, the gesture meant something different for each person in the room.

Jayla brought the clear glass up to her lips and pretended to take a sip. In reality, the liquid didn't touch her skin.

"To friends!" Roger and Molly stated, as they locked eyes. They clinked their glasses together, and then they each took a mouthful of the muddy liquid.

The strange drink tasted like blue cheese, peppered kale, and rotten eggs, and it burned as it skated over the roughness of their tongues. And as much as they would have wanted to spit it out, the slimy concoction seemed to slither down their throats all by itself.

A second later, Molly's eyes were looking around the room in alarm. She felt strange, and she knew her body couldn't handle any more fright. She wanted to run, but it felt like her feet were rooted to the spot. And when she tried to stand up, her eyelids were closing and her body was desperate to lean over.

Molly was scared, and she gasped as if she was going to scream. But instead of a noise coming out, a large amount of air burst into her mouth and it almost choked her. She cringed in terror, as if she had just seen a creepy figure spring up from behind her. At the same time, her wide eyes looked like they were begging to be released from their sockets as the temperature of her body was growing cold.

Roger was watching Molly with total surprise, but before he could ask her what was wrong, he began to experience his own reaction to Jayla's disgusting drink.

A combination of anxiety and confusion raced through his veins. 'She had done something', was his first reaction. 'She must have become enraged with jealousy', was his second. As a pall of dread was hanging heavily over his entire body, Roger could tell that he was now at the mercy of his former girlfriend. He felt helpless as his own muscles were becoming extremely tired, and he was close to tears from the guilt of not being able to save Molly.

Molly was completely passed out, with half of her face pressed into the seat cushions of the couch. She wasn't laying in a natural position, but Roger determined that nothing about this day had been normal.

Roger was fighting the effects of the poison with all his might, but he didn't know how much longer he could stay awake.

Jayla was standing a few feet away from both of her victims, and she was quietly celebrating her success. She was giddy that her plan had worked, and she could feel the excitement rising within her.

But while her victory was sweet, she remembered that there was still a little more work to do.

"Why?" Roger asked, as his body was sinking into a deep well of misery. He was livid at the idea that he was in his last moment of life, but felt that he had done everything he could to make things right for both of these women.

As his body leaned haphazardly against Molly's, a salty tear laced its way down the uneven ridges of his prickly right cheek. His heart was breaking as he realized how close he had come to bringing her home, and that the dream of having a 'happily ever after', was now fading into the frightening veil of a forced sleep.

When both of her victims had slid into the dark abyss of slumber, Jayla got all of her things together and carried it to the front door. When she came back into the family room again, she helped Roger to stand up.

Roger felt as if he had taken way too many drugs, and none of them were interacting well with the others. His senses were tainted, and the navigating tool in his brain was turned off. He could feel himself moving down the hall, but it was like he was looking out of eyes that belonged to someone else. He could feel the rush of fresh air against his skin when he stepped outside, but it felt foreign to him, as if his brain needed to figure out if this was real or a ruse.

It was an odd feeling to have his hips and back jerk for no reason, but his mind wasn't accepting the idea that he was going down the three solid steps of the cracked front porch. And when his body contorted so that he could somehow fit into something open and small, he wanted to know why someone was putting him into a box.

Once the pressure of being forced to bend was released, and his muscles were no longer moving, he was able to stretch out. As the blood raced through his veins and his mind was trying to shut down, it felt like he was in a heavy fog; everything was so surreal, that it was hard to tell if he was awake or asleep.

Jayla turned the key to start the motor. She then looked over at her passenger and approached the next task with typical cheerfulness. "Hang on", she stated lightly. Her stern voice was courteous but patronizing, and as the car rolled away from the curb, there was a definite strength in her face.

Jayla sighed with complete fulfillment, for after everything that had happened over the past few days, she was now completely content. "Nothing is going to stop me from collecting your soul tonight", she giggled. A satisfied smile appeared on her lips as a musk-rose flush dusted her round cheeks.

Roger didn't hear her words, nor did he understand what was happening. He was vaguely aware that he had been tied into something that was now moving, but he couldn't be sure of anything.

Meanwhile, Molly had not been laying properly and her body automatically adjusted itself. In an attempt to get more comfortable, she accidentally slid off the couch and bumped the side of her head against the dirty, uneven floor boards. The pain and shock of this brought her to a very light sense of awareness, and because her vision was blurred, she strained to see all that was around her.

As Molly touched the swollen area of the throbbing pain in her skull, she called out. "Hello?" The eerie silence in the house frightened her to her very core, and goaded her with mental numbness. "Roger?" With eyes that were wide and glassy, she grabbed onto the round arm of the worn-out couch with shaky hands. "Jayla?" As she tried to drag her drug-induced body into a standing position, she called out again. "Is anyone here?" There was no answer, and she was now super sensitive to everything in the immediate area.

Molly was trembling and on the verge of hyperventilating, and her heart was racing with unbelievable power. 'Am I alone?' she wondered, while apprehension coursed through every inch of her body. She felt deprived of some of her senses and wasn't entirely sure if she wanted to be there by herself or not. "Jayla?" she called again, as she took a wobbly step away from the couch. The tone of the faint echo was ominous, as if whatever evil was lurking in the shadows was growing larger and stronger by the minute.

Molly had a hundred thoughts rushing through her mind, while she steadied herself against the nearest wall. As she took one step after another, she hoped that this had all been a bad dream, and that she would wake up very soon.

When Molly got to the end of the long hallway, she looked to her right and she could see the front door. She took a deep breath and was pretending to have confidence, as she made her way towards the entrance of the ghostly home.

She turned the knob and pulled the door open, and the bizarre whining and cracking sound reminded her of a black and white movie, where an innocent girl was lifting the lid of a vampire's dusty coffin.

Suddenly, the crisp night air kissed her exposed skin, and she dared to believe that this moment was real. Her feet didn't want to move, but she also didn't want to linger in the doorway any longer than she had to. And as her gullible eyes spied the outside world, she wondered if she really was about to escape the mental and physical torture of being held captive.

CHAPTER FIFTEEN

October 31, 2000

It was 15 minutes to midnight on Hallow's Eve, and the face of the full moon was lit up like a Christmas tree. It was a brightly-colored super moon, and this one seemed to give out a vibe unlike any of the ones before it.

Mother Earth was shutting down, harvests were done, trees had been shedding their leaves, and animals had started preparing for hibernation.

During the next 24 hours, as the veil between the two worlds thinned out, everything would feel different. The dead would come alive, the alive would dress up as the dead, and all supernatural power will get heightened. The molecules in the air carried extra energy on this day, and witchcraft had a way of piggybacking off other spells. All of this created even more effectiveness for all incantations, divinations, and other avenues of magic.

As an astute witch, Jayla knew the mystique of all of these facts by heart, and she hoped that this glorious night was going to play out exactly how she had planned. She was minutes away from arriving at her destination, and as she turned to look at the listless man to her right, she took great pride in the fact that Roger was sound asleep.

For a brief second, she wanted to keep him as a boyfriend so that she would never be alone again. Sadly, she knew that that would be foolish, for she still had to feed on the souls of corrupt men in order to survive. 'Could I keep this one and continue life as I have been living it?' she wondered blindly. As she looked upon his peaceful features, she honestly wanted to, but she knew in her heart that she could not.

Jayla faced forward again, and as a tear or two slid down her warm cheeks, she commanded herself to be brave. "I need to stick with the plan", she stated firmly. She then braced herself and wished for the astonishing power of this very moment, to guide her towards the miraculous occurrence that she had been looking forward to.

Molly had been through a lot in the last 24 hours, and she knew that she couldn't take much more. As she lifted her foot to step outside, her stomach suddenly vomited all the hot vile which had been temporarily housed in her abdomen. A minute or two later, she felt a lot better. She wiped her mouth with the back of her hand, and looked around the immediate area to establish if anyone had heard her throw up. As her teeth chattered and a cloud of cold fear gathered to all sides of her, she confirmed that there was nothing nearby, but dead air. Because she was now pretty certain that she was alone, she raced out of the house.

As she rushed across the porch and onto the dying grass, she was nervous and confused but very relieved to be free. She took no time to get acquainted with her unfamiliar surroundings, and ran out to the pavement like a crazy woman who was filled with unsupported fears.

Ophelia's Curse

While the cool breeze brushed against her arm, and the clouds tried to hide behind the moon, Molly found herself alone on a very long street with darkened houses on both sides. When she looked down the road, she could behold what seemed like another world. There were bright lights and people driving around, but she didn't think that she could walk that far. With a heavy heart, she studied the neighbourhood and became frantic very quickly. 'Where am I?' she wondered, as a daunting look of curiosity spread across her worried face.

Suddenly, nightmarish images began to emerge in the many dark corners around her. She called out when she heard something similar to a garbage can tip over, and she tried to convince herself that she had nothing to worry about. 'Should I go back inside the house where Jayla left me?' she wondered. Molly dismissed that notion before she inhaled her next breath.

Her vision was now better than it had been, but she was still groggy and couldn't see numbers on any of the houses. All of the brightness which shone around her came from the moon and the dimly-lit street lights, but none of it was comforting. She rubbed her hands against her upper arms as if to warm herself up, and she looked for a way to get home. But which way should she go?

After pondering the question for a few seconds, she decided that she needed help.

It took all of her willpower, but Molly stood tall, made fists with her hands, took a deep breath, and screamed at the top of her lungs. And as she continued to scream, she took step-after-step towards the traffic lights off in the distance, and she didn't stop until people began to respond to her anguish.

The lights flicked on as people could hear her frantic cries of gloom, and one-by-one, they came out to help.

Molly fell to her knees with great relief, and made sure to look into the kind faces of the caring neighbours. They could all see that she was suffering, and some asked her what was going on.

Molly bowed her head, and through tear-stained whimpers, she slowly revealed her horrific tale.

Everyone there was stunned by the story, and while one of them called the police, another two came rushing out of their house with a warm blanket and a hot cup of tea.

By some strange luck, the driver of a police car had turned right and found himself driving towards a familiar car. The cop who was the passenger, recognized it from the last police briefing, and immediately typed the license plate number into the database. Both of them cheered when it came back as being registered to Marlowe and Molly Perkins.

While Officer Tom Sauck radioed dispatch with the good news, Officer John Wall was staring straight ahead. He had spotted a small group of people who were gathered in a semi-circle, but he couldn't tell what they were doing. Without waiting for permission, he stepped out of the car to go and check.

Officer Sauck made sure that Marlowe's vehicle was scheduled to be impounded sometime in the next hour, and then it would be taken to police headquarters for further investigation. He then exited the squad car and joined his partner up the block.

"Are you alright?" Officer Wall asked. He extended his hand, and both he and Officer Sauck helped the weeping woman to stand up.

"I'm okay now", Molly insisted. She was very grateful to have everyone around her, including the police. "But I have so much to tell you."

"How about if we start with your name?" the taller officer asked.

"My name is Molly Perkins."

The faces of both the officers went pale and blank, and they immediately turned and locked eyes. They were thrilled by this strange coincidence and took a quick second to rejoice, but not out loud. While they believed they had a lot to celebrate, they slid back into cop mode and did their jobs with dignity and privilege.

A minute later, Officer Wall led Molly to the warmth of the squad car while Officer Sauck insisted that everyone go home. "The show's over! Thank you all for trying to help! You can go home now, and we'll take it from here! Thank you!" the older cop called loudly. The handsome man had his hands up in the air, and was shuffling from one foot to the other. He was shouting at the top of his lungs and turning his head this way and that, and all in order to attract more attention to what he was saying.

Molly sat down in the back seat and brought her knees up to her chest, while Officer Wall placed the warm woollen blanket around her body.

After Officer Sauck had everything under control, he walked back to his car.

When she was ready, Molly took ten minutes to tell the kind officers about Roger, Jayla, and the old woman who Jayla said was her grandmother. She also explained how she had been kidnapped, but that she didn't know why.

As they listened to her story, Officer Wall made sure to write everything down.

He had a hard time absorbing all the dreadful details which Molly was revealing, and he wished that he could console her. He knew that he couldn't, so he continued to maintain his strict poise and vacant poker face for the people around him.

Officer Sauck had been listening to all that Molly was willing to disclose, and he too was getting angry from all that he had heard.

He decided that the fake grandmother was the lure for Jayla to get closer to Molly. Molly had been kidnapped, but so far, there was no ransom involved. Roger showed up pretending to rescue Molly, but both Jayla and Roger disappeared after she had been drugged.

The cop was quite to deduce that the facts were simple, but nothing made sense. Was Marlowe's murder somehow connected to this? Molly was Marlowe's wife, but how did that tie in to the kidnapping? Fingerprints will prove how Marlowe's car got here, but where are Jayla and Roger now?

As Officer Sauck snapped back to reality, he could hear a bit more of the depressing information which Molly was giving to his partner.

Molly was now crying beyond control and her body couldn't stop shaking. When she felt like she was done telling her story, she raised her tear-stained face. "When can I go home?"

Officer Wall wanted to take her there now, but he still had some questions which the police department needed answers to. "In a few minutes, I think."

Molly pushed her face into her knees, and tried not to make loud sounds as she continued to sob.

She was tired and cold, and she didn't want to think of anything else except going home. She imagined what it would be like to eat her own food and climb into her own bed, but that concept still seemed to be so far away.

"Is there anything else you can tell me?" the officer asked.

Molly looked directly into his kind face when she answered. "I have a feeling that Jayla and Roger are together, but I don't know where Marlowe is. I haven't heard from him all day and I'd like to see him."

Molly locked eyes with Officer Wall, but after her last statement, he deliberately lowered his face and looked at the floor.

The entire police department was well aware that Marlowe had been killed, but Officer Wall couldn't bring himself to tell her the whole truth.

"There was an accident and he got shot." Because Molly was in a fragile state of mind, he decided that that was enough for now.

Molly's eyes widened and she stopped crying for a brief second. She tried to absorb what had happened to Marlowe, and while she wanted to know how badly he had been hurt, she was suspended in disbelief and couldn't get the words out.

Another cop car pulled up alongside of the squad car that Molly was in, and the driver honked the horn.

"OH!" Molly cried out. She lowered her head and tightened the blanket around her, as if to hide herself from the rest of the world.

Officer Sauck went over right away, and filled the new officers in on what he knew so far.

Because they had signalled for him to come over, Officer Wall nodded. He then turned his attention back to Molly. "Will you be okay if I leave you alone for a few minutes?"

Her eyes had teared-up as she replied, "You'll come back though, right?" She suddenly had a great fear of being alone.

Officer John Wall's mouth curved into an unconscious smile. "Yes, I'll be right back." He then went over to speak with the three officers at the other car.

He confirmed that the woman in his vehicle was Molly Perkins, and that she had been held against her will inside of 'that house.' Officer Wall pointed to the one-story, white stucco home on his right, so they could note the address.

That information was immediately given to Officer Dytania Johnson in dispatch, by the driver of the second squad car, Officer Alberto Ruiz.

Officer Johnson gave this information to a higher ranking officer, who in turn, ordered the officers on site to search the premises. "Turn everything over, pull every drawer out, and open every cabinet that you can find", he stated loudly and with an intense voice. "We need clues and we need them now!"

An ambulance with lights on but no siren, pulled up alongside the squad car where Molly was sitting.

Officer Sauck looked over to see how Molly was doing, and hated that she had a look of fear on her face. It was his hope that she would feel better soon.

Adrenaline rushed through her entire body, as Molly watched Officer Wall going over to talk with the paramedics. She felt blessed to have been rescued, but she thought that she would have been able to go home long before now. She was scared and confused, and had tightened her grip around her pulled up knees. And while peeking over the edge of the blanket that was covering her up to her nose, she was able to observe all of the chaos that was going on around her.

Some neighbours, who had been kind enough to come out of their houses a while ago, were watching the exciting events from their front lawns or porches. The children more than the adults, found the noise and flashing colored lights amazing, and because it was usually a quiet street, it felt like the circus had come and parked itself within their reach.

Meanwhile, a helicopter with two officers, had been sent to the skies to see the roads from another angle. "If anyone is heading out of town at a fast clip, let us know immediately!" the sergeant ordered.

"10-4", they replied. The air traffic personnel were definitely enthusiastic about this situation, because they loved that they were part of one of the more dramatic things to have happened this year.

While it seemed like forever, it was only a few minutes before Officer Wall came back to the car to be with Molly. "Is it okay if the paramedics check you out?" he asked in a quiet and soothing voice. "They just want to make sure that you're ok."

Molly looked into his kind eyes with the trust of a newborn child, and she nodded yes. She moved slowly as she got out of the squad car, and reached out for Officer Wall's help. Her legs had been confined due to how she was sitting, and they didn't seem to want to reposition freely.

Officer Sauck watched what was happening, and he rushed over to help Molly get out of the back seat of the city vehicle.

She was wobbly as she stood up, so both officers held onto her until she was able to catch her breath. When she was ready, they helped her walk towards the ambulance.

A female paramedic greeted Molly, and extended her hand to show her where to sit down. She then nodded to the two officers to ensure them that Molly would be in good hands.

Both officers said thanks, and then they told Molly that they would check up on her as soon as they could. After she nodded, they ran across the street to join the rest of their team, inside of the dark and bleak home.

Not surprisingly, the police were everywhere, searching for clues as to the whereabouts of Jayla and Roger. Some were taking pictures, others were taking fabric samples in the family room and kitchen, and others were lifting fingerprints from anything that might have been touched.

By now, there was so much commotion going on in their neighbourhood, that none of the neighbours were able to go back to sleep.

It didn't take long before even more people arrived, and they seemed to come from several blocks away. The chatter was loud, and when the gossip of what might have happened started to erupt, that's when the newspapers and TV crews came on the scene.

Two more squad cars and an unmarked vehicle, pulled up in front of the decaying old house. All the uniformed officers raced for the front door and rushed inside, without speaking to anyone on the street. After finding the person in charge and receiving the proper guidance, they began their own search for clues.

The police helicopter had an image of a speeding car, which was driving along the highway that cut through the Schilling Forest. They decided to track it for a few minutes before they radioed their findings in to dispatch.

There seemed to be a lot of activity behind the cheerless walls of the old house, with lights flashing as pictures were being taken, the sound of doors and cupboards being slammed shut, and people talking back and forth on their hand-held radios. And it wasn't unexpected to see, that things which were thought to be evidence, were taken outside and dumped on the front lawn.

When someone clad in pajamas and slippers came over to examine what was in the pile of alleged junk, a police officer was immediately ordered to stand guard and shoo everyone away.

The mountain of evidence was placed into the trunks of nearby squad cars, by a different division of the city's police department. It would be looked at with a fine-toothed comb, sometime during the next day. For now, it was highly respected and being treated like the finest gold in the world.

And as if there wasn't enough noise in the area already, an announcement was suddenly broadcast over all the police car radios.

"Ten forty-nine to dispatch."

"Dispatch."

"We've spotted a southbound vehicle going faster than it should be, on highway 22X."

All officers within ear shot were cheering, for this might be the vehicle which they were looking for.

All available police cars, apart from those officers who were still inside the house, headed to that stretch of road.

Detective Katts heard the announcement, and happily drove his small Toyota hatchback to that same area.

The detective had his own reason for being part of the chase, and he wasn't about to let anyone stop him. With Molly being rescued and Marlowe's car being found, he knew that it would just be a matter of time before they all learned what had happened to Roger and Jayla. Once those two were in custody, everyone would then have the final details behind this abstruse plot, and he wanted to be there when the last piece of the puzzle got put into its proper place.

By the time Officer Wall came back to check on Molly, she had been examined by two paramedics and was not found to have any bruising or open wounds. She did have a small bump on her head, but they claim that it was nothing to worry about.

"She'll be examined again at the hospital, but we think she's overly distraught and just needs to rest", the paramedic stated.

Officer Wall thanked them and then turned his attention to Molly. He touched her shoulders with gentle hands, and looked straight into her eyes. "You're going to be fine now", he stated with complete confidence. "You go with these people and I'll check up on you later."

Molly was very grateful for his concern. "Thank you, for everything", she said with compassion, as she stared into his gold-flecked eyes.

Officer Wall melted a little bit, while showing her his cocky masculine grin. "You're welcome."

Molly let the paramedics help her into the back of their vehicle, while the handsome officer watched her from a few feet away.

When the double doors closed and the attendants walked to their seats, the officer tapped the back of the vehicle for good luck. The flashing lights were immediately turned on and the sirens began to blare loudly, so that the city van could drive safely through the large crowd of people.

Strangers – some dressed and some in pajamas - were assembled on every square foot of space on that one-block area. They were drinking and gossiping while taking in the excitement of the carnival-like atmosphere, and they loved that they had an excuse not to go to work the next day.

Before the ambulance was half-way down the road, Officer Wall had been able to make his way back into the house across the street. In that same moment, Jayla was parking her car at the gate of the Schilling Forest.

She made sure to drive inside one of the smaller openings, and purposely hid her car behind a large bush. Not surprisingly, when the motor turned off, Roger began to stir.

"Wh-what? Where am I?" he stuttered, as his eyes tried to open. As he looked around, all he could see were very tall trees. The former inmate was confused and not fully awake, and he had no idea where he was.

"Let's get out", Jayla stated happily. She was almost giddy and didn't care if Roger could see it. "I have something to show you." She made her way over to the passenger side of the car as if she was dancing. "Let me help you", she said, as she extended her hand.

"Why are we here?" he asked with a bewildered look on his face. His legs were unsteady and he was protesting the idea of walking around.

Jayla didn't care, and persisted to tug at his arms until he felt that he had no choice but to stand up.

The police helicopter had been flying above the highway which took people out of town, and they now had trouble seeing where the car in question had gone to. Neither officer wanted to call it in, but both knew that they had to.

"Ten forty-nine to dispatch", Officer Gary Douglas stated with hesitation in his voice.

"Dispatch"

"We've lost sight of the fast-moving vehicle, but we believe that it might have gone into the Schilling Forest."

There was a second of muddled silence, while the man from dispatch tried to collect his thoughts. "Keep your eyes peeled and let us know when you have any further details."

"10-4"

It was 5 minutes to midnight when Jayla guided Roger into the beautiful forest. He had never been there before, and was stunned by how attractive the multi-colored leaves and the abnormally shaped trees were. When he breathed in, there was a very pleasant scent of lavender that seemed to wriggle into his nasal passages. When the flowery notes hit his bloodstream, it put a bounce in his step and made him curious to see more.

Everything made him wide-eyed and totally aware, and while he was having trouble with the idea that he was there with his ex-girlfriend, he was even more surprised to see that the trees were bowing and parting as if they knew Jayla personally.

As they walked further down the worn-out path, Roger spotted other trails which looped off of the one which they were walking on. When he looked up, he saw a hundred twinkling stars through the branches of the old trees. While that seemed so pretty, he thought it was odd that the full moon was smiling down on him, as if to inform him of a secret message. When he looked down, he noticed that a weird white mist was covering his feet up to his ankles. It seemed to rise up from the earth with no rhyme or reason, and when he tried to step out of it, the mist became thicker and glued itself to his legs.

Roger turned his attention to Jayla, and he saw that she was marching forward as if she knew where she was going. The outline of her body was shimmering, but she was casting a pulsing black shadow on the ground behind her. Roger's mind screamed in torment at how odd this was; none of this felt real, and it was almost as if he was being manipulated like a wooden puppet.

Jayla absolutely knew the way, for she'd been down this path many times before today. She just hoped that the outcome would be the same as always.

Thunder rolled loudly in the western part of the sky, and it had startled a bird and caused it to fly out of the branches overhead. Its rasping scream frightened Roger so much, that he looked up and immediately rubbed a hand against his chest as if he was in pain. He was astounded by the size of the bird's large wingspan, and wanted to study it for a minute longer.

Jayla could feel Roger's unwillingness to move forward, but she was careful not to let anything upset her timeline. "Come, on. It's not too much further."

The couple finally came to a large clearing, where Roger's eyes spied a giant campfire. He wasn't sure what it was for, and then he noticed the medium-sized basket of food. There was also a blanket that had been perfectly spread out on the ground, and it looked as if they were going to have a picnic.

The last thing he could recall, was being in an old house with Molly and Jayla. They were toasting something, and now he was here.

Roger wanted to hit the pause button on his worries and stress for even a minute, because things were happening much too quickly for him to process. He had been swaying back and forth with what was real and what was a dream, and he was now becoming more and more concerned about all that was going on.

"We've arrived!" Jayla announced happily. With a celebratory attitude, she closed her eyes, raised the palms of her hands towards the sky, and smiled as she spun around in one complete turn.

All over the world, the dead were rising, and she was about to share in that glory by giving them someone else to play with. She was happier than she'd been in a while, and couldn't wait for this event to begin.

Roger watched her in awe, for it was clear that she was satisfied that they had arrived. His eyes went wide with a great amount of curiosity, when she stopped spinning and walked over to the perfectly laid stumps of wood.

Jayla lit the whole pile on fire as if there was nothing peculiar about what she was doing, and then she made herself comfortable on the blanket.

Roger was completely mesmerized by everything around him, including Jayla. And while a part of him didn't believe that any of this was real, another part of him was frightened beyond belief.

Jayla smiled as she turned to him, and she made sure to speak in a gentle tone. "Come here, my love." She patted the spot next to her on the blanket while she stared into his face.

Roger could feel the significant pull from her eyes, and saw that they were begging him to obey. He did as he was asked, for it didn't feel as if he had any other choice.

Detective Katts had just passed the outskirts of town, and he could see the dense forest area up ahead. He couldn't wait to learn who was driving the speeding vehicle or why it was heading here, and he hoped that what he found out, would fill in some of the gaps to Marlowe's death.

His main job was to gather information and get it typed up at the station. After he had it all laid out in front of him, he added pictures and other facts, until he was able to find the answers to the questions which everyone else was looking for.

He gave his all to this job, and he was brilliant at it. And he didn't care what he had to do in order to get it done.

The majestic woodland spanned the two sides of the two-lane highway, and from the little that he knew about this place, there were only a couple of openings where a person could go inside and have a look around.

Because he'd never been in there himself, Detective Katts reduced his speed, in order to study the remarkable foliage.

It pleased Jayla to have Roger's body so close, because it reminded her of old times. And while she would have liked to recreate some wonderful past events, she knew that she needed to live in this particular moment. "Let's play a little game, shall we?" She had murmured the question into his ear with the purr of a kitten.

Her lips were so close that her hot breath gave him chills, and his body automatically stiffened as his fear escalated. Roger was angry and chose to turn his face away, but in doing so, he spotted strange symbols dancing across the top of the red and yellow flames. Because he knew that that couldn't be possible, his heart was now pounding inside of his chest.

Jayla smiled as she reached for the rope that had been hiding under a corner of the blanket. "Look what I have", she sang, as if it was a line from a song. She then tricked him into letting her tie his hands behind his back.

Because Roger felt as if he had no other option, he began to wonder if he was under some sort of spell.

"Good boy", she cheered, as if he was a subhuman specimen. Her pleasure was obvious and it showed in her face and mannerism. "See?" she asked, once she was done. "That didn't hurt a bit."

The air suddenly hummed as if it was becoming thick with magic, while Jayla murmured despicable ramblings that were similar to the sounds that a witch in a movie would make.

Roger stared at her, as if she was a dusty tomb from ancient times. In one way, he didn't know if she was dead, undead, or something in-between. In his warped mind, however, he hoped that she was as twisted as he was, and that they would end up in a sexual position that he had never tried before.

The thought both intrigued him and scared him, but he decided that he was man enough to continue. He soon found himself becoming more and more mesmerized by how this evening was going to turn out.

Much to Roger's surprise, Jayla slowly transformed into a completely different individual. Her hair had doubled in thickness and length, and had become wiry and very dry. Her height began to increase, but stopped after 14 inches had been added onto her sturdy frame. And when her beauty had faded and her perfect features had contorted, he felt as if he had been thrown into a catacomb of utter doom.

Roger was confused and felt the need to blink several times. 'Am I seeing what I think I'm seeing?' he wondered. He wanted to believe that his eyes were deceiving him, but he wasn't 100% sure of anything anymore.

As he looked around, he became more afraid, and he was quick to decide that none of this could be real. It also made him wonder if this was some sort of delusion, which had been derived from the scent of the peculiar fire.

Jayla's nails had grown and proceeded to crack, and the skin on her hands had become old and gnarled. The cute outfit which she had worn when they had entered the woods, had turned into a long and loose black dress with long sleeves, and her shoes were now brown and decrepit.

Roger felt as if he was wide awake, but he couldn't really tell. "What the fuck is happening?" he asked out loud and to no-one in particular. His skin was moist from sweat and his heart was pounding. He was terrified and closed his eyes, and to gain some control over the panic in his heart, he took a few abdominal breaths. When he opened his eyes, it was with a brilliant idea.

Roger used one hand to inflict pain upon the other. He fought to mask the high-pitched piercing cry from the throbbing sting which he had given to himself, but now he was even more confused. "Does one feel pain in a dream?"

He thought he had kept those words in his mind, but he had unknowingly said them out loud.

The witch heard his question, and it made her silly with pleasure. 'Let him go on thinking that this is just a dream', she laughed in her head. 'He'll be much easier to control if he didn't struggle.' Jayla cackled out loud at her own thoughts, and the sound seemed to linger beyond life and death.

It was then when Roger understood that none of this was normal, and that this was in no way going to end up as a romantic evening. He began to panic, and quickly spun his head around to see if there was a way out. And while there were many paths which he could take, he wasn't sure which one would bring him back to Jayla's car.

There was a strange glow in Jayla's emerald green eyes, as if she could read his thoughts. "You aren't thinking of leaving me, are you?" she teased. 'No, he wouldn't dare', she stated under her breath, as if a second personality had come forward. The witch turned herself around and continued what she was doing.

Her coldness startled him and made him cry out. "HELP!" he screamed with great intensity. He no longer cared if this was a dream or not, for he sincerely believed that he was fighting for his life.

Jayla laughed at his babbling nonsense. "No-one can hear you out here, my dear. It's just you and me." Jayla was drunk with power and couldn't wait to receive his soul.

As Roger looked at his former girlfriend, he couldn't believe the drastic change in her. She used to be kind and loving, and now she was aggressive and quite creepy. Everything in his soul told him to leave, but how?

As beads of nervous sweat began to bleed through his skin, Roger tried to wiggle out of the ropes that bound his hands together. He knew it would be useless, but it was his best bet for right now.

Jayla was busy, but she could hear the faint grunts and moans coming from behind her back. "Be patient, my love. It won't be too long now."

While Roger paid extreme attention to what she was doing, he twisted his wrists, he moved his hands this way and that, but short of breaking some bones, he couldn't get free from the knotted twine.

Because he hadn't let up and the sounds were making her nervous, Jayla turned around to see what Roger was doing. When she saw that he was trying to liberate himself from the rope, she flew into a violent rage.

Jayla was devastated by his mutiny, and now saw Roger as a dirty little worm. He was fidgety and somewhat defiant, and the ugly fear that her plan would not be executed to perfection, choked her like a whole fish being shoved down her throat.

She now knew that she would have to perform this spell as quickly as possible, for she was not about to let him slip away again.

The witch took a few steps towards him, bent forward in a very intimidating manner, and released her venom into his face. "Obey me!" she spewed. Her tone was low and ghostly, and she made sure to deliver her next sentence as a command. "Or the consequences that will befall you, will be worse than you could have ever dreamed!" she promised. The greyish skin on her grotesque face was covered by a wild expression, and it informed Roger that the penalties for disobeying would be earth-shattering.

Roger's eyes and mouth popped wide open, and he was now looking at her with a feeble gaze. He was in shock and couldn't move. And while doom was hanging like a thick fog all around him, he had no intention of dying under her care.

Feeling that he had heard her message, Jayla moved away and went back to the business at hand.

Because Roger had been in many grave situations before this one, his mind was already conjuring up an escape plan.

Jayla was less than five feet away, and had gathered all that she needed to streamline the spell. When she was ready, she laid everything out on the ground around her.

Roger was holding his breath and watching her with glassy frightened eyes. He was well-aware that he would only get one chance to escape, and if he failed, his life would be over. However, if he didn't try at all, he felt that he would probably die anyway.

Jayla was now set to begin. She closed her eyes and breathed in the fresh air of the first few minutes of Halloween.

She loved the earthy fragrance of death, and the thought of the old souls meeting the newly dead ones in the next few hours. She also loved the idea that the power of her magic would be greatly enhanced, and that all of this happened under the bright and watchful eye of Halloween's full moon.

While Jayla was conjuring up her magic, Roger watched with great interest; he was waiting for his window of opportunity to open up.

With dramatic flair, the quick-tempered witch lifted her hands to the sky. She held them there while she began to recite the first verse of the spell, which would render Roger lifeless.

As Jayla seemed to be falling into a trance, Roger attempted to get away. He got up slowly, making sure that his concentration never left the back of her head, and without making a noise, he took his first step.

His wide eyes were staring at Jayla, and his breath was coming in short spurts as if he was in extreme pain. And even though his hands were tightly bound behind him, he began to run light-footed into the thickness of the trees.

The rope around his ankles had been tight at first, but had loosened very quickly, as he moved one step after another away from the campsite.

Jayla had been busy gathering cosmic energy and communal strength to perform the transference spell, and she didn't notice that he had left. And because the wind had now picked up, and branches were cracking and breaking from the extreme swirling movements of the relocating air, Roger's nimble footsteps were lost in the exchange.

Roger picked the closest opening to rush through, and found a tapered dirt path to run on. There were other paths that broke off into other paths, and because he didn't know which ones went around in circles and which ones led him back to the main road, he decided to stay right where he was.

In his mind, he would either get out and be free, or he would die trying – he saw no other option.

He was running on sheer wits now, and he couldn't decide what was right or what was wrong. All he could do was keep going forward. And even though his face and body were getting smacked and torn up by low-hanging branches, when the rope had dropped away from his feet, he was able to pick up speed. He then thought of nothing else but getting out of the forest alive.

The active root of the raging fire had noticed that Roger had escaped, and it hissed and popped as if to make the witch aware of what was happening. Because she was not paying attention to the normal cracks and small explosions, the inferno made an extremely loud bang. Thankfully, that was enough to bring Jayla out of her trance.

As the fire calmed itself down, Jayla turned around to see what was going on. After she determined that the flames were okay, she looked at the spot where Roger should have been sitting. "WHAT?!" she screamed. She was in total disbelief that he was not there, and her level of anger was evident in the pitch and volume of her voice.

As her enlarged eyes scanned the immediate area, she slammed her tight fists down by her sides. She immediately lifted her nose to smell the wind, in order to find his scent. With unforgiving fury blowing from her large nostrils, she could tell right away that he was heading north, and on a longer path than the one which they had come in on. "Cur-ses!" she screamed. Her eyes were sizzling and she was madder than hell, for she knew that he would eventually find his way out.

With every ounce of evil in her body, she called upon all the elements in the four corners to heed the following words:

With the powers that be, I call to thee
To help me in my quest

Sharp lightning crashed across the sky as she continued.

> Find the man with the dark soul
> And bring him to my breast

The ground shook as if a giant had stomped his foot against it with supreme wrath. This caused the trees to cringe and all animals to seek shelter.

> If you can hear me, I beg and implore
> For this has now turned into war

She spoke the next words as if she was giving a harsh warning to Roger.

> These last few minutes you have on this earth
> Will be worse than what you experienced at birth

Roger felt like a boa constrictor was wrapping itself around his body, and his lungs were suddenly not taking in enough air. These setbacks had triggered a strong bout of anxiety, but he didn't care – his only thought was to get out of the forest and away from Jayla.

Jayla lowered her arms and tried to absorb all that was around her, but she knew that he couldn't have gotten too far. She cast her eyes through the inexact lines of the forest, in order to get the impression of where he might be.

Roger was terribly confused by all that had happened, and he didn't want to die. He was being careless as he passed each tree and shrub on the ground as if they were nothing, and he began to cry with hope when he stumbled upon a way out.

Detective Katts had been guided along the only road through the forest, by the shiny high beams on his car. There were no street lights on that stretch of highway, and the moon didn't offer much support because it was obscured by the tall trees. For him to see anything of interest was quite challenging, but he wasn't about to give up.

The detective eventually spotted what he thought was an opening in the forest, and he slowed his car down to investigate. Little did he know that he was only seconds away from experiencing one of the worst few minutes of his life.

CHAPTER SIXTEEN

October 31, 2000

The wind carried the sound of Roger's breathing straight to her pointed ears, but she still couldn't place his exact location. She hated working so hard, and instead of wasting anymore time, Jayla followed the sounds of his feet as they hit the ground.

Roger had broken through the massive jungle of trees and horror, and after turning his head to the left, he spotted a car's headlights. He placed himself in the middle of the road in order to flag the driver down. "Help!" he called loudly, but he knew how it looked; a wide-eyed, disheveled man, with his hands tied behind his back, and he was out in the middle of nowhere. But, maybe that could work in his favor. "Help me, please!" he called again.

Detective Katts had just opened his car door and was about to stand up, when he spotted a male figure dart out into the middle of the two-lane highway. Because the man seemed to be injured, the kind detective responded. "Hello? Are you okay?" In that moment, he wasn't sure if he should keep his distance or not.

Meanwhile, Jayla was whisking her way through the dense forest with great speed.

"No!" Roger cried, as tears of joy appeared in his eyes. "I need help!" He was more than relieved that he was about to be rescued, and sprinted towards the stranger's car. "Thank God that you've arrived!" he stated happily. He had no idea who this man was, nor did he care; he was just crazy with desperation to escape an early death. "Do you have anything that can cut these ropes off my hands?"

Roger was now standing in the bright headlights, while Detective Katts made sure to stay at least two feet away. The detective kept close eye contact with the man before him, while he searched his pockets for something sharp.

There were so many questions which the detective wanted to ask, for this situation thoroughly intrigued him. And while he gallantly sawed the rope off with his small but useful army knife, Roger kept encouraging him to hurry up.

"Get me free and you can have anything you want!" Roger insisted. He was greatly tormented by the fact that Jayla might show up, and he wanted to get away before she caught up to him.

"Ok, ok. Just relax", the detective stated in a fatherly manner.

He might have sounded calm, but the detective was becoming more and more uneasy as the seconds ticked by.

Roger's anxiety was growing wild, and his heart was pounding like crazy. He knew that he needed to get out of there fast, but how? An idea struck him, and once his hands were free, he knew what he had to do.

"There you go", the detective announced. As he took a step backwards, he put his army knife in his left pants pocket but kept his keychain in his right hand.

Roger had a fearful look in his eyes as he grabbed the stranger's keys. He took a step forward, and with extreme force, he pushed the kind man onto the hard ground. He then jumped into the small car and sped away.

This left the detective in complete darkness, except for the light which the moon was generating. He was confused and wasn't sure if the last few minutes had been real or not, but the throbbing pain throughout his body, was sending him strong signals that he had indeed been injured.

His first impulse was to stand up and check himself out, but before he could even move a muscle, a menacing witchly figure had broken through an opening of the forest, and was now standing over him. The sudden whoosh sound surprised him so much, that he missed taking his next breath.

"Hello", she cooed, in a very witchly voice.

His eyes were straining to focus and he thought his mind was playing tricks on him. The detective wasn't quite sure what he was seeing, but it was scary enough that his heart was now in his throat.

Officer Gary Douglas and his partner were in the helicopter, and they had been watching everything from up above.

"Ten forty-nine to dispatch"

"Dispatch"

"We've spotted something odd in that long stretch of road by the forest. A second car slowed down and then stopped, and now it seems to be speeding along the highway."

"Chase it!" Officer Johnson screamed with urgency. "Follow that car!"

He and everyone else at the station, had been dismayed that the first car had disappeared. They were sure that it had gone into the forest, but they were now more intent on where this second car was going.

"Do you copy?"

"We copy!" Officer Gary Douglas replied. "10-4."

The man in dispatch turned around, and was quick to relay this new information to his superior.

It was not his job to give such direct orders to a fellow officer, but he got caught up in the excitement and acted in a manner that was conducive to the situation. Thankfully, his superior agreed to what he had done, so there would be no reprimand in Officer Dytania Johnson's future.

As she stood tall before her injured victim, Jayla looked down at the torn ropes which were now laying on the ground. Her anger in that moment was almost too painful for her to bear, and her resentment snapped.

The detective's head and back had bounced off the gravelly road when Roger had pushed him down, so he was in a lot of pain and greatly confused by all that was happening. He couldn't help but stare into the hag's angry face, and it caused him to panic. "Please don't kill me", he cried. His voice was quivering and he felt a little urine trickle into his pants.

Detective Katts was deathly afraid that she was going to grab him with her branch-like arms, and as he tried to move, an unnerving moan escaped from deep within his throat.

"You may have thought that you've escaped, but I've got you now!" she shrieked with glee. As she thrust her face even closer, she shone her cruel crimson eyes into his.

Detective Katts let out a scream of absolute terror. He had hated horror movies ever since he was little, and now he felt like he had fallen into the middle of the worst one ever.

Jayla's face took on a haunted look and her crooked nose wrinkled with satisfaction. She was under the impression that this man was Roger, and as her expression hardened, she reached her arm out to drag him back to the campfire.

"NO, NO!" he cried, as he tried to scoot out of her reach. He was using his arms and legs to shimmy away from her grip, and it was terrifying that she was still able to reach him.

Jayla stomped one foot on the ground and grabbed him by the back of the shoulder. And with one clean jerk, he was now hers.

"No-o-o-o-o-o-o!!" he screamed, but she was stronger than he gave her credit for.

Detective Katts continued to scream, as his heart was pumping like the distraught wings of a frightened caged bird. He suddenly felt the bloom of a cold moisture cover his body, and he knew that he would remember this moment for the rest of his life.

Jayla suddenly found it strange that the weight and shape of 'Roger's' body was not familiar to her. And when the detective was pulled closer to her face, Jayla was able to drink in his odor. "Wh-hat is this?" she asked, as every one of her muscles tensed with fury.

Jayla quickly arranged the man's body so that she could see the features on his face more clearly. "CURSES!" she howled, when she realized that she had been duped.

Her screech was so loud and long that it scared the birds out of their nests, and all the small animals were quickly burrowing themselves deep into the ground.

The detective saw her face when she screamed, and it was so distressing, that it plunged him into a lowly depression.

He had seen many disturbing death scenes during his long career, but he never thought he would be part of anything so dastardly. And the fact that he didn't know how or if he was going to get away, paralyzed him to no end.

"Ah-h-h-h-h-h!!" she screamed into the night air. Her clenched fists were like hard balls of ice, while bitterness filled her mouth. Rage swept over her as she choked on her own anger. Her skin crawled as she fought the urge to throw up, and because this was not the man she was looking for, she knew what she had to do.

"Please let me go!" the detective cried softly, as he begged for his life.

Fear had hit him like a bucket of chilled water, and his heartbeat was drumming in his ears. He was so scared that he could hardly breathe, but he watched her every move with gawking eyes and great interest.

As the full moon streamed through the top of the jagged tree branches, Jayla released her tight hold on the whimpering man. And while the wind was whistling and singing its praise for her good deed, the detective was catapulted backwards with enormous speed.

Detective Katts was once again, tossed into a large puddle of total terror. He was grateful that she had let him go, and he didn't dare give her any reason to come back.

The large man was frozen with fear of who or what she was. His eyes were wide, his skin had paled, and he was scared that she was going to kill him.

The detective had never been so filled with worry in his whole life; there was little to no light around them, and while he was crouching from fright on the cold pavement, she was hovering a few feet away, and a few inches off the ground.

As he wished for her to go away, he watched her pace. By the look on her face, her mind seemed to be calculating her next move. The detective was fascinated, and felt that her animated presence was commanding his full attention.

"Where are you, my pretty?" she squawked like a parrot. She looked straight into the moon's face, as if that's where she would find the answer.

Detective Katts held his breath and stayed on the ground like a frightened dog.

Because she no longer had any use for the battered stranger, Jayla ignored him. She looked to her left and then to her right, and then her instincts told her the correct way to go.

As the feeling of horror grew heavy in his chest, the detective watched as the ragged figure of the witchly female, rushed away in a hurried, floating manner. And while his eyes went even wider at that strange sight, his heart began to beat faster than it ever had before.

As she moved to catch up to Roger, Jayla's blood was boiling with the foulness of hate. "You will not get away again!" she screamed. Her face was turning bright red with fury. Her pulse was jittering somewhere between the 170 and 190 mark, while a frosty shiver swarmed over her entire body.

Meanwhile, Roger was driving like the wind while watching for any signs that someone was following him. He could tell that he was going through a fight and flight mode, and he was mentally ordering himself to calm down.

He was still not sure how any of this could be real, but he concluded that the excessive saliva in his mouth, his extreme light-headedness, and the profuse sweating under his arms and on his face and neck, was all due to his enormous fear that he was indeed awake.

As Jayla raced to catch up to Roger, her incessant frustration was swelling to a breaking point. And when she spotted the car up ahead, she snickered with relief. "I've got you now!" she cackled with vicious contempt.

Because his focus was mainly on what was behind him, rather than what was in front of him or above him, Roger was unaware that Jayla was getting closer.

Roger had been blinded by greed, but also by an idea that he could outrun the law - and perhaps death. While he was consumed by a little bit of worry, he was governed by the fact that he had been in many nail-biting situations in the past, and he had always gotten free. Unfortunately, this same destructive theory was guiding him through this hellish adventure tonight.

As the helicopter lowered itself towards the detective's speeding car, the officers inside, fed as much information to dispatch as they could.

"Excellent!" the sergeant stated. "Continue to follow it and keep me updated."

"10-4"

"And to all units on the ground, respond to the Schilling Forest, immediately!" the sergeant ordered.

Not a minute later, Roger could hear the loud whirling of a helicopter above him. 'Is that the police?' he wondered. 'Had they learn that he had killed Marlowe and Jack?' His eyebrows drew together in an agonized expression, for it could very well be true. However, he also had a horrifying feeling that Jayla would find him first.

As thoughts of his life ending in a violent death, flashed before his eyes, the image of Molly's face appeared in his mind. Roger was worried about her and wondered if she was okay. He hated that he didn't get to have much time with her back at the house, and fretted that he might never see her again.

"Damn it all to hell!" he cried, as he banged the heel of his hand against the solid steering wheel. He had hoped to have a future with Molly, but with no Plan B, it no longer seemed like it was going to happen.

Roger had many tears rolling down his face now, as he realized that he had many questions that he would never get answers to. Each one was asking why these last few days had turned out like this, and each question ended with a shrug of his shoulders and a deafening silence ringing in his ears. "Wake up!" he screamed, as he continued to agonize over his troubled situation.

Jayla was smiling with total satisfaction as she finally caught up to her prey. She pressed her face into the passenger window, and because that didn't grab his attention, she playfully tapped against the glass with a fragile fingernail. She then giggled when he recoiled and almost lost control of the car.

Roger's body jerked, as a huge bolt of raw adrenaline shot through his veins. "Wh-hat?

H-How?" he stuttered. He was driving 131 mph, and his mind was lost in the image of her flying beside his car.

Roger wanted so much to deny what was happening, but even though Jayla was partially hidden by the darkness, he would never be able to forget how her hair was being tossed and pressed backwards.

"No! This is not real!" he stated firmly. While he pushed the illusion out of his mind, he hoped that the terror of it would not slow down his reflexes. He slammed his foot even harder on the gas pedal to prove it.

Jayla laughed out loud at his stupidity, but she loved his courageous attitude. But did he really think that he could outrun her?

As the car drove faster, Roger was no longer concerned with the police. He decided that if he just kept his mind focused on how he could get away from Jayla, then he would be okay.

Roger had now decided that she must be a witch, or something along the lines of being unhuman.

He didn't know how that could be possible, but after everything he had seen tonight, he definitely would say that there was something very abnormal about her.

Because most of the police force had heard what was happening through their car radios, several of them had rushed to the Schilling Forest, while a few more were in hot pursuit of the speeding car up ahead.

Detective Katts was still sitting on the ground where he had parked his car, and he was more than relieved when he saw the familiar flashing colored lights coming towards him. He stood up slowly, his hands were high in the air, and he was prepared to greet whoever came up to him first. "I'm Detective Andrew Katts!" he shouted, while holding up his I.D. "I'm one of you guys!"

Officer Grant Morgan and his partner, Officer Adrian Morales, recognized him right away.

Detective Katts was tearful and quite grateful, as he rushed into the arms of the nearest cop.

"You're going to be ok, now", the officer stated kindly. He could see that his friend was traumatized and needed assistance, and immediately placed him into the back seat of the warm squad car.

Neither officer could believe the emotional and physical state which the detective was in, nor could they wait to hear how he got that way.

They asked him a few questions, and listened with confusion while he blubbered about a man who had ropes around his wrists. And when they asked him where his car was, he replied, "The injured man stole it, and he was now being chased by an angry witch."

Officer Morgan shared a private glance with his partner, before they both decided that the middle-aged detective needed to be taken to the hospital right away.

"I'm telling the truth!" he insisted. There was a defiance in his tone, as well as a subtle challenge to disagree.

"Ok, calm down", Officer Morales stated in a firm tone of voice.

The detective threw his body against the back of the seat, and he somehow knew that he was going into shock. 'Did any of that really happen?' he wondered with total curiosity. He sat forward and looked around, and when he couldn't see his car, he decided that something did indeed happen, but he didn't know how much of it was real.

Officer Morgan leaned to the side, and in a whisper he told his fellow officer, "You wait here, but keep me appraised of what's going on until I get back."

Officer Morales gave his friend a knowing nod. He then exited the vehicle and joined the other officers on the scene.

Detective Katts tilted his body forward when Officer Morgan started his car. "Listen, I know you don't believe me", he said, in a voice that was begging the officer to hear him. "But I'm telling the truth." He was anything but calm, and there was a great deal of audible stress in his voice.

"Oh, I believe you", the driver of the squad car replied.

Of course he didn't believe him, but Officer Grant Morgan, a ten-year veteran of the Police Force, wanted his passenger to calm down while he drove them back to town.

It was far behind him, but Roger could see several red and blue flashing lights in his rear-view mirror. 'Had they all come in pursuit of me?' he wondered. It was in that second when he didn't know what to focus on more - Jayla or the cops.

Time was running out, and Jayla was desperate to get Roger to stop the car. She banged on the glass with a closed fist in order to scare him. "I see you", she laughed, but in reality, she was trying to be threatening.

If they left now, this would give her less than seven hours to get his soul and burn it to a crisp by sunrise. While that wasn't a lot of time, it pissed her off that this was all that she was going to have.

Roger's sweaty hands were holding onto the steering wheel as if his life depended on it. And under his pinched expression, his thoughts were all over the place.

Suddenly, he spotted a sign that warned him of a hidden turn up ahead, and his brain went into overdrive. And while his lungs had involuntarily sucked in a deep breath from shock, his body was not letting it go. His eyes widened with fear over how sharp that turn might be, and his muscles were beginning to shake uncontrollably.

Roger hadn't counted on the day ending like this, but then, he couldn't believe anything that had happened in the past few days.

He had never been in that area before, and he didn't know the lay of the land, the height of the hills, or the depth of the valleys. In his current state of mind, he honestly assumed that the road would stay flat and straight for a long time to come.

Jayla could see that Roger was suddenly having problems focusing, and this amused her, but only for a second. In an unforgiving tone of voice, she implored him to pull over. "Stop the car!" she demanded loudly. She made sure to emphasize each letter of each word very carefully. "And if you don't obey, I will force you off the road!" she added with a harsh evil lilt.

The pitch of her voice had now deepened, and because her face had become stern and corpselike, the whole scenario was quite spine-chilling.

The officers in the helicopter watched in awe, as the car below them was swerving back and forth across both lanes of traffic.

They did not see anyone on the passenger side of the car, but Roger did, and the image of the furious witch was scaring him. He knew he had to be callous if he wanted to be free of her, so he steered the car directly into her body. Unfortunately, it didn't seem to faze her or slow her down.

Jayla had been able to fly out of the way of the bumps and bruises which Roger was trying to inflict, but it wasn't making her happy. Brutal hate and bloody devastation blazed behind her angry eyes, as she explored how this scenario was going to play out.

The hidden turn was coming up, so Roger had no choice but to place all of his attention on the road. He held his breath while his hands were tightly gripping the steering wheel. His eyes grew large as he tried to focus on all that was before him. He took a deep breath, prayed that he would make it, and then prepared himself for the car to go around the very tight turn.

With dazzling determination, Jayla forced herself to calm down. Her plan was to bring him to the campsite as she had done with 98% of the other men, but another idea suddenly crowded her mind.

The turn was upon him, and it was a lot sharper than Roger had expected. And because there was no roadside barrier along the edge of that particular stretch of road, it made him sit up straighter and take more notice of the situation.

Roger panicked when he felt both passenger tires kick up the dust and stones from the gravel shoulder, and even though he let his left foot rest against the brake pedal, he was not about to stop the vehicle.

Several police cars were speeding to catch up to Roger, while the officers in the helicopter continued to watch him from overhead.

Jayla needed to take Roger's soul when he died, but she wondered if it would make a difference how his life would end. After taking a quick second to think about it, she agreed that it probably wouldn't matter. So with very little doubt flowing through her icy veins, she rose herself up above the car and watched in anticipation for what was about to happen.

Roger was not equipped to make such a tight turn in a strange car, and he was filled with worry. He was facing danger head-on, and he was now prepared to make whatever demands either Jayla or the police had.

Ophelia's Curse

He was fearing for his life and anxiously muttering useless promises into the air. He was in denial that he would die, but then he felt the car leave the familiarity of the bumpy pavement.

With a racing heartbeat and a heightened level of desperation, he tried to readjust the direction of the wheels. But when the vehicle tipped onto its side, he cringed with hope that he would make it out of this alive.

Jayla was wide-eyed and speechless, and marvelled at how this chase was spinning in her favor.

The police watched in absolute horror, as the car which Roger was driving, slid off the road and began to go sideways down the 10 storey, treed embankment.

Roger panicked when the car began to fall, and his gaze was completely unfocused. He felt an overwhelming feeling of dread spread throughout his body, and his hands began to flutter in the air as if that would make the car fall slower. His mind was shutting down from extreme anxiety, but it left him with one thought. "MO-LLY!" he shouted. His voice was trembling and had risen to a high-pitched screech.

Even over the whirling blades of the helicopter, the police could hear his deathly scream. The ghastly sound sent chills up everyone's back, and it cast a shadow of bewilderment to all who were near.

"Mol-leeeee!" he shrieked as loud as he could. That was the last sound anyone heard, before Roger died.

Jayla watched in total bliss, as the car plummeted towards the bushy plant life on the uneven ground. She made a hasty decision to recite the transference spell right away, and afterwards, she made her way to where she thought the car would land.

As this hour of the day doth die
Wolves will howl and spirits will cry
On Halloween his soul will resign
When Roger lands,
Our souls will entwine

She looked up to the heavens and watched the night sky turn darker. And while she continued to speak, she could feel the energy in the air change.

> With the full moon up high
> And all the stars in the sky
> Leave his body, reside in mine
> Heed these words and all will be fine

Meanwhile, the police watched as the car bounced against the side of the hill, over and over again.

And when it finally found its resting place, Jayla was there and ready.

She opened the car door and stared into Roger's lifeless face. Because of the powerful transference spell, his soul knew what to do, and it instantly left his body and sailed into hers. Three minutes later, the car exploded, and Roger was soon burned to a crisp.

Everyone who had been watching, gasped in horror at the unfortunate accident. They instantly removed their hats and rested them against their chests, and then they lowered their heads in a moment of silence.

In the meantime, Jayla had hurried to the campsite to put out the large bonfire. And after grabbing her basket of food and tucking her blanket under her arm, she raced to her car and made her way back to the safety of her simple, one thousand square foot home.

The senior police officer wrapped his fingers around his car radio, and gave all the information to dispatch. As the details were quickly spread to the rest of the police department, all the sirens were turned off and all the squad cars had slowed down their vehicles.

Detective Katts had been examined in the emergency room of the Regal hospital, and was ordered to stay overnight for further observation. And it was just as well, because he was so unsure of what had happened in the Schilling Forest, that he wouldn't have been able to write his report, anyway.

As an added bonus, he was overjoyed when he found out that Nurse Jasper was on duty, and that she was assigned to his room. When they saw each other, their eyes locked with a happy familiarity. And while a quiet passion simmered between them, their hearts found a new reason to keep beating.

Officer Morgan was heading back to his partner, when he heard the disturbing news on the police scanner. He was admittedly shocked by the horrible outcome, and couldn't wait to be with his fellow officers.

There were nine police cars parked on the edge of the hill that night, and under the full moon and a thousand twinkling stars, all of the officers watched the remnants of the devastation in silence. They had a feeling that their regular lives would be forever changed, and they surmised that even the strongest of men would be turned into timid forest creatures, once they learned the gruesome details of all that had happened prior to that moment.

Since the helicopter was the only vehicle that could get down to the burning car, it descended without getting too close. The flames were high and hot, and the only thing that the two officers could see, was smoke.

The helicopter rose a few minutes later, and it was easy for everyone to predict, that this was going to be a very busy place when the sun came up in the morning.

After Officer Morgan arrived, he let his eyes skim over the overwhelming damage of the horrific crash. He then listened as everyone filled him in on the newest details. After that, he allowed himself to be part of the silent parade, when everyone drove away from the fiery scene.

CHAPTER SEVENTEEN

October 31, 2000

It was 9am on Halloween morning, the sun was up and the majority of the world was awake. Some were going to school, others were going to work, and a small group of die-hard Halloween enthusiasts, were busy decorating their homes for the big event. Everyone was excited and could hardly wait until suppertime, when the kids came out in elaborate costumes, to fill their bags with candy.

Jayla was safe and sound in her own home, and after destroying Molly's purse and everything in it, she went onto her computer and looked for her next victim.

This whole thing with Roger had been a new, and at times, difficult adventure, and it was not something which she wanted to do again; the chase at the beginning was easy, but then Roger kept slipping through the cracks and it was hard for her to keep track of him. And while she eventually received his dark soul, she lost a great deal of energy because of the elaborate details in the extra spells which she had to perform.

Jayla had learned a lot in the past week, and she vowed to do things a lot differently from now on.

Detective Katts was very happy to be back in his own home again, and surrounded by his personal possessions. He was also happy to have been reunited with Arlene Jersey – the nurse from the Regal Hospital. But for now, the detective was typing out his stimulating report, and he hoped that he could work through some of the emotional grief which he had encountered in the past 24 hours.

He had been kept in a hard, twin bed at the well-lit hospital, and it had been more than comforting to be under the hundreds of florescent lights in Triage. He had been examined by two different doctors, and was found to be thoroughly and mentally exhausted. He had also sustained some major bangs and bruises, but was assured that those would heal over time.

With a little coaxing from Nurse Jersey, the aging detective had taken the strong medicine which she had offered, and he had been able to get some sleep. However, he woke up startled and anxious around 4am, and when he found out that she had gone home after her shift had ended, the detective begged the doctor on duty to release him as soon as he could.

As he sucked the last bit of cold coffee from his large porcelain mug, Detective Katts stared at the black letters which had magically appeared on the white page before him. He was pleased that his report was now finished, and after inserting a clean piece of paper into his typewriter, he began to type the first page of his novel.

Despite the fact that his car had been destroyed in the crash, and that he would forever be scarred by what had happened between him and the witch, the detective had been quite intrigued by the entire story of Roger and Molly. And while he had been sitting in the hospital bed waiting to be released, he had decided to write a murder mystery story, using yesterday's crime as the plot.

As he continued to click his sausage-like fingers against the full-length keyboard, he was loving how the story was connecting together. He made sure to use some literary license to fill in the blanks, but the parts which were real, were quite captivating:

Roger's fingerprints had been lifted from a glass at the dreary house where Molly had been held captive. Not surprisingly, the police had been able to match those fingerprints to the ones which were found on the outer frame of the back door of the hardware store. After the police typed that information into the data base, Roger's lengthy criminal record jumped off the computer screen.

It was the handsome detective who had deduced that Roger was the brains behind the now-famous, bloody crime scene on Leiland Avenue. And while

it was not certain why Marlowe had died or why Adam had been shot, the detective surmised that it looked like a well-thought-out robbery that had gone horribly wrong.

And then there was Jayla – no last name. She was unearthly, and definitely not delicate. She was ghostly and strong, and she had strange powers. She left no fingerprints, or any other clues which could identify her, but both Molly and the detective swore that she was real. And because of her involvement with Molly and Roger, she was undeniably someone who should be questioned by the police.

But did she play a part in the carnage at Jack's store? That was the question on everyone's lips.

> - An excerpt from
> 'The Murder on Leiland Avenue'
> - by Andrew Katts

* * * * * *

Molly had just walked through her front door, and she hated the feeling of being in that big house all alone. It was in total disarray from all that the police had been looking for yesterday, and while they had promised to pay for a cleaning company to help her straighten everything up, she had no idea when they would arrive.

She had been in the hospital until an hour ago, and had been informed that Marlowe had been shot and killed. They also told her that Roger had died, but they didn't say how. While she was struggling with sorrow for Roger, she was terribly crushed by the news that her husband was gone.

Molly was full-out crying as she stood in the middle of her disorganized living room, and while her heart was breaking into a million pieces, she was in total disbelief of all that had happened in the past 24 hours. As she looked around, her arms were folded tightly across her stomach, as if to protect her from whatever else was about to jump into her life.

Her statement had been given out in bits and pieces throughout the night, but around 1am, the doctors ordered everyone to stop their brutal interrogation; they could see that she was tired and had been through so much already, and they wanted her to get some rest.

Molly was quite certain that she would sell the house and move somewhere else, and she understood that it would take time to get it all figured out. In the end, she decided that it would be worth it; the memories of her life with Marlowe would haunt her too much if she stayed.

Officer Wall had volunteered to check on Molly and record the damage which had been done to her home, and as he thumped his strong knuckle against her front door, he hoped that she was there.

Molly was startled by the loud knock. "Who is it?" she called sharply. She was still frightened by all that had happened with Jayla, and she could feel her anxiety rising.

The handsome man could barely hear her, so he leaned into the door and stated his name. "Officer Wall."

"Oh!" Molly was happily surprised that he had come over, and used her hands to wipe the moisture off her face. "Coming!" she called. She took a second to check her clothing, and then she opened the door.

He tipped his hat and said Hi.

"Hi", Molly replied. After she saw his familiar face, she jumped into his arms as if they were old friends.

Officer Wall hadn't been prepared for this kind of welcome, but he clasped his arms around her back and held on tight. He was aware of all that she had gone through, and he was more than eager to give her some moral support.

"Would you like to have some coffee with me?" she asked kindly, as she ended the spontaneous embrace.

He knew he was blushing as he checked his watch, and hoped that she couldn't see how he truly felt. "I'd love to, but I can't stay too long."

"That's ok", she sighed. She felt slightly embarrassed as she led him into the kitchen, but because he was quick to make her feel comfortable, she didn't hesitate to remove her mask of awkwardness.

The two of them sat and talked after she placed the fresh cups of coffee on the table. And even though there was a huge mess all around them, it didn't take long before Molly realized that the house had suddenly taken on a strange sense of calmness - it was a feeling that had never been part of her home before.

After a few long minutes of friendly chatting, the police officer patched the broken window in her back door. After jotting down the other places that needed attention, he told her that he had to go to the station. "Perhaps I could check in on you later?" he asked with hope in his heart. "I could call you, if you don't mind."

The expression on the officer's face was priceless, as if this was the first time he had ever asked a girl out.

Molly nodded, and her face lit up brighter than a sunny Sunday afternoon.

She loved his compassion and how attentive he had been, and because she hadn't had butterflies in her tummy for more than 20 years, she felt like a teenager again.

Molly handed him a piece of paper with her phone number on it. She stared into his eyes as he folded it in half, and then watched as he pushed it into the small pocket on the front of his shirt.

"Thanks", he said softly. "I guess I'll talk with you later."

"Ok." Molly exhaled a long soft sigh of contentment, for she had a feeling that this was the first day of the rest of her life.

* * * * * *

Louise had woken up in the middle of the night, and was surprised that she had fallen asleep on the couch. She was disappointed that she didn't get to see Jack when he came home, and she went upstairs to find him.

Jack was sound asleep on his side of the bed, so Louise stood and watched him for a few minutes before she crawled in next to him. As she lay on her pillow, she listened to him breathe and snore, and she praised the heavens that he was still alive.

As she moved her body closer and cuddled up beside him, she felt horrible that she had even thought about running away. And as she realized what could have happened had Jack been shot instead of Marlowe, she cried herself to sleep.

Jack woke up next to Louise, and it was the best morning that they had had in years. And when they stood at their front door as he was going off to work, they pushed their past aside and made plans to celebrate their future.

"I love you!" Louise called as she watched him walk to his car. And for the first time in years, she really meant it.

"I love you, too!" he replied. He blew her a kiss and then opened his car door. "See you later!"

They both smiled and waved as he drove out of their driveway, and each one couldn't wait until that night, when they could both make up for past mistakes.

When he was gone, Louise went to the kitchen to clean up the mess from their unhurried breakfast. When that was done, she went upstairs to get herself ready for the day. The music was playing gently in the background, and she could hear children laughing and a dog barking outside in the yard across the street. She only had one thought on her mind in that moment, and that was to make things right with Jack. Now that she had a second chance, she promised herself that she wasn't going to ruin it.

Meanwhile, Jack was at work and not feeling very well at all. His head had been banging from the inside out for about an hour, and he was now weak and very nauseous.

Jack had had a lot to drink the night before, and decided that he was in the throes of a violent hangover. The hot water which had pierced his skin in the shower, didn't take away any of the brutality of the pain in his head or tummy. He questioned if black coffee would work, and decided to drink as much as he could tolerate.

Jack had to be at the hardware store this morning, to meet with the police and a representative from the insurance company. They were all there to assess the damage and to fill out some forms, while other people were on site to clean up or fix what was broken.

He didn't usually like to take any time off from work, but because of how he felt, today he would have made an exception.

Jack was usually guarded about his private life, so it shocked him when one of the police officers asked him if he was ok.

"I'm fine", he replied lightly, and he brought his right hand up to the side of his head where it hurt. "It's just a headache, and I'm going to go home as soon as we're done here."

The officer made a face as if he didn't agree that Jack was ok. "If you're sure…"

Jack nodded, and he hoped that the officer would stop worrying.

The uniformed man shrugged his shoulders and walked away.

Not long after that, Jack's body leaned to the side, and it took less than a minute for him to drop to the ground.

Because of how many people were milling about and how much work there was to do, nobody saw him for almost an hour. When someone happened to find him laying on the dirty floor of the crime scene, they rushed over and asked him if he was ok. When he didn't respond, even after a few minutes of intense prodding, an ambulance was called. After the paramedics arrived, they reported that Jack Chisholm had suffered a massive stroke.

Unbeknownst to Jack, he had been enduring high triglyceride levels for some time. He had also experienced quite a lot of stress in the past week or so, and yesterday's events had raised his blood pressure enough to bring his body to a complete standstill.

A taut silence fell over the entire crowd of people, when they learned that he had been declared dead. And once the news had sunk in, loud sorrowful gasps could be heard from nearly everyone's lips. Some were crying, some fell to their knees, and others were trembling in complete disbelief.

They all needed to stop and grieve, but not because they were being told to; there had been a murder and a robbery yesterday, and now there was a death today. It was all so unexpected and very distressing, and no-one felt like they could continue with what they were expected to do.

Detective Katts had learned of Jack's death, when it was broadcast over the police radio to dispatch. He had already written bits and pieces of his report since early that morning, and he had been able to jot down 50 quick notes for his upcoming novel. And with the news that Jack's body was being taken to the morgue, this ultimately changed the last page of his police report, and the first page of his murder mystery story.

The entire police department, and those of the surrounding areas, were astonished to learn that Jack - the man who had escaped death yesterday - had died today. Nobody could have predicted that to happen, and now someone needed to give this bad news to his wife.

By the time the doorbell rang, Louise had had her hair and nails done, she'd gone shopping for that night's supper, and she was preparing their celebratory meal.

After opening her front door, she was very surprised when a somber-looking police officer said that he needed to talk with her.

She was immediately stricken with panic, because her first thought was that they had somehow found out about her connection with Marlowe. But because there was only one police officer at her front door, she decided that he hadn't come to arrest her.

The officer was quick to place his hat over his heart before he spoke again. "Could I have a moment of your time?"

"Of course." She moved aside and made a sweeping motion with her hand. Meanwhile, her eyebrows were sitting high on her forehead while her other hand had dropped down to her side. Her lips were parted as if she was going to say something else, and her eyes were wide with worry about why he was there.

"Thank you." He made his way to the couch and waited until she sat down. "I know you're aware of what happened yesterday, but there's another piece of news that I have to share with you."

As Louise listened to the depressing details of Jack's death, she wanted to faint. She was stunned and now sobbing, and she could feel that her eyes were not blinking nearly enough.

"I'm so sorry for your loss", the officer stated kindly.

Louise was frantic and wanted him to reverse everything that he was saying. As she lay a shaky hand against her breastbone, it felt like she was unable to fill her lungs with air.

'This is Karma', her soul whispered.

Louise closed her eyes with sorrow, for although she knew that this was true, she wished that none of this had happened.

"It's not the part of my job that I enjoy, but it's one that needs to be done from time-to-time", the officer was quick to point out. "Here. Perhaps this can help you." He handed her a small card with the phone number for a chapel and grief counselling.

"No, no! This can't be right!" she argued as she stared at the words on the card.

Louise couldn't hear her own voice, because her heart was thumping so loudly in her chest. She was terribly distraught and it showed, and the muscles in her body were ready to fight or run.

"Again, I'm so sorry." The officer put his hat back on his head and proceeded to walk to his car.

Louise was left standing at her front door feeling empty and abandoned, and she was being consumed by an overwhelming sadness that filled all the crevices in her broken heart. 'This is not how it was supposed to be', she cried inside of her mind. 'They had a chance for a new beginning. How could Jack die now?'

Tears were falling down her cheeks as she watched the squad car drive away, and she honestly didn't know what she should do.

When Louise eventually closed her front door, she automatically fell to her knees. Without thinking, she leaned forward and laid her forehead onto the soft curl of the knotted fabric beneath her feet. She grabbed the grey carpet in clusters with her fingers, and squeezed them as hard as she could. She then allowed her tears and frustration to pull her soul apart.

As she was screaming with emotional pain, Louise felt a tremendous amount of guilt for what she had done with Marlowe. Through her heavy sobbing, she had said sorry a thousand times, but her misery could not be soothed. And with Jack dead, she was now writhing on the floor in psychological torture.

It took a while before Louise had been able to slow her sobs down, and when she was ready, she rolled onto her back and looked up at the ceiling. A large warm tear slid off the side of her face, as she realized that she had no real friends. However, she knew that Adam and some of their customers would give her pretend comfort in the way of words and cards. It was not something which she was looking forward to, but she wasn't sure how she could avoid it.

With this clear but embarrassing revelation, Louise stood up and forced herself to go to bed. She stayed there for the next few days, and after Jack's small but impressive funeral, she decided that it was time to make some changes in her life.

CHAPTER EIGHTEEN

January 31, 2001

It has been three months since Halloween, and with the start of a new year, comes an exciting new thread of life.

Detective Katts had finished typing out his murder mystery novel, and while he made sure to embellish a few parts of the story, he made sure to connect the witch to the devilish crime. It was a bold move, but one that seemed to work quite well.

He sent the first two chapters of his book in the mail, a little more than a month ago, and everyone at the Lord Chandler Literistic Agency loved what they read. In fact, they signed him to a contract without waiting to see how the story ended.

Andrew Jonathan Katts was about to be known as an author – a career he had always dreamed about, but did not pursue until recently. He is completely overjoyed with this new adventure, and can't wait to see his hard-cover book on the shelves of all the popular book stores, all around the world. He also couldn't wait to begin writing his next novel – Witches: fact or fiction?

On a personal note, he is very happily dating Nurse Arlene Jersey. They have a sweet relationship, one of kindness and lots of love, and while they don't share a home yet, he will be proposing to her on Friday night. If she says yes, he hopes to make her his bride on February 14.

Molly Perkins has been spending a lot of quality time with Officer John Wall, and they recently classified themselves as dating. After he and his friends helped her move out of the home that she had once shared with Marlowe, the charming couple celebrated Christmas and New Year's Eve in her new place.

Molly and John make sure to have a date night at least once a week, which was something she'd never had in her marriage to Marlowe. John is five years younger than Molly, and he treats her better than she has ever been treated before in her life. And no matter where this relationship between them is heading, it was already better than either of them have had in the past.

Jayla has found her next victim on the Prison Chatline, and was using all of her womanly ways to keep him interested. They have been emailing since the beginning of December, and he called her on December 17 – one week before Christmas Eve. She is looking forward to meeting him in person this week-end, and if all goes well, a conjugal visit could be scheduled for the middle of February.

So far, Jayla has not been seen in the real world, and no matter how much the police and FBI have searched, they haven't been able to find any information on her. She is an intelligent witch, after all, and she knows enough to disguise herself so that she is totally untraceable.

Witches live by magic, but magic has many rules, and none of them are governed by man. And even though she understands all of this to be true, Jayla continues to look for a spell that will remove the misery which rains down on her head, every single day of her life.

She has been relentless in trying to unearth an incantation which can heal her aching heart, but deep down, she knows that she will always be shackled by the curse, and live submissively by its rules.

Still, that doesn't hurt her as much as the agony of losing Roger.

While a hot tear of shame slid down her warm cheeks, Jayla's skin grew pale as she faced the sad truth that she couldn't bring him back to life. She gulped back regret which her eyes couldn't hide, for though she didn't kill him herself, she begged him to forgive her, for her part in his early death.

"I'll never fall in love again", she promised through unsettling sorrow. And after she allowed her body to collapse into a nearby chair, she put her face into her hands and cried.

She had always felt safe nestled in the protective cage of his arms, because without even trying, he made her fall in love with him. That was something she couldn't say about any other man she'd ever known. And now he was gone.

Jayla predicts that she will always have very little interest in being with these useless men in prison, however, she needs their souls to survive. She blames her appalling way of life on Ophelia, and will always remain haunted by the mental pain of losing the one man who made her happy.

THE EPILOGUE

March 1, 2001

Louise had inherited everything after Jack died, and she also collected all of the insurance money. She sold the hardware store to Adam on New Year's Eve, and that same night, he asked his girlfriend to be his wife. A week later, Louise put her house up for sale – furniture and all - and moved away.

In truth, she had gone to a flattened mountain top in Iceland for about a month. The tiny village is called Tomechulo, and its purpose is to refresh witches and warlocks in an intergalactic rejuvenation coven. A strict meditation regime, experimenting with herbal, candle, and crystal magic, and getting acquainted with new techniques and channels, were activities that were greatly encouraged.

Honing one's intuitive abilities and getting a better grasp of lunar timing, were also ideal ways to spend your time.

It's been four months since Jack had died, and a woman resembling Louise was spotted in Paris, France. She was having a cozy dinner with a tall, very wealthy, dark-haired man named Alexander.

While this woman looked quite similar to Jack's widow, there were a few subtle differences. But upon closer inspection, you might even believe that this was Louise.

In secret, she was, but she had had a physical make-over done. She had also been able to strengthen her life force and natural powers through potions and independent undertakings.

Being in Iceland had been a luxury, but it was also a delightful haven for all witches and warlocks. Many trekked there to get away from the humdrum inequities of the common people, and she was one of those who needed what they could give her.

Her name is now Daphne. Her hair and make-up had been altered, and she was speaking French as if that was normal. She had invented a new background for herself, but it was all a cover-up for the person who she truly was inside.

A long time ago, she was a child from a broken home, and after her mother had gotten re-married, they moved to a village which she hated. Because of her turbulent childhood, and with a new man coming in as a stepparent, she had matured faster than other kids her age. This didn't make her wise, but it did make her clever and sassy.

It didn't take long before she had been able to make friends with a little girl named Jayla, and for a short time, she was honestly happy. However, with the pressures of the teen years looming before her, her feelings of abandonment from her father came forward.

As her body formed into a woman, she suddenly felt angry that he was not around. It was challenging, and because there were other children born after her, she wasn't given the attention which she felt she needed. This caused her to be jealous and demanding, as if she had a craving to be seen and liked all the time.

She eventually turned into a wild child, and was no longer someone who her mom was proud of. She then focused on boys to get what she wasn't getting at home. This in turn, caused a rift in her friendship with Jayla, and when they were 16 years old, their relationship began to unravel.

Back then her name was Ophelia, and after she had killed Rune, she was sent far away from the village without the ability to hear or speak. She soon ended up in the arms of a Garden Witch, who lived a little more than a hundred miles away. This small-framed hag took pity on the teenage girl, and turned her sorrows into happiness by changing the formula of the spell which had been placed upon Ophelia's head.

The young woman had to relearn how to speak and make sentences, and by using wax candles and herbs, the witch had restored Ophelia's hearing. It was a very long and tedious process, but the end result was worth its weight in gold.

The Garden Witch had become Ophelia's best friend, but when she died and her body had withered away, Ophelia was once again left on her own.

She had gained a lot of self-esteem while living with her mentor, but before too long, it was time for Ophelia to venture out into the world again.

She made friends easily, much to her delight, and she even ended up getting married. The man was nice at first, but then became nasty and withdrawn. She wasn't used to this type of behavior, and after three years in an unhappy marriage, she left him with nothing but the clothes on her back. Ophelia was then on her own, and it was much harder because she didn't have a job or any money in her pocket.

Ophelia decided to get married again, but this time she would make sure to walk away with all the money that she could get her hands on. Not surprisingly, the new relationship floundered not long after it started, but this time, she made sure to have all that she needed in order to survive for the next twelve months.

It was when Ophelia was on her third relationship, that she found out that she would get even more money, if her partner or husband died. After doing some research on that information, she quickly followed through with some bleak missions.

Throughout her many relationships, she had loosened lug nuts to cause car accidents, she cut a tree branch so that it was weak enough to fall onto a man's head, she added a little too much sleeping powder into her boyfriend's nighttime tea, and she nudged one man down the escalator at the mall, after he had had too much to drink.

When she was in the beginning of each of these relationships, she felt wonderful because somebody loved her. When the man in her life died, she was rewarded with money and possessions, but she was also left emotionally empty and couldn't wait to bring a new man home.

Those bumpy voyages had a way of crippling Ophelia's inner happiness, but because she was strong in spirit, she could usually bounce back to her former self, a month or two after she became newly-single.

Sadly, a small part of her would always lay dormant, and she may never be able to recover.

She met Jack when she was Louise. When he died, she fell into a deep depression. He had always loved her, and she was just learning how to love him back. And while it hadn't always been smooth sailing between them, she honestly believed that her marriage to Jack was the best relationship that she had ever had.

She was now Daphne Moore, a widow and a middle-aged student of the arts, and she was living by herself in Paris. She had just begun to date Alexander Hotte, a famous pastry chef at Gâteaux Thoumieux in the Eiffel Tower District, and he was making her very happy.

Unknowingly, both Jayla and Ophelia were living very similar lives. They were both witches in disguise, and they had been cast to the same fate – killing men in order to survive.

Neither knew of the other person's lifestyle, and neither knew how close they had come to meeting again after all these years. But because their futures were long and paths have a habit of intertwining, who knows what might happen down the road?

CPSIA information can be obtained
at www.ICGtesting.com
Printed in the USA
LVHW011122220819
628505LV00001B/1/P